Father Sleep

Stephen Short

Published by Green Crow Publishing, 2024.

This book is a work of fiction. All references to real people, events, establishments, or locales are only intended to advance the fictional narrative. All other characters, and all incidents and dialogue, are drawn from the author's imagination and are not to be construed as real.

FATHER SLEEP
Copyright © 2024 Stephen Short

All rights reserved. No part of this publication may be reproduced, stored or transmitted in any form or by any means, electronic, mechanical, photocopying, recording, scanning, or otherwise without written permission from the publisher. It is illegal to copy this book, post it to a website, or distribute it by any other means without permission.

Published by Green Crow Publishing, LLC
www.greencrowpublishing.com

ISBN: 979-8-227-03420-5 (ebook)
ISBN: 979-8-227-45401-0 (paperback)

First Edition: October 7, 2024

0 9 8 7 6 5 4 3 2 1

To Mimi, the sleepiest girl I know, and Wednesday, the wiggliest dog of my dreams.

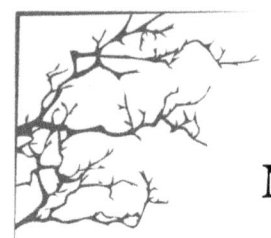

Night Four

Sliding his key into the front doorknob, Jeff heard Kate's snores gurgling through the house, and then, just under that, the quiet growl and crackle of an engine halting behind him. No, he told himself. A car door clunking shut. Jeff refused to turn around. He hurled the door open.

"Mr. Vickers!" shouted Gilbert, clomping up the snowy sidewalk.

Jeff visualized Kate's old golf clubs in the nearby closet. She wouldn't notice a Gilbert-shaped bend in her 7-iron; she hadn't played in years. And then his shoulders clenched, his hands morphed to granite, and he flexed his gravelly fingers. Finally, after three nights of terror, this was a nightmare he could seize control over, and it only required thumping that slimeball trespasser Gilbert Finnegan.

"Mr. Vickers, I'm sorry," and Jeff spun to see Gilbert, wheezing, extending a clammy hand, just like last night, "I think we got off on the wrong foot."

"I think you should go." Jeff sloshed spit around his teeth.

"I think we can still do business, sir." Jeff's temper burned with the suggestion of "business."

"Is this the Society of Dreams or whoever's (Jeff talked over Gilbert's correction) idea of 'business?' You stalking me? Taking photos of my home without my permission?"

"Mr. Vickers, you gave us your permission." Jeff gave him a blaring look that encouraged him to continue. "When you sent us the inquiry, you checked that little box before submitting that says we can commence surveying your primary location of sleep upon acceptance." Undone by a checkbox. Jeff recalled his dream of the charging bull from the other night. This is what he feared, that the dreams were somehow a premonition, a prediction of the future, with Jeff consumed by the fury of a raging bull, sentenced to electric death for murdering Gilbert Finnegan on his front porch. "I'm sorry that's not what you expected."

Jeff's massive torso swelled in an attempt to calm himself. "Cancel it. I didn't dream last night, this was a mist—"

"Well, yeah," Gilbert said. Curious, thought Jeff. So curious his anger fizzled and his fist unclenched. Gilbert responded as if Jeff asked an incredibly obvious question and Gilbert was the reluctant and unfortunate party that had to answer. *You mean to tell me that if I look into the sky I might see clouds? Well, yeah!* Well, yeah. Jeff asked what he meant, and Gilbert answered, "Of course you didn't dream." Jeff felt the bleary-eyed and crooked droop of his face. "You called the cops before I could explain."

The anger trickled back up his elbows to his balled fists. "Maybe you could explain in an email or a phone call instead of slinking around my house at midnight."

Gilbert closed his eyes, defeated. "I'll move it up the ladder." They stood silent for a few moments. The cold bled into Jeff's house and swirled up his knees and chest and neck. "I guarantee you'll dream tonight." Jeff had to admit his continued curiosity. After his dreamless sleep last night, he spent the day convincing himself everything was, ironically, a dream, and that he had never stopped living his normal life.

"Will they be like before?"

Gilbert cleared his throat. "That would be my bet, yes. It's cold out, Mr. Vickers."

Jeff knew it before he said it, but Gilbert was coming into his house that night. His hope, his delusional fantasy, that he never dreamed at all, shattered. It was late. Kate, his wife, an Olympic-level sleeper, wouldn't be bothered. Jeff stepped aside, and Gilbert lunged past the threshold. No handshake.

Gilbert's tent-like suit hung off him like old curtains. It wasn't quite tan, wasn't quite yellow, but was in prompt need of hemming. He had dark grey eyes and too many teeth in his mouth and a crooked scar that streaked his upper lip like a crackle of lightning. Something on him made a clinking, jangling sound at any mid-sized movement.

They went to the kitchen. Gilbert asked for a cup of coffee. Jeff snarled. Started the pot. The kitchen was the furthest room from the bedroom. It would have been more comfortable on the living room couch, but leading Gilbert closer to Kate seemed wrong, like a shameful perversion, or a poison that would blot her out if he got too close. They sat on opposite ends of the small, squared table.

"You smoke?" asked Gilbert, fishing around in his blazer pocket. Jeff shook his head, recalling his father's lifelong chew habit, his jowls red and blue like flowery veins. "Me either," Gilbert said with a smirk, and brought his hand back to the table. Jeff noted Gilbert's lie, recalling him hunched inside his white van roiling in cigarette smoke, right before calling the cops on him; the useless, blue state cops that took an hour to arrive and sauntered away with only a few notes and a phone number. Disgrace to the badge. Jeff's brain drifted to Kate's golf clubs.

"Thanks for the coffee." Gilbert took it with more sugar than Jeff ingested in a week and sloshed the maximum amount of milk the cup allowed. He slurped it past his scarred lips. "Nice house."

Jeff didn't care. "Who are you?"

Gilbert shrugged. "Gilbert Finnegan."

"Yes, Gilbert. Why are you in my home right now? Why did you come back?"

He laughed with big teeth, chuckling around the room to no one in particular. "*What am I doing here* he asks." After noticing Jeff's stony scowl, he sobered himself. "Look, I'm a little afraid that if I bring up an email, you're gonna lose it like last night." Beneath the table, Jeff's hands cracked like stepped-on glass. "But did you read the email?"

"I read it." The email he referred to went to Jeff's spam folder, so the unexpected flashes of Gilbert's camera outside his bedroom window at night boiled him over.

"Great, then you're up to speed."

"The email said someone would survey my house, not that you'd come into my home."

Gilbert drummed his coffee mug. "That's what the first email said." Gilbert smirked with a fat face, a little afraid to meet eyes with Jeff. "Did you check your spam folder?"

"You've got to be kidding." And there it was, about 20 messages down, from the Society of Divine Dreams: "*What to Expect When You're Divining.*"

"Not the first time it's happened." Jeff noticed a whip of righteousness in Gilbert. He cocked himself to the side and leaned way back. Jeff expected him to drop his ugly feet on the table and recline. "Well you can read it if you want, or I can just talk at ya, since you don't seem to be properly apprised of the situation." Jeff scanned the email; it thanked him, yadda yadda, visitor, yadda yadda, quality of dreamscape, yadda yadda yadda yadda....

Gilbert jumped in, "What do you know about oneiromancy?"

Jeff glared daggers. "Never heard of it."

"It's plastered all over the website you visited to get our contact info."

"Do you mean 'honor-o-mancy?' Guess I didn't know how to pronounce it."

"Oneiromancy—o-nye-ro-man-see. More or less, the study of dreams. Well, not really. That's more oneirology. It's the 'mancy' that brings me here, this late at night, drinking your coffee." He drank the coffee.

"That means magic, right?"

"No, Mr. Vickers." Gilbert draped out his hand, cradling an invisible cigarette between his fingers. He resisted yanking his arm up for a drag. "The 'mancy' bit means 'divination.' You heard of that one before?"

"I read a book with it once, but it didn't paint it in a good light."

"Ahh, a reader. Very good. Well, yeah. It's not exactly a 'science' but more of an 'experience.' I have a lot of experience with oneiromancy. The Society of *Divine* Dreams, yeah? That's where it comes from. We divine your dreams."

"So what, you predict the future with them or something? That's insane."

"Well you reached out to us, Mr. Vickers—Jesus, can I just call you Jeff? Jeff, you didn't think it was so crazy the other night, did you?"

"I was scared." He didn't know why he told this stranger, this interloper, about his feelings. Gilbert leaned his greasy, pocked face forward. Jeff imagined cratering his knuckles into it. "I never had dreams before." And it was true. For 50-plus years, until a few nights ago, Jeff slept in empty bliss the whole night with nary a flash, image, or sparkle at all. But lately he woke gasping and screaming. "These scared me."

"Yes!" Gilbert hollered and smacked the table. His coffee stirred and slopped over the edge of the cup. Most husbands would tell Gilbert to shush, but Jeff knew Kate was out for the count. "Of course, sir, yes sir, Jeff sir, yes! That is the key! You're a Shark."

"I'm a man."

"We call them 'Sharks,' people that don't dream." Gilbert did that thing with his hand again, pulling it up to his mouth and aching when there wasn't a cigarette. "'Sharks'—comes from Charcot-Wilbrand syndrome, it's this disorder where individuals who've suffered brain damage lose their ability to dream." Jeff's face had to be a panicked blur. "Not that you have brain damage, Jeff, no. You're dreaming! Hmm! Sharks is just a name thing, you're fine. Probably fine."

Thankful for the reassurance, Jeff recalled scrambling over the internet in a frightened buzz, looking for any explanation for the new terror hounding his sleep. One website mentioned Charcot-Wilbrand. The disorder raked its claws over his mind with every dizzying turn of his head, every sharp, sandy clench of his fists, when he looked back on getting clobbered in the face repeatedly as a middling college boxer. The potential for brain damage certainly existed.

"The thing is, Sharks like you don't come along very often. We call people 'Sharks' when they've never had dreams before and then they suddenly do. Like you." He smiled tall and overhung. Jeff pondered the definition, and the sudden blast of dreams haunting him where before there was nothing for decades. Hopefully he reached out to the right people.

"I think you really reached out to the right people, Jeff." Was he in his brain?

"I just don't know what any of this means. So what if I'm having dreams, what does that mean for you? What does the Society do?"

"Well," Gilbert settled around in his chair, boneless. "All sorts of stuff." Gilbert's grey eyes fell on Jeff. He thought Gilbert was going to stop right there as if he would just understand, but thankfully, he pressed on. "We're a company, or a business, corporation—no, not a corporation, but—you know, we're an *entity*, there, that specializes in oneiromancy. We help people, we talk to them, we divine their dreams and help to make their lives better, yeah?"

"Just anyone that reaches out, or only Sharks?"

"Anyone, yeah. But most people don't do much for us or our research. Most people have dreams all the time and they aren't special. Yours might actually *be* special, Jeff."

"You mentioned business. How much will this whole thing cost me?" Jeff couldn't believe the words leaving his mouth.

Was he believing this whole thing? Jeff felt like he was anteing into a poker hand, just to see where the river took him.

"So you're in, huh?" Gilbert grinned again and leaned forward. Grease pooled at the tip of his shiny, hooked nose. "You're smart. You understand these things." Gilbert winked at him with words.

Jeff wanted to believe he was as smart as Gilbert said, so he chose his words carefully. "Maybe spell it out so you confirm what I'm thinking." Perfection.

"Well, we're a research entity with a unique opportunity in front of us; a Shark! A *whale*, even. No, you're not a whale, but it's a reference to the White Whale of Moby Dick fame, literature classic, you know, a famed prize or a highly sought-after trophy. A whale of a Shark. We'd like to work with you, Jeff. For us and for you. Mutually beneficial. No charge."

"What's the benefit for me?"

Gilbert shifted crooked-like. "Well, what prompted you to contact us?" Jeff almost answered, but then Gilbert said, "You were scared. We can help with that. *I know*, Jeff, I know. You are wondering *how*. Again, you're smart, I don't need to go all super in-depth with you right now, but basically, the Sharks I've worked with before were able to do incredible things with their lives through the power of oneiromancy. Incredible." There was an uncomfortable pause. Jeff stared straight ahead, urging him to continue. "Life-changing things, you know. Better dreams, better life. Usually people contact us thinking their dreams are a sign of what's going to happen in their lives, like some sort of prediction or premonition, you know." Jeff hoped he wasn't blushing or sour. "But it doesn't really work that way. In fact, it's quite the opposite; most people aren't special, aren't smart. Their lives are so," and he flopped his cigarette-less hand about, "so jacked up they can't help but have nightmares. But when they spend approximately 30 percent of their life sleeping, dreaming, and it's *shit*—or even worse, trauma-inducing—people get pretty motivated to make some adjustments. They feel powerless, you know." He sucked at his front teeth. "They want to control some aspect of their life; why not their dreams? But we actually *can* control them, Jeff. It's my job. I've been doing it for decades."

This made Jeff think of what *he* had done for decades: work at his terrible job, mostly. He watched a bit of news for the least popular party in his region. Plowed through hundreds of e-books and couldn't even sell them to make his money back. Played nickel poker with people he hated.

And Kate. What of Kate? He and Kate married decades ago near a quiet, trickling stream, and their love, as was natural, trickled away over the years with it. Kate, ever leery of responsibility, didn't allow for much change or development in their relationship as far as building a family. Children were too risky; they could be born with terrible disfigurements, be shot up at school, get riddled with vaccines causing mental impairments—all of which could be attributed to the liberal leanings of the last several decades. She also specifically noted the chances of having twins, naturally about 1 in 250, but given her family history of women birthing twins (her mother was a twin and her least favorite sister had twin boys just out of high school), she feared her slight frame would crumple under the strain. Outside of children, even pets weren't welcome under their roof. Kate feared bonding with and losing them too soon, only amplified by her mother's sudden death about a year ago.

These fears, all expressed from the same person who encouraged him to think positively, meant it was just Jeff and Kate for years and years.

And Jeff, admittedly, didn't have a ton of ambition. The last time he felt driven to better himself was in his college days, boxing on weekends for less money than he won in jangling nickels at poker. That is, of course, until he got sucker punched after the bell while stumbling back to his corner of the ring. He won the bout due to misconduct, but it spelled the beginning of the end of his boxing career, a result of the clanging concussion; Jeff's reactions slowed, he became leery and paranoid of his opponents. He fought from a place of fear rather than true enjoyment, and in a panic a couple of fights later, got wholloped alongside his head and his brain mushed against his skull once more and the doctor forbid him from boxing anymore. After that he kept working for Colson and getting fat and his hands crunched when he flexed them, his eyes took extra time to adjust to movement, and he got dizzy when he turned his head too fast.

"With the Society's help, you can make changes in ways that nobody else can. That's where the whole Shark thing comes in. Most people have a hard time enacting change in their life. Present company excluded, of course. Obviously. They're stuck in their ways, doing the same old thing because it's comfortable. They're content. Even if they're content sitting in a bowl of garbage that scrapes against their back, it's what they know. Sharks can use their *dreams to change their life*, and that's much easier than just changing their life."

Jeff might as well have been transported to another universe; the unusual man in the kitchen going on and on about his dreams, or lack thereof, and how this meant power; his own thoughts on his life, his wife, his job, his future and past; using the power of dreams to change his situation.

But Gilbert was right: Jeff did think the dreams meant something, whether good or bad. They were the entire reason for contacting the Society in the first place, right? The concept shouldn't seem that strange. If he drove to the grocery store for oranges he wouldn't suddenly be alarmed and shellshocked when they had oranges for sale. Yet here he was, stunned that Gilbert had oranges available in the form of oneiromancy.

"Can you prove it?" he stammered.

Gilbert chuckled again around the room, laughing and motioning to no one in particular, "*Can I prove it*, he asks." He thumbed the elbow patches on his not-yellow, not-tan blazer. "Let's see—I knew you didn't have any dreams last night, huh? Is that enough?"

"Lucky guess." Jeff was not confident in this answer.

"Sure, lucky. I *guess*, then, to put it simply, I *made it so you weren't going to dream.*" Gilbert launched his legs up and rested them on the corner of the table, then crossed them. Jeff saw gum on the bottom of his shoes, smashed to brownness. "Let's see. You wouldn't have noticed, you wouldn't remember. Your brain noticed, but you're not your brain, obviously, so there's a little disconnect there. I needed to survey your house, where you slept, what the lighting was, the angle of the bedroom; again, oneiromancy isn't a science, but that doesn't mean we just leave everything to chance, okay?" Gilbert shuffled in his seat. "So, using that information I was able to gather about where on Earth you slept, the longitudinal values of your brain during slumber, etcetera, etcetera," waving his hand, "I gave you a sign to silence the dreams for a night. Or really I gave your brain a sign, like I said, you wouldn't remember."

For what must have been the hundredth time that night, Jeff's eyes felt blank and wobbly. "Was that before or after I called the cops?" Gilbert grinned and leaned back. "Is it like a hand signal?"

"Don't worry about it, Jeff. Don't worry about it at all."

"I don't understand why you think I'm special, a 'Shark.'"

"Like I said before—no dreams, now dreams, yeah?" Gilbert scratched his chin with his long, yellowed fingernails. "That, and you didn't dream last night, and I knew it. Your average Joe wouldn't have been fazed." Jeff stared at Gilbert, at his faded eyes, wondering if he was giving him some sort of sign now, or what it would even look like. "You wrote in your inquiry that you dreamt of a bull, right?" Jeff nodded. "But it's not always a bull?"

"I guess I don't know, I don't remember everything. Maybe it's too early. Only had a few dreams. One of the others had a deer and some jaguars in them, or cheetahs."

"But you're not sure? Jeff," Gilbert said, shuffling forward and clasping his hands in front of him on the table, "this could be very important. You've got to know what you're seeing, because communicating that accurately to me will determine the efficacy of our results." Gilbert took a big breath in and out and slurped down the last of his coffee. "Well. You know honestly most of my clients are stuck so far up their own ass they don't question these things all that much. Most of them think they're God or something so they just kind of roll with me." Jeff almost felt like Gilbert was expecting an apology. He was in his house, drinking his coffee, smearing old convenience store gum on his wife's kitchen table and acting like Jeff was in the wrong. "Okay, how about this—I can tell you're getting tired. All you need to do is what you normally do. Just go to bed. Nothing special. When you wake up, write down what you see. *Exactly* what you see. Obviously the sooner you do it the better, the clearer the picture will be. We're looking for as much recollection as possible. Accuracy, Jeff. Accuracy is key. David didn't take down Goliath by whipping a stone at his fingernail. You've got to be clear and exact." Gilbert rocked up to his oversized shoes. "I'm gonna head. We can talk more tomorrow. You've got my email. Tonight, I just need you to sleep. Just go to sleep, Jeff." Gilbert thumped his hand down on Jeff's shoulder.

Surely his jaw drooped low. He floated to the bedroom. He levitated down and his head weighed soft on his pillow. Kate remained a log. Such a simple command. Just go to sleep. But the things Gilbert spoke of were not so simple. All at once he felt concerned from the dreams he already had, and hopeful there might be a shred of help for him around the corner. The whole situation was odd, though he was indeed the instigator; Jeff reached out to them. The Society of Divine Dreams didn't arrive, rejected from the neighbors, on his doorstep like religious fanatics selling dreamcures. He had the visions and the terror and dread and sought the Society out himself. They weren't asking him for money, at least not yet. Seemingly only details, but the textbook slam of information Gilbert just dumped on him was sorting into its proper brain crevices for analysis.

Jeff opened his eyes but felt nothing. His phone showed about two hours had passed since he laid down, but no sleep, and no dreams to remember. To his side the cavernous rush of breath hurled from Kate's throat. With her gifts combined with his, the Society would certainly have their hands full. He did his best to clear his mind and fall asleep.

A Shark? Was Jeff special in some way? He always feared his noteworthy days were passed, and, admittedly, if he was special, he assumed it would be from his physical form, the ferocity of calculated jabs and uppercuts, not from something latent in his mind. After the sucker-punch, any dream of boxing withered into the dirt. The idea of having a dream to chase—ironic now—was an albatross. For someone with little drive to apply himself, having someone knock at his door with a solution, a focus and direction, seemed like the answer to a problem he had hidden from for years.

And he supposed in some ways that very thing just occurred.

Two or so hours later. No sleep. No "somnolent vision" as the Society's website put it. And to boot he rattled at just how alert he was. The night whipped by, and he would soon have to get up for work. Perhaps he would be able to address his loathsome job via dream intervention. Gilbert seemed to be twirling around a question when he talked about some people not being able to change their lives to alter their dreams. Was this a common trait of so-called Sharks? A meandering life of non-events? He thought of folks at NA meetings being told "it's not your fault" when really Jeff figured if they didn't jam tar into their veins with their own twisted thumbs they might not be in that room. But his undirection might have an explanation, something that really *would* make it not his fault.

The slightest edge of the razor carving his nerves dulled just enough.

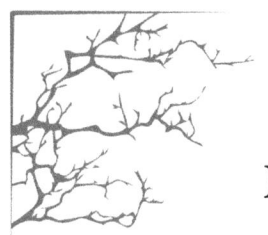

Night Five

He warbled open his soft eyes and it washed over him. The vision. Jeff scrambled from the comforter and broke for the writing desk in the hallway. Shaky, sweaty hands in the drawer snatched a crumpled yellow legal pad and the first pen they could. *Fool*, he thought. Should have had this ready. It was simple.

Pink. Solid, deep pink. Circles of pink. And a frog smack in the center.

Yes. That was the vision. Admittedly, he found it odd. The last dream he remembered was a fair bit more dramatic than this one. He decided to appreciate the fact he wasn't terror-stricken or unsticking his shirt from his back. Positive thinking, just like Kate suggested.

Pink frog-circles, huh? What does the Society do with such information? Do they evaluate the color? The shape or creature? And now he wasn't sure of the etiquette. Did he need to reach out or would Gilbert come calling? Maybe he was sly in his van crunching curious numbers about his REM cycles. Kate shuffled her feet across the carpet to the bathroom. It probably wasn't the best idea to chance that Gilbert would just come knocking on the door, perhaps when Kate might answer, so he decided to strike the first blow.

The chair groaned as he shoved up and went down the hall. Despite the poor sleep he had, he picked his feet up a bit higher when he stepped, his mood brighter despite no food or coffee. The prospect of fixing things, his life, lightened him, and for the first time in a long time, he *wanted* to kiss Kate.

Her toothbrush buzzed in her mouth. He slid behind her and wrapped his hairy forearms around her waist, leaned his head down on her shoulders and swayed. Her free hand fell on his wrist. She spit.

"We should do something together," Jeff said.

Kate doused her face with water from the hot tap. "What kind of something?" She patted a hand towel across her forehead and eyelids. The fringes of her wet hairline shimmered.

"I wanna go on a date with you," he said. She turned to face him. "Let's get dinner."

Kate swished her hair back into a grey ponytail. "We can get dinner," she said, "but we can't go to Charlie Fuskie's." Jeff was pretty sure they deep fried everything at Fuskie's down to the front doors.

"How about Audette's?" Perfect. Smaller, dimmer, rotating weekly specials that the waitstaff expounded on at each table.

"You make the call." The drawstrings of Kate's green scrubs seared together with a snap. "Let me know what time," she said, shuffling out the door to the kitchen to grab her bagel before heading out to work.

Jeff told himself, *This is the last day she doesn't kiss me out the door*. He partially blamed himself for their distance. Takes two to tango, they say. He took the first step toward closing the gap through his request of a date. Almost a starting over, a renaissance in their decades-long relationship. Kate was, due to his many failures, the biggest source of pride in his life, and to lose her would mean unimaginable things, unbearable shame. It had been a strange week, and though the previous season wasn't unusual, he couldn't remember the last time he felt optimistic. Jeff could look in the mirror (not too low, though) and say honestly, I feel good.

At work, Jeff's boss, Colson, was distracted by an IT meltdown instead of breathing down Jeff's neck, so he enjoyed the absence of screaming. He checked his phone every few minutes, being sure to look in the spam folder. Nothing yet, but he tried not to let it bother him. All things considered, the day was going well. He made the reservation at Audette's and texted Kate, who responded with a heart emoji.

Their dinner table bloomed with tea candles floating in water dishes peppered throughout their spread of bread, olives, and cheeses. Jeff noticed a distance in Kate, her chocolate eyes bouncing to other tables, inspecting the saltshakers. She twirled a carrot stick in honey dip on a charcuterie board. The waiter came by for their entrée orders and Jeff ordered the cod special and mentioned that their table didn't have flowers like the others.

"Please," said Kate, "don't bother yourself. We're perfectly fine. More space for our dishes." She took a sip from her cocktail, a brownish number with a pineapple skewered into it. "I'll have the avocado and fingerling salad." The waiter left.

Jeff had less to talk about than he realized. Every ounce of him wanted to share the dreams, the somnolent visions, to mention he hadn't slept well in days because of them, but he knew that Kate couldn't relate. "How's your dad doing?"

She looked down and bobbed her head. "I think he's doing well. He's still getting used to the space." Her father lived in the same farmhouse since her mother passed. "It's hard to imagine," said Kate, "not having your person there." She brought her drink to her pale lips. "All that time together."

Jeff hadn't thought of it that way. He hadn't thought of it much at all actually. This was the first time in almost a year she mentioned her parents outside of her dad's occasional visits. Jeff kept his face neutral but kicked himself internally for not checking on his wife. He took her phrasing as a good sign though, as Jeff was, by default, "her person."

"How's Claudia?" he asked.

Kate grinned, the candlelight melting her chocolate eyes. "I think she's fine. Pretty hungover from our night out." Kate chuckled and sipped her wine. "I'm glad you agreed to join us. It's good we're spending this time together."

"Yeah, I was just feeling a little..." Jeff searched the room. Waitstaff tucked their hands behind their backs and carted trays to each table with one hand. "...off. I'm sure I didn't make a great impression."

"Something at work?"

"You know Colson," he said. "Always coming by, hollering at me like it's a 'hello.'"

"Maybe that *is* his hello?"

"That's optimistic."

"As I always say, I think you could use a little more optimism."

"I'm not too optimistic about retiring."

"You're a long way from that, still."

"Even less optimistic."

"How's Howard?"

It was Jeff's turn to chuckle. "Still an ass."

"Don't you enjoy betting all your nickels away in his garage every week?"

"I enjoy the rare win when I see his stupid face drop." Kate grabbed her glass. "You know he had his motorcycle out? Without the cover. That giant black thing, all shined up in the dead of winter."

"Maybe," Kate started, plucking positivity from her secret stash, "he's just proud of something." Jeff tried to think what he was proud of. "And maybe he wants to share it. Maybe he considers you a friend?"

Jeff mustered only a "Maybe," before their food came and the talk died. Jeff's mind drifted to his next meeting with Gilbert, the frog in pink circles, and what that might really, truly mean for his future. And what it meant for Kate.

"What do you dream about?"

Kate looked up, slurping greens past her lips. "Like a topic?"

Jeff smiled, a real, genuine one. "I dunno, do they have a topic?"

"I guess not. Let me think." She twirled her fork, stabbing at a potato. "Mostly colors, I think. Shapes." She brought her fork up to her mouth, and before shoving the bite in, "What about you?"

"Oh," Jeff said, looking down at his mostly empty plate. "Normal stuff."

Jeff's phone buzzed with a message from Gilbert as he left the restaurant. Stepping onto the street, Jeff glanced down the block for a white van but didn't notice one.

To the surprise of neither party, Kate crashed once she stepped through the front door, her toes scuffing the carpet on her way back to the bedroom. Jeff flipped on the news about the farce of climate change (obviously there was snow out on the ground, where was global warming now?), welfare fraud from freeloading pot smokers (Jeff dreamed of quitting his job and lounging around all day, lost in a haze), medical malpractice from secret abortions (yet another reason not to trust the doctors in town). He loathed the quiet. Needed distractions. Empty moments allowed for thinking that brought the loud parts of his brain to the driver's seat. They took charge, and shadows of doubt cracked over his head and leaked in soggy drips. Doubt about his career, education, marriage, friendships (or lack thereof), location, and basically every avenue his forward feet had led him down. Surely being an accountant at a small tech firm wasn't the most fulfilling prospect for him. He wished he could tell people he was a quarterback and threw the longest touchdown pass in his college history. He would even take professional poker player, professional indoor sunglasses wearer, liar by trade, river rider. Were the decades spent cringing under Colson's abrasive shouts truly anything other than the first rebound he found? And Kate.

Did Kate even love him? He knew it was normal for couples to grow distant, but he feared it was a welcome distance on her end, feared she didn't care to be closer, feared a lonely contentment shrouded her side of the bed. Jeff shared years back that he wanted a child. Kate made it clear she was less than enthusiastic. Maybe he ignored the sign of distance to come? Jeff blamed his lackluster education, plus a few lousy concussions, for his current thornbush of a job. He hobbled into work every day because he couldn't be bothered to do anything else. Perhaps Kate felt the same way about their marriage? Settling, why not? In love because she's supposed to be.

Gilbert Finnegan rapped his dry knuckles on the door and Jeff let him in. "Lookin' a little blue, buddy." Jeff hoped his face didn't show his emotional snarl like it showed his depressing thoughts. They fashioned themselves at the same table as the night before. Gilbert hoisted his legs up and crossed them. "You smoke?" He asked, digging a tan and white pack with the plastic wrap partially undone from his baggy jacket pocket.

"I said no yesterday."

His eyebrows tilted. "You mind?"

Jeff hated any smoke; cigarettes, cigars, even campfires. The smell often welded to the back of his nares. One time, while heading to his car from work, he walked past Greg from HR as he leaned against a concrete pillar, dragging fire through the winter air. It was weeks before the creeping stench left him. "I'd rather you didn't, thanks."

"Hell." He stuffed the pack away. "Seem like you could use one tonight." Gilbert's stringy hair raked across his shiny skull. The scar on his lip looked bigger than he remembered, crawling up near his right nostril in white cracks.

"I prefer to sort my problems, not drown them," Jeff said. Gilbert enjoyed this comment. He magnetized to Jeff's eyes and a lip-only grin smeared over his face. The kind of smile that said *pants on fire*. Gilbert asked for coffee. Jeff dumped the sopping grounds and replaced them, then threw the switch on the pot. "You might drink me out of my home, Gil."

"It's Gilbert."

Jeff poured the coffee.

"Tell me about the dream. How did it go?"

Finally. "I almost couldn't get to sleep at first. And then I kept on waking up. But eventually I saw a pink background. Deep pink, and circles of different shades of pink spreading out like ripples in a pond. And a frog in the middle."

Gilbert nodded his head. He had the coffee cup in one hand and two fingers at attention, missing a cigarette, hovering near his mouth. "Go on."

Suddenly he had a flashback to sixth grade when he was out sick and mistakenly glugged a few extra doses of cold medicine. He returned to school the next day with a smogged brain and couldn't elaborate on the Seven Years' War when the teacher grilled him.

"That was everything."

"No good, Jeff. No good." He rocked back and pulled deep from the coffee cup. "We need a little more."

"Do you mean there's more to the dream or what, what more do 'we' need?"

"Okay, something along the lines of like," and he settled both chair legs back down on the kitchen linoleum, "what the frog was sitting on. Did it ribbit or hop or tongue a fly? Any markings, textures. The pink, how many rings did you see? I think it's a bit nutty to expect you to know the exact tones but at least gimme something like lighter or darker."

"So you're not wondering why I dreamt about a bull goring me a few days ago and a boring frog last night?"

"No, I knew you'd dream about the frog, Jeff. I told you. I'm giving your brain signs. You dream what I want you to—for now at least. Like I said last night, accuracy is important."

Oddly, this made sense. Jeff's prior dreams were more visceral, in first person, it was *him* in the dream along with the bull, with the deer, the maybe-jaguars. The frog dream was just a picture, moving, like a screensaver washed over his brain. Jeff, the man, wasn't present at all. "So you make me dream what you want?"

"Couldn't well verify your knowledge if I hadn't read the textbook first."

"I don't understand why we can't just do what will help me. What does the bull mean?"

"The bull means that you were scared something was wrong with you. But that fear was so irrational that you couldn't go to a doctor about it, and so your solution was to go online and send an email to the Society of Divine Dreams."

Jeff ignored the possible insult. "The bull really doesn't mean anything?"

Gilbert rocked his feet down and leaned in, spilling some coffee past the brim and it dragged down around the base to a semi-circle. "It's not that it doesn't mean *anything*, it's that, well, frankly, dreams can be fucking weird. And I can't confirm that you really saw what you think you saw, Jeff." Gilbert's harsh shift in tone knocked Jeff off-balance like a stranger bumping into him at the grocery store. He didn't speak. "Look at it this way. You ever see *Karate Kid*?" Jeff nodded. "Yeah, so wax on, Jeff-san. Wax on. Pretty soon you'll be sweeping that bull's leg."

Jeff felt oddly assured by the implication that improvement was likely. He was used to Colson covering his glasses with spittle over nothing at all, but Gilbert seemed to possess a noticeable amount of faith in him.

"Wax on?"

"Wax on. Okay, same as last night. Just go to sleep. You should be having the same dream again. It's already done on my end. But you really need to get there, really need to pay attention, give me those details." Jeff felt like a "champ" was coming next, but alas. "I'm not trying to nag you here but also please kindly use your internet skills to look up the difference between a frog and a toad. I'm gonna take off." Gilbert rose, skidding his giant-sized shoes along the laminate. "Same time tomorrow night?" Jeff knew if Gilbert kept coming by at the hour he did, Kate would always be asleep and unwakeable. And if his dreams kept haunting him like they had been, Jeff would be more than happy to avoid sleep and stop them.

Again, Jeff felt almost weightless. He teetered through the off-white hallways of his home, some color that Kate picked out, but now he felt he should know what it was. Was it beige or taupe, something like that? He could probably look it up, but unless it appeared in a somnolent vision, he'd let it go. The toothbrush wound around his mouth and tickled his mustache. He spat and washed and laid down next to Kate as she grinded the air.

In the winter, the only things Jeff appreciated were an excuse to stay inside and the shimmering reflection of the moon on snow crawling over the slats of the bedroom blinds. A positive thinker would find more to be appreciative of.

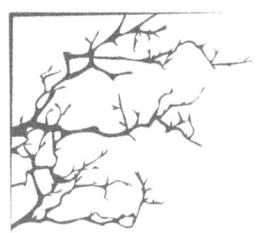

Night Six

Jeff woke in quiet and lurched his heavy top half up. Out from under the covers. Down the hall. The legal pad. Be specific.

Pink. Vivid pink, deep. Circles of pink that went light dark mid, light dark mid. Three circles in the pattern. A frog or toad in the center on a burnt tuft of grass. The frog/toad was white or beige or taupe on the bottom and had green—hunter green!—spots speckled along the top half. On its side was a tattoo of a heart with an arrow through it.

Brilliant.

He kicked out of his chair and stammered down the hall and noticed the clean air in his ears. In the room, the bed was empty; Kate was gone. Jeff thought it impossible. Kate never woke early for any reason ever, like she was sleep's captive and the ransom was simply time. Then he realized he took so long being absolutely sure about the frog dream that the sun smashed over the hills and through slits in the blinds. She may have had an emergency at work, he told himself. Probably some wealthy guy got his front teeth knocked out and he's got wedding photos at noon. Jeff licked his lips, missing a goodbye kiss.

As he stepped each trunky leg into his greyed slacks, he thumbed a message in his phone to Kate saying *Missed you this morning* and threw a heart in there for good measure. If she was gluing some moron's canine back on he shouldn't expect an answer for a while, but her exit sloshed at the bottom of his skull like swamp spray. He should take care not to let his new focus on being a Shark distract him from Kate.

Strange as it was, Jeff liked being something—a Shark—it was like an accomplishment or a proud title. He had issues with his others: accountant, being that he wanted to knuckle in Colson's skull every day. Ex-boxer, as along with this phrasing came to mind the words "washed up" and "has been" or the dreadful "not good enough." And husband, in that Kate felt more than arms reach away despite their scraping heels and clacking knees in the night. The downside was he couldn't picture himself sharing with anyone. *Hey Howard, guess what this weird guy told me I was!* Probably not going to win him any admirers at the poker game. He needed to go withdraw some nickels for this week's session.

His day at the office was 50 percent printing out Colson's berating emails and chewing pieces of them to spit in his mailbox, 25 percent checking and re-checking his phone for messages from Kate, and 25 percent learning the difference between a frog and a toad for tonight's meeting. The dumpy Kate-pond sloshing at the bottom of his brain had a stick tossed into it which rippled away scum and torn lily pads: he was likely spending most of his evening with a bald smoker rather than his wife.

Frogs, it turns out, are the more athletic-looking of the two. They typically have smoother skin, smaller, more pointed noses and wonky long legs for evasive sproinging. Often brighter. Toads are the great dumpy ones. Often larger, wide noses, tend to look lumpy and dull. Jeff's vision was almost certainly of a toad, and photos lined up with the colors that he noted—at least the hunter green part. And it must be a toad because Gilbert specifically made a comment about it, unless the suggestion was a trick to make him mindlessly vacillate and warble. Now to sort out that white/beige/taupe problem. Jeff quickly learned that taupe was more of a greyish brown and decided it wasn't the one. He'd stick with beige.

He didn't get an official reply from Kate, only a "heart" over the message he sent her. Jeff hated this. He tried to convince himself it was just her being busy, but his swamp brain swirled and tormented, wondering what was so hard about typing a message. Fool of a man, he told himself. Back on that positivity, now. Perhaps a bottle of wine would play it right. A nice gesture, an out-of-the-way gesture, with the potential to loosen her up a smidge. Jeff slipped into the store for a bottle of red from the middle shelf, then swung by the bank for a few clunking rolls of nickels. Class.

The wine bottle waited. Kate came home late enough for Jeff's mind to circle the drain of doubt and destruction for miles. By the time she spilled through the front door, blurry, he already hated, loved, re-hated, then feverishly adored, worshipped, and idolized her patient footfalls and longed for the howling snores she whirled out every night. "Sorry I was gone so long." Her voice sagged and rumbled. "I'm so tired, Jeff. I'm just going to go to bed."

"Yeah, sure. Rough day?" but the door already shut. At close to 7:30 p.m., Jeff was surprised Kate hadn't slammed her car into some ditch after passing out behind the wheel. He poured the whole bottle of red into a McDonald's cup and slurped from it, grating.

Jeff leaned heavy on the door as he swung it open at Gilbert's knock. He dropped into the chair and it buckled from the shock. Gilbert slipped a tan and white cigarette pack from his jacket. "You smoke?"

"I don't care," and waved it away when Gilbert pointed a filtered end out to him. Jeff conceded that the nagging smoke smell in the kitchen would perhaps give Kate a reason to talk to him. Gilbert struck his cigarette up and reclined in the wooden-backed chair, his coat jangling with tiny clinks of metal, tossing his legs up to the corner of the table and crossing them. Jeff settled on it now: Gilbert's suit was the color that fingertips turn after they'd pinched cigarettes for years.

"How'd it go last night?" He wasn't dragging yet, just watching Jeff's eyes, dull.

"Well," he tried to siphon the wine from his brain to his liver for a proper recount. "Think I can get it right. A pink background, pink circles flowing out from the center. Three shades of pink that go from lightest to darkest to middle and repeats with the ripples. In the center on some brown grass is a toad. It has a beige underside and hunter green spots all over its top." Gilbert's eyebrows raised one percent, just enough to let Jeff know he was interested. "And the toad had a tattoo on its side of a heart with an arrow through it."

As he said it, Jeff leaned back in his chair, kicking his feet up on the opposite end that Gilbert did. He felt satisfied. Confident. Gilbert gave nothing away. He pulled his feet down and stepped to the coffee machine to make his own cup. He knew where the grounds were, where to find filters, and slapped the switch over. He leaned on the counter. He, finally, smoked, with a smushed up mouth and squinting eyes daggering Jeff's.

"I got it, didn't I?"

"Beige, huh?"

Wasn't it?, he thought.

"I would have gone with off-white, but beige is pretty good. And it seems you now know what a damn toad looks like." Another drag. The coffee was ready. He piled a mountain of sugar past the brim. Jeff expected him to start chewing the drink any second. "I'll say you're getting there." Getting there? How many more nights could this last, waxing on? Jeff, perhaps encouraged by the wine dampening the sting of grit in his finger joints, wanted to fight; fight his life, his dreams. Fight for his wife. "But that bit you gave, that's not bad." As Gilbert's lips clamped on the filter, his lip became more pronounced in color as his unscarred flesh brightened.

"Thank you," Jeff said.

Gilbert shoved one hand to his hip, brushing his yellow blazer to the side, and there was that metallic jangling again. "What color was the arrow?"

Oh. "The shaft or the feathers?"

"Feathers, huh?" Weren't they? He thought so. "Yeah, what color were the feathers, Jeff?"

"Yellow." Probably.

"And the shaft?"

"Brown." Seemed a gimme. But now he wondered if he should have said black. Gilbert's eyes flared him over his coffee cup which read, "Opinions are like assholes, everyone's got one."

"Anatomical or cartoon?"

"What?"

"The heart."

"It was a cartoon shape, like a butt with a point at the bottom."

Gilbert laughed at this and paused before chewing into his coffee.

"What did the heart say?"

Jeff tried not to give his lie away. He was so close. "Mom."

"*Not* good enough." Ashes drizzled to the laminate. Jeff's drunken brain swooned. He didn't understand. He couldn't remember, didn't even realize, that the heart was so detailed. "But we're getting there. I bet after tonight you hit it right on the head." He dragged. "Then we can move on." He puffed.

"What are you doing here?"

Gilbert shuffled in the seat. The pop of his puckered lips trading the cigarette to his fingers stung in Jeff's ears. "I guess I'm listening to you tell me your *somnolent visions*, Jeff."

"No. What do you do all day here when you're not here with me?"

Gilbert squared his eyes to Jeff's and smirked. "Paperwork." Jeff's reaction urged him forward. "Hell, you know, it's just like what you do. Buncha shit, buncha dumb stuff." He waved his pluming hand to and fro at an invisible audience. "What do *you* do when I'm not here with you?" His head bobbled like it would teeter off his neck.

Jeff thought of his interactions with Gilbert so far, his perfectly timed coming and goings, the van, how he left exactly when Jeff called the useless cops, and returned to his curb once they left; how he knew where things like coffee were in his home. "Surprised you don't know that already." Gilbert grinned, showing his yellow-kissed teeth.

"You got me. I know what you do. But I don't know *why*. And that'll all come," he shifted forward, "in time," he was standing, gnashing the last of his coffee, "once you can tell me what you see."

"Another night?"

"Another night. Just like last night. It's already been done, the signs and whatnot. You'll dream of the frog—toad—and the pink and the grass and the tattoo, just pay it some good attention, really get in there."

"Yeah."

"And once you do, we can do what everyone loves about oneiromancy." Gilbert took a deep breath, "*Therapy*," and sighed it out. Gilbert stepped into the gross snow, melted and refrozen over the cloudy days and white nights. He climbed into his van and spun his cigarette butt to the neighbor's curb.

Jeff zombied to the bedroom, still half drunk, and laid down.

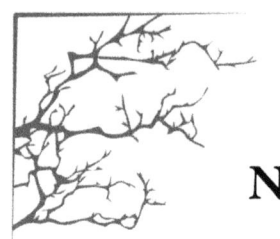

Night Seven

He woke up. The background wasn't pink anymore, it was bright, drinkable orange. Yellow feathers on the arrow. Black shaft. The tattoo read "Frog."

Kate spent most of the day out with coworkers, helping to plan an anniversary party for Claudia. Jeff didn't ask how long they'd been married, as it occurred to him that he and Kate never had an anniversary party despite several major milestones rolling on by like bumbling tumbleweeds. Despite the dream last night being so simple and, admittedly, very non-threatening, he couldn't help but picture Kate's weedy arm with a heart tattoo on it that read "wife."

Poker with his old coworkers; Jeff had been looking for a comfortable way out of these gatherings for months. The regularity of it smothered him like a chore he needed to complete, yet he showed up week after week. Depending on the game, six or seven men, not including Jeff, huddled in Howard's warm garage, roasting from a bulky space heater glowing in the corner. Howard's glistening black motorcycle still uncovered despite the snow on the ground, possibly just polished again since last week. The bike hulked like a reclining chair with a highway destroying engine nailed to it.

Peter, a pointy-faced man with leathery skin sent cards around the table, then paired them up on a second lap. Blinds went in. Jeff always offered a blind bet to stay in the game. Just enough to see where things go.

Howard also operated under this principle. His big face loomed under his trucker hat, mustache wide, blanketed his upper lip. Howard was a smiler, a grinner, a laugher. And naturally, as a regular poker player, a damn liar. Jeff was used to Howard trying to scare him off, tossing nickels into the pot like a flex. Jeff needed to look for tics. Howard scanned the room. Remarked on the shine of his bike. Leaned back on his chair, cupping his cards like he was trying to fold them into an envelope. Jeff would raise. Howard would laugh and motion to the table with his big smile, lurching forward with his big teeth out. The boys around the table, usually not so forward with their coins, grimaced and exchanged winking eyes.

"Boy I'm gonna sleep good tonight," said Howard, as Jeff incorrectly called his bluffs. Jeff lost hand after hand after hand, until finally he bluffed aggressively on two of a kind (threes), and the lie swept most of the table's winnings to Jeff's cookie tin. They slid, clanging against each other and the side of the tin like a broken tambourine.

Gilbert arrived when he always did. The night was frigid, but the day had been warmer than expected, and flat grass crept from under the snow's oppression. Gilbert crossed his legs on the table. He brought his own coffee, snapped up from a local favorite café. It said "Finnegan" on it, scraggled in watery-black pen. It didn't surprise Jeff that Gilbert would be wary about giving out his real name. The type of man who slinks in the woods and drives an unmarked van likely wouldn't share his life's story with strangers. Jeff would call him Gilbert until he learned otherwise.

"You smoke?" He lifted a tan and white plastic-wrapped pack from his jacket.

"No, but you may." Gilbert thanked him and burned the end of one with a cheap green lighter. The singed tip crawled along the stem towards Gilbert's scarred mouth and yellow teeth.

Speaking loudly, comfortable in Jeff's kitchen, Gilbert asked, "So what's the good news?" and blew out a heavy burst. "Did you see the whole thing?"

"I think I did." It was a matter-of-fact statement, shoving aside Jeff's doubts. Jeff clasped his hands together at the center of the table. Jeff was bothered by the last two nights; Kate's absence, despite his declaration not to let her drag away like rope through his glassy palms; the simple pettiness of Gilbert, who, just days ago, flashed photos from outside his bedroom window, who told him of oneiromancy and the ability to change his life, who told Jeff he was a Shark, that he was special. Who snuck dreams to him like fingers behind his head in a photograph, like a "kick me" sign slapped to his back. "Should I start from the top?"

"Yeah Jeff, you should. Go ahead and start with the pink circles." His hands were cupped at the base of his head, displacing what remained of his spare combover. One side of his oversized jacket sunk with pocket-weight. The pink circles, the clanging idea in his brain all day, and Gilbert dropped bait for him. Or had he? Last night, Gilbert introduced a new layer to it all by telling Jeff what he would dream. But he didn't. Not exactly. The vision played out like it had the previous two nights, plus Jeff's attention snapped to certain details Gilbert deemed important, but the entire background was different.

One of two things happened: either Gilbert lied to him about what his dream would be, or Jeff wasn't seeing what Gilbert wanted, some wires crossed in Jeff's somnolent mind, the signals Gilbert sent him. Maybe Gilbert hasn't fed dreams to people with a history of concussions? This process grated on Jeff, and he didn't feel as encouraged or inflated by Gilbert's small optimism anymore. He wanted to get down to business, to make his life better. He hated this inane process, this game Gilbert was playing. Or seemed to be playing.

"What's the point of this?"

Gilbert's face fell. "I told you the other day. Need to make sure your brain is tuned right. Like a gee-tar." He sat up. "Your hands might be forming the shape of a G chord but if the tuning's in drop D—or worse—it's not gonna be a G. We gotta play G's, Jeff. G's when the sheet music calls for it. Wax on, remember?"

"Yeah." Something wasn't right, but with whom? Was Jeff's own brain out of tune? He bluffed at poker, maybe a bluff now would win him the pot. "There were feathers on the arrow, like I said last night, and they were yellow, like I said last night. But I guessed last night. I made sure today. Yellow feathers. A black shaft on the arrow—you knew I guessed last night because I said brown." Gilbert grinned with half of his mouth. Yellow teeth simmered smoky behind his lips. "The tattoo didn't say 'Mom,' it said 'Frog,' which explains why I thought the toad was a frog. And that's that."

"So you told me about the tattoo. What about the rest?" Jeff sensed Gilbert sniffing out his annoyance. "Just for formality's sake. Be specific."

Jeff committed. "Vivid pink circles emanating out in rings of three, going from lightest, neutral, to darkest, from a toad with a beige bottom half and hunter green spots spread along top. The toad is sitting on a burnt patch of grass. The tattoo of the cartoon heart with an arrow through it is on its side. Its left side."

Gilbert bobbed his head, tossed smoke past his lips and smiled. "Yes! I mean, I would assume you called it a frog because Americans, by and large, refer to that particular brand of amphibian as frogs across the board. You'd think they forgot about the Princess and the Toad. Ha!" Jeff nodded in agreement, hoping the lie was the right choice. "But that's good. Very good. The tattoo; that's the thing I'm talking about. Details. Subliminal details will get you there. You won't always notice them, but they affect you. Intensely." He leaned in. "Your brain will unlock massive potential."

Jeff wasn't sure that statement meant anything at all. "Should I have mentioned that the toad had two eyes, too?"

Kicking his chair back to all fours, Gilbert laughed and said, "No, no. That's expected. If a man has a pointy nose, it's not necessarily important unless it's *really* pointy, or it's broken, or he's got septum piercing or something, you know, like a bullring? Two eyes; normal. One eye," and he said this, gesturing the cindered end of his cigarette at Jeff with each word, "extremely important detail." He took a long, quiet drag and relaxed back against the wood of the chair.

Jeff was relatively certain his bluff worked. However, this introduced the snag that his visions weren't quite what Gilbert intended. He got the big picture, but clearly some aspects didn't jive. Would the color of rings blaring out from a toad really be that big of a deal? Once they fell into the full swing of oneiromancy, what would the ultimate consequence of this lie become? Jeff pictured the *Challenger* rocket bursting in a bouquet of torrid smoke, the result of some faulty plastic seals. Possibly the smallest detail aboard a billion-dollar investment blew the whole thing. Jeff needed to be careful, pay as much attention as possible to his dreams. Gilbert was vague discussing what could change in his life, but Jeff needed to be sure he didn't sprout a third arm or something even crazier.

"Jeff, it's time we talked a little bit about what the hell you're doing."

Maybe it wasn't the best bluff? "What do you mean?"

"You contacted the Society. Your dreams scared you, you said. Most of my clients aren't exactly hitting a ten on happiness, you know what I mean? Hell, half the time I come over here you look like somebody shit right in your morning cereal." Gilbert upended his coffee cup and a caffeine river gushed past his lips.

"I guess there's some things I'd like to change with my life." He just said it.

"Go on." A tremendous pull on the cigarette, almost to the filter.

"The reason I emailed. I want the dreams to stop."

"Hmm, no. Not true. You thought your dreams might mean something—and they can mean something, in time. But stop, no, they won't be stopping anytime soon. And trust me, you don't want them to. The potential is too great to waste. What else?"

"I hate my job."

"Welcome to America!" he guffawed and rested with his shoulders jammed to his ears on the back of the chair. "But you don't quit." It wasn't a question.

"I'll be able to retire soon."

"Oh? You're not *that* old, Jeff."

"I've worked there a long time. It would be early retirement, but only just. I probably wouldn't be able to scrape by forever. And I don't want to put that on the wife."

"Mmhm. Jobs suck, Jeff. If they were fun, they wouldn't have to pay you to do them. Like this! You're not paying me because I like sitting in kitchens with middle-aged men that give me shit." Jeff's eyes jerked up, but he played off like he saw a fly at the back of the room. Gilbert slipped another cigarette from his pack and lit up. He stuffed the butt of the other in the pack. Jeff appreciated this, didn't want Kate to see evidence if she couldn't already smell it. "But I get it. So the job could be better. Boss breathing down your neck all the time."

"Literally breathes down my neck. Just always seems to have it out for me."

"Yeah, we can see about that. And you know, we're getting a bit on, you and I. Not ready to retire or anything but high school, hell, college was a long time ago. Each day has to count. You're smart, you know that." Gilbert stood from his chair, squeaking the legs along, and walked over to the coffee station. He knocked the remainder in his cup back down his throat. Jeff thought he saw him chew. "You can't let time get away from you. We should make it a priority to address your employer aysap." Gilbert filled his cup and dumped most of the container of sugar inside as well. "What about the fact that you've spent most nights this week hanging out with an ugly bald guy?

Think that could maybe improve?" Gilbert stabbed, going for nerves.

"I suppose." Jeff tried to remain calm. "Kate and I have been together a long time. It's probably natural for couples to grow apart, but I guess I just want to be closer. We don't have any children or pets or anything, and she's all I've got." Admitting there was an issue with his life at all felt like ripping off his own skin for show, but he *knew it*, and somehow the act of saying it out loud to Gilbert Finnegan tossed his stomach in loops but lightened him like a pressure valve cracking open and whooshing.

"Jeff. Jeffy boy. That's not true!" Gilbert hurled his ugly legs back to the table and crossed his feet over. "You've got me." And he exploded into terrible forward laughter. His palm slammed the table, loud enough to wake a normal wife. "You've got me, buddy! And we trust each other. Of course. And you're a Shark! You've got more going for you than you might think. You've got friends aside from ol' me. How'd poker go today?"

Another detail Gilbert knew that Jeff never mentioned. How much of this dance was a test? Was just tuning the gee-tar? Jeff felt like Gilbert was a dark circus tent swallowing the air over him and soon it would just be elephant shit and popcorn butter. "I won so many nickels my cookie tin weighs almost ten pounds, I'm sure of it." He laughed.

"It's heavy. Yeah. Hard to carry around. I get it. You haven't talked to a guy or heard of a guy named Jericho Dillinger have you?"

"No, should I?"

"No!" Stern, another heavy slam on the table that almost bounced his coffee cup to the laminate. "No. I'd hope not."

Jeff hesitated to press him about it, but another sudden mood swing from Gilbert seemed suspicious. "He's from the Society. Asshole. Said he was thinking of taking on some work in the area and *you* are the only lead here so he must have meant you. Just wanted to make sure."

"Never heard of him. You're the only one from the Society I've been in contact with. What's the deal with you all anyway? Is there like a big building or company picnics or something?"

Gilbert chortled. "Hell, I'm surprised you didn't look that up yourself, ya little googler! Thought you would have found the business license and seen what type of entity they were, found the headquarters address and maybe even done one of those street view things where you might see someone picking their nose on the street corner. Heh."

"I didn't, no." It was odd, admittedly. Jeff couldn't remember the last time he saw a doctor, instead googling his symptoms and handling it himself. He did the same whenever the washing machine failed, spilling over with scummy water, or if the oven needed a new element. He could fix them himself just as well. Maybe he should give himself more credit.

"Honestly, guy who runs the business is kind of an ass, but I'm a specialist, Jeff. Worked a long time at this stuff." Gilbert just looked at his cigarette like he was inspecting it for quality assurance. "Not a lot of places hiring oneiromancers." He smiled.

"So what now?"

Gilbert settled back into his seat, both feet planted. Jeff could tell Gilbert's coffee cup was empty due to the hollow plunk it made when he patted his fingers along the side. Jeff was a little jealous that Gilbert hadn't smashed his own hands to pulp in the past and could painlessly do something as simple and mindless as drum on a coffee cup. "We're not wasting any more time."

Did Gilbert think the last several days were a waste also? All the nonsense about tuning his brain like a gee-tar, the frog and the toad and the circle background. Rather than prepping for the show, would Gilbert rather have kicked the amps up to 11 and blammed away? If what Gilbert said was true—and Jeff somehow both doubted and sincerely hoped things could change for the better—then Jeff supposed his life would be better molded by careful hands rather than those of a madman. This realization unsettled him, given his recent choice to lie and derail the tuning process. Orange background.

"Tonight, It's all up to you. We'll know more tomorrow. You're in the driver's seat now, Jeff. But the process is all the same. You have a sweet ol' dream and write it down. If you're specific enough, then we'll have some direction."

Jeff heaved a stale breath out. He realized his chest was strained and taut for some time now. "Do you know if it'll be bad or not? Like before, with the bull?"

A quick grin, almost meant as a condescension, "I really don't. If I was a betting man, but really that's more your style it seems, then I'd say yes. And I say that because those types of dreams are what brought us both here in the first place. Who knows? Maybe the last couple days have given you some perspective or inspiration, and your brain won't have to be so aggressive in grabbing your attention. Maybe you're capable of making the changes you want with some more subtle hints."

Gilbert's optimism pleased Jeff.

"—But I doubt it," he added, before Jeff's mind could stroll too far down that path. "Besides, for me personally, a Shark is useful because of the potential for their dreams to affect reality, and in turn, for reality to affect dreams. It's at that point that we follow the trail of breadcrumbs, adding a few of our own to the mix to see if we can alter the path, even slightly. That's why I'm here."

"So you think I could change some things?"

Gilbert blew a plume of smoke from the side of his mouth. "Some things, yeah."

Gilbert said he wanted to meet somewhere else the next night, which Jeff agreed if for no other reason than to keep Kate from noticing the smoke scent dangling near the refrigerator. The slog back to the bedroom carried his mind to frantic places. Jeff ping-ponged between commitment to the current plan and a crawling, hooking fear that pushed him to email Gilbert about the orange background. Maybe he could still pass it off as a mistake? *Sorry Gilbert, I think the biggest part of the vision was actually a completely different color than what I told you, ha ha ha. What now?* But was it better to fake it 'til he made it or beg for forgiveness? *We trust each other*, Gilbert said. Did he know? Was this an underhanded dig? Gilbert dealt a lot with the subliminal, given that he'd guided his dreams to very specific places the last several nights via "signs" Jeff hadn't been able to recognize.

Jeff stepped through the door frame to a sound like ripping chainsaws coming from Kate's side of the bed. He stripped and slipped under the covers while the snowshine bled over the blinds. The bedroom was harder to observe that night. Immense darkness and his aged, failing eyes made it so that if anything was displaced, he often stumbled over it. Kate never woke, though. Jeff laid his head down and tried to relax the wadded knot in his stomach.

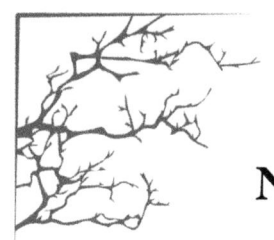

Night Eight

It wasn't as he expected. He woke confused, wondering if something was wrong in his REMmed out brain. Still, Jeff made the trudge to the writing desk and the folded sheets of the legal pad. His pen slithered in his wet grip.

Three equal, flat, matte columns. Plain white, plain red, plain yellow, from left to right. The columns loomed forward, closer and closer to my POV. The closer they got to me, they started to vibrate. Their shaking bled them together. The dream whited over and repeated to the tune of hundreds, hundreds.

The dreams he experienced earlier, even the ones brought on by Gilbert, had a focus; the frog—toad—with the tattoo. The circles. The bull charging, the jaguars hounding the deer. This dream was just lines of color.

And it fell over his head like a black bag, mugging him and kidnapping his pride.

Gilbert *had* fed him a dream that night. The shaking columns merging their colors. White and red make pink, red and yellow make orange. Jeff didn't need to feign recognition of goldenrod or fuchsia; these were plain primary colors. Gilbert mocked him in his sleep. *A lie for a lie*, he thought. Jeff was at once annoyed by the waste of time—a whole day, lost, though Jeff tried not to focus on years lost as an accountant—and echoes of last night's conversation wormed their way back. And at the same time, he couldn't help but be impressed with Gilbert's ability: something Gilbert did triggered these effects, such specific visions Jeff experienced. And all before, he dreamt of nothing at all, not even blackness. Jeff always comforted himself with the audible of pulverizing Gilbert should the situation call for it. But now, seeing this, he thought Gilbert was right; the potential was too great to waste. Gilbert's *power*, for lack of a better term, to show Jeff exactly what he wanted while he slept was like a dragging weight plummeting in quicksand. How deep could this go? Was Jeff prepared for whatever Gilbert could do for his life? If he could feed him dreams to make fun of him, he could certainly do so to make him even more miserable. Jeff felt like a guinea pig for science. No exchange of money. Gilbert told him this little exercise was all in the name of good research and the benefit of other people, but here he was, overstretching his reach and playing coy. Jeff would have to come clean. There was no way around it. Likely Gilbert had some fantastic prank lined up to spring on him at the meeting tonight, as if he wouldn't expect someone as thick as Jeff to figure the signals out.

Jeff pondered this for so long that Kate swept through the hallway straight out the door in her scrubs without acknowledgement. It happened again. His head fell to his hands, and he would have massaged his temples if it didn't feel like micro-knives poking into his finger joints.

Kate blew back through the front door later than usual. Jeff had been bouncing between concern, frustration, and dread with every minute that ticked by without a follow up message to his *Where are you?* he'd sent an hour before. For some reason, when he saw her, smearing tears with the heel of her hand, he thought of the name Jericho Dillinger—likely a sick plant from Gilbert—and clenched. Regardless, he shoved up from the couch, not bothering to mute the news he was too distracted to listen to, and dog-earing his copy of *Catcher in the Rye*, wondering why the liberals had it banned—he'd have to look it up when he finished—and went to her.

Kate explained between sheer breaths and wails: "Claudia's at the hospital from a car wreck, some drunk driver." Claudia, her coworker, her friend even, who talked with Jeff at the bar the week before, was hungover when he and Kate went to dinner, whose anniversary party was now on hold.

"I'm so sorry, honey." In truth, he was only mildly affected. He didn't know Claudia that much aside from their brief talk. He recalled her name jumbled in the blender of things Kate prattled about over the years when she got home from work and yacked her dreadful day out on him. But these days he thought her spilling her work beans would be a welcome change. For all Jeff knew, she might have hated Claudia once, but sometimes people get in the habit of feeling comfortable, like bad things only happen in third-world countries and on the news to other people. "How can I help?" He impressed himself with his support.

Kate threw her arms around his neck, and she sponged her wet face against his shirt. Her head, her soft, greying hair, nudged up and down with her gasps and he kissed it at appropriate intervals while swaying in a quarter-circle like a slow dance. In light of his hopes to repair and cultivate their relationship, Jeff decided it was best to let this ride as much as possible. As long as his knees didn't go numb, he would stay here, swaying. Fortunately for his knees, she pulled back and looked up, chocolate eyes walled in pink. She kissed him, genuine and full. Jeff answered, and his hands found gentle ways to comfort her shoulders, her back. It could have taken an hour and Jeff wouldn't have realized it. Aside from spare morning pecks the two of them hadn't kissed like that in recent memory. Surely a good sign. He would do his best to follow it to the T.

"Should I make some dinner?" he offered. He could tell she was initially a hair flustered that it wasn't already in the works, but something quelled her, and she nodded, scrambling for a tissue. Jeff bumbled through the kitchen, hoping now that she *couldn't* smell the cigarette smoke lest it derail the conversation. He clanged a dented pot from under a larger, Russian doll setup of pots and started water to simmer. "Do you want to talk about it?" It was the right move to be sensitive. Allow her to come to him.

Kate dropped into the same seat Jeff spent hours in this week and looked at nothing in particular across the room. Jeff rumbled through the fridge. "We just didn't see her today. She didn't show up for work. And Dr. Teague got a call from her husband from the hospital. He just stomped in the staff room and said it to all of us right before patient care started. It's been up there, above my head, all day." She sipped water from a faded glass. "I'm just processing everything right now. They said she might not make it." Jeff thought that sounded a touch dramatic. No, no, he didn't know the situation, he just needed to be here for Kate, with whom nothing was wrong, and no car had crunched over. Positive thinking. "Can you believe some asshole was drunk that early? It happened as she left her house."

"Some people just don't know how their actions can hurt others. They think only of themselves." A positive, helpful partner would be supportive yet condemning at just the right moments, especially when dealing with a wrong such as this. Kate slurped again. He discovered an opened box of pasta and remnants of a brick of parmesan. The pasta was at the foaming stage in the jumping water. He let a few silent seconds air over them and decided to put the gas pedal down. "Are you feeling okay?" Pure emotional combusting power.

"I'm not sure. I want to talk to her. I could call her now. Her name's right here." She waved her phone, glowing, between her fingers. It brushed over her wedding ring. "But I know it's dead on the other end." Jeff raised his head to her.

"Not dead, surely."

"That was a bad choice of words," Kate said. Jeff resumed stirring, keeping the noodles from gluing themselves to the bottom of the pot and blowing bubbles away from the top. "I want to push this button to reach her, to ask her how she is. I just know better."

"Do you know her husband's number?" She shook her head. "You could call the doctor—your boss, Dr. Teague, and see if he's heard anything." Jeff regretted this as soon as it tumbled off his tongue; maybe it wasn't wise to suggest she seek reassurance from another man. Not Claudia's husband, whatever his name is. Not her boss, Dr. Teague. Not Jericho Dillinger, the phantom oneiromancer.

Thankfully, "I think he's got it worse than the rest of us do. It's his office, his insurance plan. You know how those things are." Kate did that thing where she tipped her cup fully vertical, hoping to eke out one last drop trickling to the rim. "I think I'm better off letting him be. It can happen to anyone."

"To me, to you, yeah." Kate's hands hugged the desert-dry glass. Jeff dumped pasta straight to two bowls from the strained pan, flung a pat of butter in each, and sprinkled some grated parmesan on the top. The dish mushed and melted in pale cream. Jeff wondered if Gilbert would consider this beige. He forked each bowl and brought them to the table, sitting in Gilbert's spot. Kate thanked him. Jeff nodded, silent. They clanked and ate. A salty swell spread through Jeff's mouth. Kate thanked him again, added it was delicious, but left about half.

It was true, that *things* could happen to anyone. Part of Jeff's id-level fear circled around the possibility of terrible tragedies. With his dealings with the Society, at this moment, he only hoped he didn't make things worse. On the surface, his life seemed safe and secure. He had a house, a job, a wife; It was just barren of true pleasure and happiness. He hated his job, felt his wife hated him at times, and the house felt like a crinkling fire blanket unfit to drown either sadness out. The life he wanted to change wasn't tragic on the level of drunken car wrecks, but in terms of a lifetime spent wanting more, it might be a complete waste if he didn't act soon. He shoveled noodles into his mouth.

Jeff didn't float to the bedroom but walked behind Kate on his own two feet. She held his hand for the first time in recent memory. Thumbed his knuckle. They passed the threshold of the door and didn't turn the lights on.

Jeff slipped from under the covers, both those heating the bed and the cover of Kate's droning airway. He climbed into clothes and snatched his keys from the kitchen counter and drove to Shelley's Café on 14th Street.

Gilbert waited, half-shining in the overhead lights, seated on a puffy diner bench, near-finished with his first, or maybe tenth, coffee. That's why he wanted to come here, Jeff thought. Better coffee. This nighttime hangout was the only one like it in town, peppered with college kids studying and laughing and drooling over each other. The artsy crowd hung out here. Lots of English majors, poets, musicians. Kids in black, ripped jeans, jackets that said *SLUT* on them, or ironic pajamas with garlic bread patterns.

"Hey-hey, champ!" Gilbert greeted. He lifted his foam-crusted mug by the handle and gestured towards Jeff while he slid into the bench across from him and clattered the table askew.

"It was orange." Jeff fessed immediately.

Gilbert took half a beat too long before, "What was?"

"The circles around the toad were orange the other night, Gilbert. I'm sorry." Two college girls prepared to wrestle across the room.

"Are you serious?"

"I'm sorry I wasted your time, and mine, in turn. I lied."

"This is serious, Jeff, serious stuff." He swung forward, hunching, clenched, snapping the folds of his brow together in worry.

"I wanted to get past the wax on phase, and I thought that was the fastest way."

"Jeff, Jeff, listen—orange is serious. ORANGE? You're sure it was orange?"

Jeff tried to calm himself with a deep, belly bloating breath. "Yes, it was orange, Gilbert."

"Oh my god," he said, "do you know what this means?!"

Jeff knew better, in this particular moment, than to worry. "It means I lied and I wasted our time and I'm sorry."

"You just aren't any fun. I was about to really turn it up. I've been waiting for this all day." Gilbert genuinely looked a bit dejected. "Wait here, I'm gonna get more." He dragged his cup off the edge of the table, his yellowy blazer clanking like dampened wind chimes, and warbled over to the counter for a refill. Jeff stared, but not too much, at the girls diving into each other's laps. He wondered what he would think if they were his daughters. If he would be angry, if he would think *Hey, they're just being kids*, or if he'd be supportive and give them huge, dad-armed hugs. If he'd be able to save enough for tuition, or to get them a car, or a perfect dress for prom, and if he would have plowed through the slicing in his hands to pin a chilled flower to the front of it. If he'd have encouraged them to chase their dreams, like being a homeless poet or a painter, or forced them to be a doctor or a lawyer or a boxer, or worse, a goddamned accountant. He wondered if they'd be Sharks like him or air-plowing windmills like Kate. Wondered if Kate would even be the mother.

Gilbert slid back into the bench. His cup tossed some of the foam over the edge and it dragged down, staining brown. "So, just for formality's sake, go ahead and start with the pink circles, Jeff." He winked a greasy lid at him and tossed his legs to the side so his over-big shoes dunked into the walkway.

"Three columns of flat color, plain white, plain red, plain yellow. The columns shook and their edges combined to form pink between the white and red, and orange between the red and yellow. This repeated on a loop several hundred times."

Gilbert slapped his knees, motioning and laughing in directions around him to no one in particular, his laugh too gawdy and overloud for the occasion. None of the college students cared. A perfect setting to talk about oneiromancy. "God damn I got you good, huh? Whoo!" He dramatically punched his legs again and again, then abruptly stopped, swerved forward, "You don't seem to find this very funny."

"Sorry, Gilbert, I don't. I made a mistake, I understand."

"Yeah. Well. I'm not going to waste the line that I came up with for this occasion so buckle up: 'A lie for a lie, now a truth for a truth.'" He grinned wide and dumb. "You know, because you told me about the pink circles but I knew better and so I told you that you were going to have your own dreams and... you know?"

"Yes." The girls had crawled off one another and laughed, traded drinks and showed each other things on their phones, glowing in the iLight.

"I told you you were smart! Ahh. So, the truth is, I'm not giving you any signals tonight. Now I know, *I said that last night*, however, we trust each other again, we can actually get on to the science. Or, you know. The fun stuff."

"Why am I here, Gilbert?"

Not the response he expected, his shoulders shifted sideways. "You're scared. You're scared of your dreams. You dreamed, finally, and—"

"I think I'm depressed."

"Sure."

FATHER SLEEP

The girls in the corner winded down. They huddled back-to-back, necks craning their vertebrae in links to the next. The kind of position that Jeff would hate himself for even considering at his age. "This is a bad idea." Jeff continued to look over at them.

"Little young for us, don't you think, partner?"

"Gilbert, I'm gonna go home." Jeff tucked up to his feet and straightened his clothes.

Gilbert's face and voice morphed to stone, "I can't guarantee the dreams won't come back, Jeff."

"Yeah."

"Was it the light dream, was that too far?"

"Maybe." Jeff stepped to the counter.

"Sorry, Jeff—Mr. Vickers. You know how to reach me if you need to. I'm still willing."

"Sure." Jeff paid the barista at the till for the drinks of the sleepy girls in the corner and got swallowed by the snow.

The drive home pulverized his eyes, snow spilling over in endless breaths from the dark white. In his head he thought only of home: home and Kate. Beneath the tires, the streets threatened with freezing spite. Jeff's eyelids never raised over halfway, tranced by some kind of vulgar absence. The car never slid, slipped, or skittered, only rounded turns in heavy arcs hauling him forward like he was towed behind the swollen sail of his failures.

Entering the front door, moon pressing through the quartered window, Jeff's footsteps empty, barren, missing, he discarded his ice-blown boots and lurched in wet jeans to the bedroom. Kate's dream-drunk heaves like caverns engulfing him. He stripped and stepped into bed. He held her, arm over waist. He thanked whatever god might listen for Kate.

The night drank him.

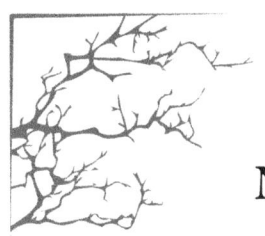

Night Nine

He made it through. Kate's skin seared. Jeff rolled away to seek a cold spot under the sea foam of blankets. He didn't dream.

Thoughts sunk over his head like a cracked, dripping egg, slowly, drying. Gilbert was not the answer. The Society of Divine Dreams was not the answer. He couldn't say for sure what the question was, but he was here, awake, and had a dreamless night of sleep. He knew, in the dark, cobwebbed, and slatted-over sections of his thoughts, there yelled a drowned voice that said *Gilbert's last favor*. Jeff's quiet night wasn't a mute from the oneiromancer. Things were getting better.

Kate stirred. Jeff put his lips to her back, her shoulder blade. She rose from the bed and slunk to the bathroom, not facing him. *She'll come around*, Jeff thought. How long had he been absent or neglectful? How many days, months, years had he spoiled? The coffee shop washed him in the cold breath of perspective. He realized what he had by venture of what he did not, and he did not want to conflate or combine the two.

"Have you heard about Claudia?" he asked when Kate walked, naked, back through the door.

"Her husband posted she's still alive. She lived through a hard surgery."

"Amazing. That's great news."

"Yes," she said. There's a chance, Jeff thought. A chance that this would all work out. He reached for her, but she stepped past him to the closet and into a black pair of scrubs. Before cinching them tight, Kate traded them out for a bright blue instead. Jeff figured it wasn't just simple preference that prompted the change. She'll come around.

While his solution to the Kate dilemma was to care and empathize, his solution to the Colson attrition was to avoid it altogether. Jeff sent an email, the most impersonal of alerts, that he would be out. He didn't give a reason, didn't say he was bedridden or that a family member died. Just said he wouldn't be in. Not every problem can be solved with care and empathy. Some problems need space, he told himself.

Jeff still collected his things as if he were going to work, and when Kate stepped out the front door with only a quiet wave, he waited a few beats until she was down the road a bit and climbed into his own car.

He drove to the hospital and found, far from the front sliding glass doors, a cramped parking spot and entered the walk-in clinic. The open layout of the room let subdued murmurs wash around the walls. Rattling clacks of the receptionists and forever ringing phones (a muffled tune Jeff couldn't place, perhaps "Frere Jacques"?) thankfully covered the whispers of patients clutching towels to their faces, tipping to one side of their faded cushioned chairs, and hacking hard into paper medical masks.

It took over an hour before an overweight nurse dragged Jeff back into a blaring room, and she mentioned his own weight. She checked his blood pressure and told him a combination of numbers that he didn't understand the meaning of, and she clarified, "The doctor will go over it." She sat at a computer and, with a voice attempting to sound happy and energized, "So you're having trouble sleeping, Jeff?" Jeff nodded his head. "How much sleep do you get each night?" After each question her eyes never turned to Jeff, and instead hung on the screen like half-drawn curtains.

"Maybe three to six hours."

"How long has this been occurring?"

"A week or so."

Her eyes finally left the screen to pierce his own for a brief beat, then sucked back to the monitor and she clacked her notes on the keyboard. The nurse had short fingernails painted a gagging red. Jeff realized he didn't know what Kate's nails looked like. She asked more questions he didn't think were relevant or was ready to address, about his diet, vitamins, exercise, libido, caffeine intake, tobacco, alcohol, and drug use. Jeff felt his jaw stiffen and the tendon at the back of his knee clenched. He should have done this himself with a google search.

When the nurse finally left, he pulled out his phone and checked. He stumbled upon things like "nightmare disorder," which typically affected children, but could also lead to suicidal thoughts. Jeff didn't think he had those but also couldn't picture a child having them either. Jeff saw a fake bouquet of purple flowers leaning in a clear vase without water. He wondered if Kate would like them, and decided he'd pick some up when he was done. The posters on the wall were of cross-sections of spines, brains, organs, elderly people smiling in fields with blocky text that read "DEMENTIA" across their necks.

The doctor, who introduced herself as Dr. Williams, finally rushed in 20 minutes later than the nurse said she would. She was young, with a ponytail that was dyed some warped brown color that he didn't like. He looked at her pale hands and saw she had blue nail polish on. Mental note to look at Kate's nails.

"So you're having trouble sleeping, Jeff?" Deja vu. Jeff nodded. "How much sleep do you get each night?" It was all Jeff could do to keep from wrenching the computer screen around to see what the hell the chunky nurse typed out.

"Between three and six hours, it's been going on about a week." And then Gilbert's sneering voice rattled in his head, *A lie for a lie.* "I don't sleep much because of bad dreams." The young doctor looked over, her ponytail swishing behind her. "Nightmares."

She set her jaw and chewed on her lip. "You're concerned about nightmares?"

"I never dreamed before. Ever. Now I'm afraid to sleep."

"Any big changes lately?" He could tell she was giving him the benefit of the doubt, trying not to laugh a grown man out of the office.

"Just the dreams."

"No deaths in the family, no stress? Work okay?" Dr. Williams paused and adjusted in her seat. "Marriage?" She covered it up quickly with a breath and, "Anything?" Jeff's forehead hurt and he realized the top half of his face was clenched like he just had a bucket of ice water sloshed over his head. "Sometimes things like this can come from anxiety or depression, you know. Your heart rate is a little high." Dr. Williams crossed one leg over the other. "But that can sometimes just be from being at the doctor, being stressed because of that."

"You think I'm depressed?" His hands sweat into the paper on the bed.

"I don't know, Jeff. It's possible. This is the first time I'm seeing you, so I'm just presenting some options. It's possible that you could have a genuine problem, but it's only been occurring a short time, so I'm hesitant to prescribe any medication or run any major tests." Jeff wondered what tests there could be for dreams, and pictured a toad nestled on burnt grass in a pink pond. "There's also your history of concussions. There are still studies ongoing regarding the long-term effects. My recommendation for now would be to refer you, either to a therapist or to a somnologist, for a sleep study. We could also discuss a neurologist, but I don't think that's fully warranted yet. I'd say the therapist might be better. There are several in town, usually covered by insurance, you could be seen in a few weeks most likely." Jeff's nostrils flared like bats were ready to fly out of them. "The sleep study is expensive and you'd have to go to Seattle. Your insurance might not cover it."

Jeff had his phone at the ready and squinted his eyes in the fluorescent lighting. "What do you know about," squinting further and preparing his tongue, "Charcot-Wilbrand syndrome?"

"Never heard of it."

"What about nightmare syndrome?"

"Have you heard of hypochondria?"

"Do you think I have it?"

"There's a good chance. The cure is a therapist."

"Sleep study, please."

Jeff left the hospital shaken and airy. He suspected they would feel differently about his heart rate now than they did then. He turned on the radio and heard about corporate giants polluting public lakes, a recently reopened nostalgia mall lit up with automatic rifle fire, and overcrowded school systems. This was all between intrusive thoughts of Kate and their strained relationship, and Colson's crowded forehead squished together in a tirade with spit littering his monitor. And then again, the furthest crawlspace near his occipital, the teetering hope that his dreamless nights would continue sunk into the folds of thought, a quiet pollution fogging his meninges.

The recurring thoughts of Kate and the implication that his inner thoughts were visible even to strangers meant that when he made it to the grocery store he couldn't exactly remember driving there. Plows stacked last night's snow into the corners of untrekkable intersections, pocked with gravel. Jeff bought a pre-made lasagna and a bouquet of white lilies.

Kate came home a bit later than usual (the lasagna near cool) and Jeff refused to allow the name Jericho Dillinger weasel into his head. Her scrubs were blown out with white and damp under the armpits.

"I wish you'd said something," she said after a quick and cool greeting. "A few of us are seeing Claudia tonight. But thank you." The lilies lay untouched and found their way to a McDonald's cup leaned against the refrigerator.

She'll come around, he thought. He hoped. He tried not to focus on the slight accusation from her suggestion, that *he* should have said something. Perhaps *she* should have said she was planning something, that she would be home late.

And there it was again, the lazy husband tendency, the negative thoughts. They weren't going to help. They were not caring and empathetic. The truth was that their marriage was fractured, and such things take time and tenderness to heal—healing he could handle himself, without a nosy shrink judging his every breath. The damage that years of neglect inflicted upon them wouldn't be undone with a frozen lasagna. Not only frozen lasagna, anyways. He dumped the lasagna into three different Tupperwares and tossed the tin.

Jeff scrubbed dishes crusting over in the sink. He made it to the living room and folded couch blankets up into stacks. In the bathroom, he cleaned the sink of his trimmed beard hairs and emptied the trash, even put a new liner in (but he eyed the trees behind the house when he lifted the can lid, seeing not a greasy man with a camera but a few small deer, a pack of them that wandered the neighborhood, now used to the passing cars and blaring headlights). He tried not to feel tired. The last week of minimal sleep dragged him down like his boots were inches deep in mud. Even Kate was still awake, he assumed, as she hadn't come home yet. There was the possibility she collapsed in a hospital chair next to a heater in Claudia's room. It was still early, though dark thanks to winter's relentless choke. Jeff gave up and decided to go to bed.

It was the first time in a long time that Kate's sawing snores didn't penetrate the air. The bed was a slab of ice, dipped in the center where their combined weight settled over the years. He wrangled the covers around his legs and feet and neck for maximum insulation.

A flash pierced his periphery. All at once, the visions of the bulls, the jaguars, the emanating circles of varying colors spilling from a toad blasted his brain. The tangle of blankets blew off him as he darted to the windows and split the blinds. The trees in the backyard were silent and moving only with the heartbeat of the wind. He smashed his glasses over his face and squinted his eyes, looking for a man in an oversized suit.

Gilbert had many tricks, and something told Jeff he wasn't exactly thrilled to lose a subject. A patient? An acquaintance? No. He was a guinea pig for Gilbert's morbid interest in oneiromancy. Foolish. The dreams didn't exist. Changes to his life would come from his own doing. His own changes from within. His job, his wife, his life could be improved with the right attitude, the right actions and gestures. He was getting on in age, but an old bull could still learn new tricks.

The trees remained empty. Jeff's legs dragged him back to bed, somehow still scared of the dreams that wouldn't come. If Gilbert had some sort of power, he never knew what it was or what it looked like. If it was so subliminal, a subconscious shotgun blast to make him dream such specific things, it could very well be happening right under his nose and he'd be none the wiser.

No. The dreams weren't real. He was. Kate was. He grabbed his phone and messaged her, *Hope you're doing well.*

As the night was still young, Jeff's body was in the atypical sleep position several hours too early. It wasn't used to this behavior, and thus, reluctant to allow sleep. Perhaps this habit breaker was to blame, or the bottomless desire to eye out the window into the trees behind the house. Perhaps he knew it wouldn't, couldn't be, two nights in a row in dreamless ignorance. It could be that his mind spun every which way with stresses both real and imaginary. No, he told himself, the dreams aren't real, but the stress is. The shaking grind of your stomach is real. The ping-ponging dodge of your mind wondering about Kate is real. This is okay.

Kate. Why had he let things stale for so long? This is what every stand-up comedian had warned him about: marriages fail. Things get tired, get old, you can't become complacent. And here he was. He didn't even let her slip loose for anything else in particular. Instead of coming home to his beautiful wife he crushed his molars into plaque dust seething over the day's work. Instead of spending time helping with housework or asking how her day was he plugged his brain into the television and gawked over a losing football team and the weekly school shootings. Rather than take her out dancing or to a pottery lesson or wine and paint nights, he daydreamed about the glory days with his sweaty fingers squeezing the gloves, waiting for something fortuitous to fall into his lap.

The hallway door clunked, and careful footsteps crept in the dark. Kate opened the door but didn't remark on Jeff's unusually early evening. She slipped into pajamas and crawled on her side. She smelled like bleach and fabric softener, but not in a cloying way; like in a Kate way.

"How's Claudia?" he asked, checking the box for empathy.

She rubbed tears in the snowlight, facing away from Jeff, back nudged against his belly. "She'll be fine."

It was too good to be true, he knew. The night plummeted into day, and Jeff dreamed.

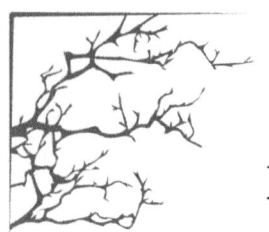

Night Ten

When he woke, he was still huddled around Kate's curved body like flesh armor. He was a deep, comfortable temperature. His foot crawled out beneath one of the blankets and he tucked it back in. He wrestled with each of his brain lobes. Should he write it down? All things considered it seemed rather mundane. In fact, it wasn't bothersome at all. Didn't even make sense. And the further he vacillated, the more he sifted the thoughts of documentation, the less of the dream he recalled. Just like that. Last night brought an empty, blackless sleep, and tonight was harmless, something involving a tortoise (turtle?) and a swing set, but even now the colors sank into some reckless drain, like littering in a city he'd never go to again.

He didn't want to move away from Kate. Wasn't that the point? The heavy epiphany he stumbled upon last night when nipping off early to bed? Spend time with Kate. He wasn't chasing dreams anymore, and they weren't chasing him.

Jeff crawled into slacks for work. The sun broke away beyond the rolling hills and slammed yellow over the town. Asphalt and gravel crackled beneath his tires. He spent most of the morning beating people away from him who offered feigned concern for his absence the day prior. Then he could finally get to work. His mountain of unread emails seemed to curve forward, peak scarved with everblacks groaning and lilting down, snow billowing and cracking off with gravity, to bare down over him. He hadn't missed a regular day of work since he could remember and wondered how many more he'd miss when the sleep study picked up. He knew his banked time off was higher than anyone else's, to the point that the company paid him out for his excess yearly. It wasn't much. The small bonus usually went toward coffee or a pizza or the pot at weekly poker. Thinking harder about it, it wasn't worth actual time in the real world that could be spent pursuing a hobby or wooing his wife.

Kate came home a bit later than he did, "Wow, the kitchen looks great."

Jeff bit his tongue's comment, not mentioning she'd walked through at least twice since he made it look great. "Yeah, how was work?"

"Busy. Dirty. Clean now." Her cheeks flushed from the grey winter air. She washed past Jeff and closed the door to change clothes.

Jeff leaned towards the door and hollered loudly to crack through, slightly annoyed she shut the door on him for as long as they'd been married. "What are you doing tonight?"

Her muffled voice sank through the door and peeked under the cracks, "Nothing. You?"

What a question. Truthfully, he hadn't thought of it. His only concern was to spend time with Kate, but he hadn't really considered what they'd be doing. "Maybe make some dinner?"

"Sure," she said. Sure.

"Didn't want a repeat of last night."

"I'm sorry." She bit her lip and dipped her head. "That wasn't fair."

"We can have the lasagna from last night if you want."

"Why don't we make something together?" she said. *She's coming around*, he thought.

Jeff and Kate scoured the cupboards for something they could cook. After gathering materials, it was determined that tomato soup and grilled cheese sandwiches (plus or minus cheese) were on the menu. Kate cranked open the can and heated it in a small orange pot. Jeff wondered what their pots would look like if they were pink, and imagined a frog leaping from inside the Teflon. Jeff buttered bread, checking each edge for signs of mold.

"Making grilled cheese reminds me of my childhood," Kate said. Jeff couldn't think of a single thing to respond with and hated himself for it. *She's trying*, he thought. *You should try, too*. They sat together at the Gilbert table—no, their table, their own kitchen table that belonged to them. Kate cut her sandwich in diagonals, while Jeff kept his whole but folded it in half to fit in the bowl.

A mangled crash rocked their glass side patio door. A deer, one of the small ones from last night, separated from the group, had dashed full into it, and crumpled at the base. Jeff and Kate leapt up from their dinner. The deer again jumped towards the glass, and the pane thundered under the weight. Looking beyond, two coyotes loomed. It seemed like they were at once trying to catch the deer but apprehensive about the presence of humans. Kate grabbed the closest thing she could think of for a weapon, the warm grilled cheese pan, and dashed to the front door. Jeff wasn't feeling as brave. He opened a small window above the sink and shoved his thick torso out. "Hey!" he yelled. He felt like an absolute idiot.

A deck of cards comes factory-sealed with two Jokers inside, and right now he was both of them at once.

The patio door boomed again as the deer continued to bash its unhorned head against it. Jeff continued to yell, unintelligible gibberish. As long as it was loud, that was his goal. He could see only one of the coyotes around the side of the house. Kate's strained shrieking split the air, and a frying pan flopped into the snow. The coyotes made their escape. The deer saw them leave and darted around the house the opposite way.

Kate came in through the front door, hauling the snowy pan. Jeff squished himself back inside the kitchen window. They met back at the table. Smears of blood spread along the glass door, ragged scuffs of hoof and face scrapings spilt along the glass and the cement patio, but it wasn't broken. If the coyotes had any sense about them at all they would be able to follow the deer, and it would likely take them to the rest of the pack as well. Maybe Jeff and Kate's interference would bring more harm than good. But the glass wasn't broken and a problem not had is a problem avoided, so says the positive mind.

"Did you—are you—" said Kate.

"Are you okay?"

"Yeah," through panicked gasps. Her hands fisted to her hips like Superman and her chest blew big and small with each breath. "Can you believe that? I've never seen anything like that."

"No," Jeff lied. He had seen something like that before—just last week in a dream. Granted, it was jaguars instead of coyotes, but unyoking the two was impossible. Between the swirling of the frantic kitchen and the scrapes on the patio window, Jeff's mind conjured Gilbert, his mockery of clients believing their dreams were premonitions. Gilbert's insistence now seemed like another plant. And if this one happened, Jeff feared the next where he was cornered and gored by a bull. Crazy talk, he told himself. They lived on the outskirts of town. They had almost an entire damn forest as their backyard. "Actually, I'm amazed it hasn't happened before."

"You're kidding."

"No! Think about it, we have almost an entire damn forest as our backyard. We see deer all the time, dawdling across the road. Coyotes, too. Makes sense they'd be on the chase."

"You're crazy."

"I hope so."

Jeff took photos of the window, the bloodstains and scuffs, on his phone. He wasn't sure why. He threw on a coat and cleaned the outside as best he could with a bleach wipe, which gave a cloudy appearance like smeared cooking oil. Kate declared she was opening a bottle of wine to calm down. This tied into another declaration she made years ago (Jeff remembered) that if she drank wine at home, it would be paired with oil painting. She joked this was because oil and wine didn't mix. It wasn't a very funny joke, but Jeff respected the combination of a bad habit with a good one, a hobby. She disappeared to the side room and closed the door.

Jeff never went to the room Kate painted in. He viewed it as a buffer, a way to make it so they didn't become one of *those* married couples that did everything together, that never sneezed or bought coffee without asking the other's permission. And suddenly, watching her thin body vanish into a room obscured from him, while he nestled into his comfortable armchair, he wondered if that wasn't a mistake.

This entire time, Jeff blamed only himself for the disentanglement of their marriage. He viewed the situation as the fault of an individual, a puppeteer, waggling strings along on wooden crosses. But it washed over him like suds from the first rain slapping the street during a long, dry summer, that this idea of a sole responsible party, a lone gunman, if you will, was itself a selfish thought. Noble, perhaps, bordering on martyrdom and sacrifice, but denying the influence of an entire human and her wants, thoughts, and actions. Jeff was not to blame. Kate was not to blame. They both allowed this, both wallowed in the comfort and contentment, both watched the sun set slowly on love, legs crossed on lawn chairs, huffing the pollen.

The realization of this, however, didn't make their marriage suddenly snap back together. In his mind, Jeff assumed the role of surgeon. He clasped the curved needle, strung through with wire, ready with a staple gun on the tray. Kate was the patient, afflicted, perhaps even unwilling, unconscious following some terrible mishap. Jeff could mend the wound with a careful hand, but Kate's body needed to accept closed flesh and build new cells.

He hoisted his heavy frame from the chair and stepped down the hall. Approaching the white, wooden door with rectangles carved in fours, he felt an odd foreboding. The house he'd lived in for decades had an unknown room to him. He remembered, many decades ago, when they toured the house to buy it, the room quietly on the side, perhaps big enough to be a child's bedroom, smeared in sunlight from the dusty windows. Only in passing, in a quiet sideways glance, had he ever observed it. Perhaps that made him a bad husband. Either way, it was too late for that. He wrapped thread through the curved needle and knocked with quiet knuckles on the door.

Kate opened up, surprised, and possibly still shaken from the deer mangling itself against the window.

"Can I join you?" He waited in the hall, making sure she allowed him inside the space that was de facto hers.

She waited just a beat too long before, "Sure." Kate stepped aside. She wore a heavy white apron, devastated by years of ill-flung oils. Jeff recognized the wooden floors. They clunked beneath his shoes. He stepped through to drop cloth, white only at the very edge, similarly a massacre to every other centimeter like her apron. The room felt sunken in, lined by years of paintings tacked and scattered to the wall. Kate was typically well put together, very "adult" for lack of a more appropriate label, but this room revealed a reckless and wild side, an experimental pulse, an ugly and messy mind, splashed on canvas. In his own home.

The paintings were darker than Jeff expected. Many of Kate's paintings went to the dentist's office and hung in the lobby for customers to lose themselves in while they panicked about root canals. Those were the forests, canyons swimming in moonlight, rivers sprawling through mountain slopes and muddy, crowded with critters. The paintings here were abstract, garish, blackened.

"What is it?" He pointed at the easel, so flecked and marred he wasn't sure what color it initially was. His brain sparked and he imagined Gilbert, grinning through a bitten cigarette, quizzing him on color theory of *somnolent visions.* The canvas rested on top, splattered and smeared in oils.

"Not sure." She brushed a loose strand of hair from her brow. Her arms fell like a locking safe over her chest. Kate never shared this part of her life with Jeff. It was probably something like wifely duty and obligations of marriage that prodded her to say more. "I saw something like this in a dream the other night."

In a dream, she said. Jeff, in a fit of panic after his own dreams hunted him down, previously asked her what she dreamed of. She said she didn't remember, but this was something he'd never forget. Whatever it was supposed to be was hazy, blotchy, loose. He thought he could almost make a face out of it, swollen and black. Some things could almost be eyes. Kate was a hobby painter, probably wouldn't be able to pay people to display her work. But these hauntings, these diagrams for the insane and babbling, were of an unknown quality to him. He wasn't one for art. Didn't get it. Maybe they were good, maybe she'd be laughed at by other artists. But something about these yanked his eyes in like swirling black quicksand.

"Kate, this stuff...."

"I know."

"I think these are incredible." Her eyes stretched and sharpened. She dug her face into her wine glass. "Would you want to hang some around the house?" She spit her wine back into the caved bottom.

"You want *these* around the house?"

"Maybe not these ones, you know, but something you paint. It doesn't have to hide back here if you don't want it to." Care, empathy. He could add encouragement to the chanted list.

She flashed a simple smile and then covered it up. *She'll come around*, he thought. "What do you want me to paint," Kate asked, "a deer or something?"

They crept into bed that night at the same time. Jeff turned to her back and slid his hand along her hips. He kissed her soft shoulders. Kate reached back and took his hand and threaded their fingers together, then held it there in place, in silence. *She'll come around*, he thought.

She fell far away, a blaring drag of breath, and Jeff closed his eyes over and over again.

Night Eleven

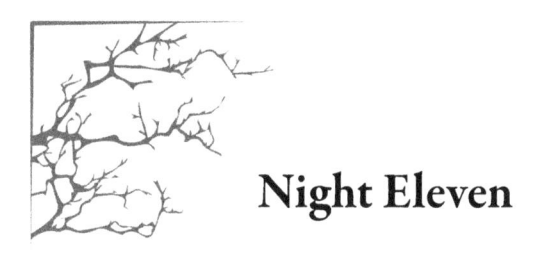

The dream shook him, ripped him from comfort and he jolted alert when his face fell back to the pillow. The final moment of the *somnolent vision* accompanied the real-life action of smacking his hand to the bed, enough that it launched him. It wasn't a question this time. He rose, robed, and rushed to the writing desk, dug out the legal pad and pen, and scribbled:

Massive eagle, brown feathers, white head, orange legs and claws. It has me gripped between each of its feet, flying high above the clouds. It drops me. I fall through clouds to see open air below me. The earth below is desert-like, red and brown and yellow, plateaus, intermittent greenery. A river snakes across the land as far as I can observe. I aim for the river. I miss, and wake up.

Jeff dropped his head to rest in his damp hands and massaged his temple. It was hard to judge whether this one was worse than the bull dream, but it was certainly worse than the deer and jaguars. Unfortunately, that dream brought an odd reflection in his living world. They're coming true, his heart yelled. They're coming true.

Jeff had a run of terrible dreams before this one. The deer dream manifested and involved Kate as well. She could have been hurt, how she sprung out to the yard slashing a frying pan at near-wolves. Jeff flipped back through the notes in his legal pad. He wished he wrote them down, every single one, to remember those little details, the things Gilbert grilled him over: the bull, the deer, and now, the eagle... but he had more, just refused to believe that *he*, Jeff Vickers, could have something so bizarre occur.

What were those dreams? Despite such a now fantastical impact on his life, he couldn't bring up a scrap of them into his squeezing brain. And if his dreams really were manifesting in his life, if the deer crashing into the side door hunted by coyotes wasn't just the Russian roulette of unlucky events, were they happening in the order he dreamed them? If so, the very first dream, whatever it was, before the bull, before the deer, had already happened. He just didn't realize it. Thinking of recent trauma, the only big things were his encounter with Gilbert in the trees and Claudia's car wreck. So either his dream was about a greasy man slinking behind his house or they could ruin people other than him. Kate, or an analog for Kate, wasn't in the deer dream as far as he could remember, so it wasn't a sure sign. Or he was completely crazy, letting his bonkers dreams control him again, keep him up, shaking in the early morning jotting insanities onto lined yellow paper.

Still, the blackening feeling that things were getting worse stormed over his brain. The bull, up until that point, was the worst. Thankfully, eagles that could soar through the air with Jeff, even at his svelte figure, simply did not exist. But things weren't 100 percent accurate: instead of jaguars it was coyotes, and Kate was present in the real world but not in the dream (probably). He couldn't be hoisted by a huge bird. The only option would be an airplane or helicopter, barring the existence of saucer-like UFOs or otherwise. But what could a bull be?

FATHER SLEEP

He wasn't a farmer—he didn't live near any cows let alone charging bulls. In a strange way he was both fearful of rushing objects that could run him through and slightly comforted by the unlikelihood of that outcome. However, the last week or so was nothing but surprising and strange, so logic should be discarded entirely.

Jeff spent the drive to work only in the right-hand lane and quadruple-checking each intersection.

Jeff stayed late. Colson shouted so loud and wide that Jeff counted the fillings on his teeth. And he didn't once swing his clenching, painful fist up at his swinging jowls. Kate would be proud. He must remember to tell her later.

When he arrived home, blinking under streetlamps, jerking his head every which way checking for traffic, he saw that Kate's father, Hank, was visiting, with his shapely, faded red pickup looming in the driveway. Hank was a good guy, didn't seem to hate Jeff all that much despite stealing his daughter away. He felt their relationship was just north of neutral, but not so friendly that they spent time together outside of these visits.

Jeff entered and greeted the room. Kate's smile beamed, its brightness unfamiliar, but carried a wrinkle of sadness resting on her lips. Unsurprising with her father visiting. Hank sat, nestled into Jeff's usual chair, tall even when sitting, bony, a trait Kate inherited. Faded blue jeans, pale blue button down, unmistakable off-white cowboy hat, bent just so at the edges.

The cowboy hat. Jeff tried, *tried* to act natural. Set his coat and bag in the kitchen. Kate's dad was a farmer. Jeff looked out the filmy, oily, glass patio door he wiped down yesterday. Through it, waiting in the driveway, was the unique decoration on Hank's truck he hadn't noticed walking inside the house:

grill-mounted steer horns, jutting out and curved, bone sharp. Impossible.

"Jeff, Daddy brought by that hutch of Momma's we talked about." Jeff didn't recall this talk or fully know what a hutch was.

"Oh good, need any help getting it in?"

"Nah, we got it," Hank said. "I'm done for the week now, but we got it."

"Probably would have broken it anyway."

"That's why we took care of it." He gave a gentle smile that magnetized eyes in any room.

"Good day at work, Kate?"

"It was fine."

"You know I counted Colson's fillings while he was shouting today. He has four on the bottom. Didn't get to see the top. They're silver."

"You like that job, Jeff?" Hank interjected.

"Sure, it's fine." He wasn't sure why it was impossible to just say it. He hated his job. He wondered how anybody liked their job at all. They wouldn't have to pay workers to work if it was enjoyable, and a bell of recollection gonged in the back corner of his brain. "Always on the lookout though." Why did he say these things?

"You know, all these years, being my own boss and all that; not too bad. Nobody yelling at me. Not like that, least." He shifted in Jeff's chair and took an angle that directly faced him rather than the room in general. "I know you said you like it fine, but I sense that's a nicety you feel you need to say. It's none of my business what you do, but if you do something every damn day and hate it, it'll take its toll on you." He tilted his head around to touch eyes to Kate and then back to Jeff. "Trust me."

Jeff was surprised at this. Over the decades Jeff knew him, Hank didn't tend to delve into these more emotional and logical (what a contradiction) topics. He was always a smooth talker, a loud presence in a quiet body, grey eyes cooling, but generally, when he did talk, people listened. "I've thought a lot about that lately."

"Well, keep on thinking," Hank said. "Kate here found something pretty decent, right honey?"

"Yeah, Dad."

"You start to think of how much time you spend at work, son." Hank called him "son." "You wonder if it's a waste." He licked his thin lips. "Lord knows we don't know how much we got." The room went quiet as church. This discreet reference echoed, a quiet nod to Annie's passing the previous year. Kate lowered her eyes and brushed a strand of greying hair over her ear. Jeff hadn't asked her how she was doing in quite some time. He didn't understand the loss of a parent. Not like that anyway. His own were off in the Utah mountains somewhere and sent weekly emails he didn't often read. He feared they were being lulled into conversion by the slew of eager Mormons. Kate used to remark that her mom was still the number one recommended contact by her phone whenever she went to send a picture. Hank stood. "You wanna help me with something out at the truck?"

The truck. The truck with the horns. "Sure." Jeff whirled his coat back over his shoulders. They stepped into the snow, now peppered with hail, heavy and solid, scattering on the pavement. Hank leaned smack in the middle of the horns, one leg crossed over the other, not bothering to wear a coat. Jeff elected to lean on the passenger door behind the extended mirror.

"She doing alright?" The question held unwieldy, lopsided, and unquantifiable weight.

"Sure, seems to be, yeah." Another lie in this quick visit. Jeff had no clue how she was doing regarding *this* because it hadn't crossed his selfish mind in months. Again, he just couldn't understand. He remembered from boring movies over the years that "it never leaves you."

"Yeah, she don't really talk to me much about it. I think she wants me to know she's okay. But look at me, not talking to her about it, heh." Hank's insight pierced Jeff and he felt naked despite his wintry layers. Hank's hand dipped habitually to his faded jeans pocket and slid along his hip for a lighter; he didn't carry a lighter ever since Annie was diagnosed due to secondhand smoke. Jeff wondered if Hank noticed any lingering scent in the kitchen.

Kate came through the screen door in her brown, puffy coat. "What's going on, guys?" Jeff tossed his gaze between father and daughter.

"Well," he said tilting between the horns to face her, "we were talking about you." Kate's eyebrows jumped. "I guess," and he chewed at the inconceivable air inside his mouth, "I just want to know you're doing okay."

He just said it. Just like that, out in the open in front of God and everyone. Kate crunched over the snow and gave Hank a tip-toed hug, arms latched around his neck like she might bring him down. Jeff panged with jealousy. Hank, in that moment, appeared to be about twelve feet tall and blotted out what little sun shunted over the mountains. Jeff wondered why he himself couldn't just say these things, why he wouldn't simply ask Kate about her feelings, about him, about their marriage. Slow, doubtful needles nipped at his feet, reminding him that Hank was considerably older than he was, and might have been spurred to express emotions like this around his daughter. It seemed to go well.

Hank's red taillights bled over the floating snow. Jeff followed Kate inside. He took off his coat while she stood blank in the doorway.

"Wow."

Jeff ran her coat off her shoulders. He tucked it away in the closet.

"Just wow."

Maybe another night.

Night Twelve

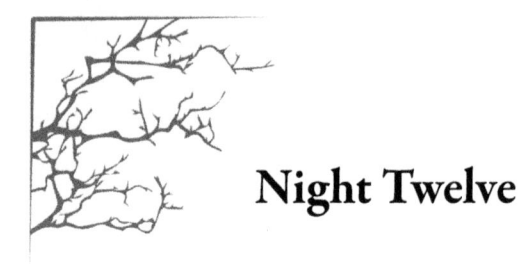

Jeff choked awake.

At the writing desk, on the yellow legal pad:

I'm swallowed headfirst in one gulp by a giant snake. It's got a yellow belly and the rest is so green it's almost black. Somehow inside its mouth, I grasp at its fangs like bars on a prison cell, and scream and scream and scream. It sends me down.

Jeff reread the passage, written in a calmer penmanship than before. Despite the squeezing inhale when he woke, this dream wasn't as traumatic as the rest. His throat stung a little, but Kate still sawed an echo around the walls, so if he actually screamed it didn't affect her. Swallowed by a giant snake. Gilbert would want him to specify an anaconda, or great boa, he was sure. He chose, with intent, to let "giant snake" stand on the legal pad. Underlined.

But he avoided the bull, at least for now. Or maybe he's delusional and "deer day" was still a rotten coincidence and these dreams meant nothing at all. Nothing, aside wondering what their meaning was endlessly, writing more than his college days, every dark morning when he startled awake. It was easier to dream of a dark warm place, even inside a large reptile, than it was to scream through frigid, slapping air and greet the dirt.

Kate shut the bedroom door behind her, stepped with quiet feet on the carpet toward him, and kissed him good morning.

Jeff drove to work without any concern of goring from t-boning traffic. At the office, when he saw Colson, Jeff greeted him with warmth and asked how he was doing. Colson said he was okay. He left Jeff alone.

At the poker game, nickels shimmering in his cookie tin, Howard bet soft, bet scared. He kept his motorcycle cloaked by a crinkled black cover with reflective tape on it. Jeff bet, not wild, but harder than usual. If he had a king in his hand, then nickels spilled to the table. Queens, too. Aces, well hell, let's live a little. He left hauling his cookie tin rattling a bit heavier that night.

Jeff got home late. Too late for Kate. She dragged impossible swathes of air through her nostrils. Jeff sat at the kitchen table, in his spot. He too sucked air into his nostrils, but quietly. No trace of smoke. No contact with Gilbert in half a week or so. If not for a spam-filtered email it might have all been a figment of his imagination, a bad dream he might have jotted down on his legal pad at 4 a.m. in jerky ball point pen. This was a good thing, he supposed. He had awful dreams the last two nights, but not *every* night. Perhaps this was all just a strange chemical imbalance working itself out. Yeah. He tried to ignore the thought of Dr. Williams recommending he go to therapy, and the bright pink and orange shutters of toad circles that flashed behind his eyelids.

Jeff didn't consider potential violation of trust when he walked into Kate's painting room. The surely permanent drop cloth was a swimming brown rainbow with occasional highlights of purple or yellow dropped from heaven. The painting leaning on the easel was not of a deer. Jeff didn't know what it was. It leaned. It sank. It dragged and drooped. It had voids for eyes and an angular, scratchy head. It was bloating and bent and towering to the ground. Kate had cleaned her palette off, but Jeff found a still-wet drop on the drop cloth. He fingered it up, rippling midnight blue, and smeared it on the figure. It looked about the same as far as he could tell.

On the way to bed, he passed the hutch in the hallway, empty save for a small, framed photo of Kate and her mom hugging on a lush baseball field. Everything inside the photo was gone, Kate's mom, her childhood, and gorgeous gleaming summer. Maybe one of them would come back.

He lay his head on his firm pillow, jet engine growling in his ear, and hoped for no dreams, no dreams at all.

Night Thirteen

Jeff dreamed of a Great White barking on a yellow beach, smashing its tail to sand. When he opened his eyes, the only thing he saw was the looping vision of Gilbert laughing, legs crossed at his kitchen table, cigarette pluming in hand.

He couldn't decide if he should write it down or not. Despite not being directly about him, it might be the most "Jeff" dream he could have. Gilbert called him a "Shark" for Charcot-Wilbrand syndrome, which he assured Jeff he didn't have, at least anymore, and Jeff believed him, because he dreamed only of not having another dream as long as he lived, and yet continued tumbling and rolling in terror and oxytocin.

He decided right there, still in bed, dream drunk, to try Gilbert Finnegan again.

But why? Things were improving through his own volition. Kate kissed him good morning, let him see her paintings. Colson waved him goodbye like an acquaintance rather than slam the door behind him. He didn't lose every nickel he owned at the poker table. But it wasn't right. He dreaded suffocating alone near the ocean, even though the Pacific of Pacific Northwest was hours away. He buckled at every deer on television or picture of a coyote at a department store. He thought the six-ish feet of his skeleton was somehow a little too tall these days, and feared tripping up a curb, spilling into a brick wall, skull caving in.

Jeff drafted an email, right there in the dark. He wanted to be absolutely sure Gilbert got it immediately and flushed these dreams away. He did it before. Jeff expected, however, that Gilbert wouldn't want his test subject—*associate*—to stop doing the thing that made him relevant and useful. Jeff's sudden appearance of heavy, vibrant, ecstatic, and shocking dreams after decades of blacklessness was key. Jeff wanted to go back to less-than black. Gilbert sought the terror in Jeff's somnolent visions. In his email, Jeff indicated he changed his mind and wanted to resume their trials and hoped he would meet him that night. Fingers crossed and crossed and crossed.

Kate, in wrinkled, crinkled, blue scrubs and a loose ponytail, waved goodbye as she walked out the door. She's coming around, he told himself.

Colson stomped down the hall, steaming toward Jeff's cubicle. He flashed radar eyes and wet teeth, angled forward and accelerating. Jeff, sensing the horns sprouting sideways from Colson's bald skull, gave him a friendly wave and a "Hey, Dave!" to cut him off. Colson shrunk. The bulge on the side of his head calmed and siphoned out. He talked to him in an annoyed, but understanding manner, about expense reports. Jeff left on time.

He started dinner when he got home, and Kate stepped in long enough to change out of her sweaty scrubs. "A couple of us are going to visit Claudia. Sorry about dinner."

"It's okay. Be safe."

She closed the door behind her, crunched into the snow, and Jeff pulled a pair of steaks out of the oven. He expected to hear from Gilbert by now, which is why he contacted him at 4 a.m. He dragged, tired and soggy, from the week of interrupted sleep, and dreaded laying his head down for what blazed over his eyes in slumber. With Kate gone and Gilbert unresponsive, he found himself, once more, alone. Habit led him to the living room where he reached for the remote control, and the thought of another school shooting, another rigged election, another gob of protestors salted his brain over, and he seethed.

Jeff felt every wrinkle across his frowning cheeks when he thought this, but it was far past time he got a real hobby; not just poker once a week, not just reading the free offerings on his e-reader; something to do that could whip him out of his pattern of negativity. He considered passing through the white door to Kate's painting room but thought better, given his recent, probably unnoticed, venture inside. Maybe joining Kate would be a good idea? Would it help their relationship to have a common hobby? Thus far, the separation of interests only served to split them, but that might be because Jeff's interests were relatively nonexistent.

As a baby step, he pulled up to the writing desk and shuffled around for a spare notebook, likely unused for decades, its original intent lost to days of repeated work-slog and drowning in depressing nightly news. He found one, spiraled, green, and the cover bent over at a diagonal. Never written in. On his phone he searched for beginner drawing tutorials and found one that guided him to draw circles and shade them as spheres. Gripping a bitten pencil at first felt like lighting sparklers in his knuckles. After a couple tough, loosely focused hours, his wrist ached like it was jointed with sand, his fingers dented from pinching the pencil just so, and the lined, aged paper riddled with oblong, ocular, cord-less eyes lined up like obedient soldiers.

Gilbert emailed him back around 8 p.m.:

Jeff, glad to hear you changed your mind. I'm not in the Northwest anymore. I'm not going to tell you WHERE I'm at, but it'll be a while before I'm inhaling snow. I'll let you know when I can come back and tap into that beautiful brain of yours. Until then, write EVERYTHING down. We'll meet and figure it out.

Best – G

Crushing. For some reason, Jeff had the psychotic delusion that an oneiromancer whom he rebuffed was simply going to wait in the wintry Pacific of the United States, hoping he changed his mind. Jeff never actually considered where on earth Gilbert lived, as he appeared as sudden as his violent dreams the very next night when he first reached out to the Society. Jeff imagined him lounging on a beach in Florida with only sunglasses and swim trunks in the heat, a vision frightening enough for one of his dreams. *Write everything down*, he said. Gilbert wrote nothing down, didn't take notes. He just knew things. He somehow gave him "signals" that altered his dreams. What were the chances that Jeff could get a signal via email?

Come to think of it, what were the chances that Gilbert's manipulation didn't urge Jeff into these thoughts, these incessant horrible dreams, in the first place? Maybe this was all a test. Jeff thought he should keep an eye out for an unmarked white van parked in the snowy night.

Kate came home, a sloppy stumble of smeared mascara. She came to him, quickly. She threw both arms over his neck and dangled like Jeff was a thick, stud-driven nail she could hang all her weight on. Her cheek drenched Jeff's old t-shirt, and she sobbed, throaty and low, so long that Jeff's calves tingled down to his toes. He waited. He stroked her greying hair and rubbed along her back, massaging layers of undershirt and bra and skin with warm, wide hands.

He hesitated to speak, not sure how many tears Kate could possibly squeeze out. "Is Claudia okay?"

She peeled herself off his wet chest and dragged her hand along her face. "She's fine." This was unexpected. "They said she'll be fine." That's good news, right?

"That's good news, right?" He pulled back and she looked up with raspberried chocolate eyes.

"She talked. She finally talked." Kate sniffled and slid more black streaks away. "She said her husband's name. She said 'Danny.'" Jeff nodded. He wasn't sure why. Clearly this was profound to Kate, or at the very least moving in a lovey kind of way.

"That's great, honey. Wonderful news. I'm glad she'll be okay." And he still doubled his thoughts, folding them in over themselves like samurai steel, smashed hundreds and thousands of times until the outside was the inside and every side.

"Mmhm." She stepped back again.

Jeff figured it out.

"If it was you, or if it was me in that hospital bed, Kate...."

"Mmhm."

"Kate, I've been missing you. And I'm sorry. And I am afraid to tell you this, but I know I've been a bad husband to you." Her eyes swam in his and they dilated. "I want to fix this. I was just hoping, I guess, that I could do it without you knowing."

She grabbed his hands. Hers were rough and cracked. "Okay," and she snagged on her own words and got lost in a valley of tongues and teeth.

"And I'm sorry, Kate."

"Yeah." She locked to him, nodding.

"If I try, Kate, if I try, and if *we* try, really," and his feet shook and his lips iced over, "can you ever love me again?"

The dam of guilt and hate and torture that cemented his ribs and tacked up his stomach and pumped his frightened blood shattered, and gorgeous, peaceful, electric air washed through.

"I do love you," she said. They kissed, precious and sweet, gentle, tickling. He knew it was a lie, but also understood that her being there, her coming home and crying and hugging him, latching her lovely eyes up to his and following him along this path he was too afraid to walk about—it meant she was willing to try.

Night Thirty-Eight

Weeks of slow, dripping progress followed. Winter was dying away. Grass under melting tufts of snow learned to stand once more. A nearby pond showed fractures dividing it into sections where it thawed, re-froze, and partially thawed again in the indecisive spring winds. Smiling blue skies sported a plain white sun most days, and nights crept in later and later. Jeff left work in the daytime and spent most nights re-courting Kate like they were nervous teens. They tried new recipes together instead of defaulting to Jeff cooking everything, like things that started from a roux, a slow combination of melted butter and flour, sneaking handprints of white residue to chests and asses. Jeff's poker games remained about the same, winning some, losing some, but no windfalls like before. As a symbolic gesture, he cashed in some of his cookie-tin nickels he tired of lugging around and bought an unruled spiral notebook, a few nice pencils and a fancy malleable eraser that the online videos said was good for fixing foolish errors.

Tonight, Kate sprawled nude on their blue couch, partially under a tasseled blanket, and Jeff practiced drawing her figure. He asked her to pose for a life drawing and she stripped and said it would be like *Titanic*. "I don't have any French girls, so you'll have to do," he said. He still struggled with the shading. He adjusted the pencil often to shake away the stabbing pain.

Despite his ambition, he was still too new and too terrible. She came out angular and misshapen, particularly her nose and stomach, respectively, the latter of which appeared distended and hazy after dozens of erasures.

"Let me see," she said after he closed the book and stretched his old knees.

"You really don't want to, trust me."

"I think I do, you're doing a great job." It wasn't a question anymore. She snatched the book and flipped it open. Her lips formed a cruel s-shape, and her chest buckled. "We'll keep this one for comparison later."

A safe deflection. Jeff's drawing was terrible, but it didn't matter. He enjoyed himself, learning a new hobby, learning Kate's love again; her quick, quiet kisses in the morning when she rolled into him, her delivery of snacks to his office once a week or so in the middle of the day, her sparking and bright smile after he made a bad joke. Her quiet gasps when they laid down together at night.

Kate sauntered back to her painting room, which Jeff was now encouraged to enter at will. He sometimes sketched there, watching the muscles at the back of her shoulder pulse, her wrist bend, the bony dazzle of her knuckles. She gave her previous painting a rest (the one Jeff altered, seemingly unbeknownst to her; it leaned in a corner near a stack of unbroken canvases) and started a new one, jokingly, of a deer. Jeff propped up on a four-legged stool sprinkled in paint flings behind her and began another life drawing in secret. He worked in shapes, mostly. Drew an oval, curved out the top to another oval, a curved rectangle. Shaded lightly, then heavy, heavy in dead zones. It was still terrible, and that was okay.

FATHER SLEEP

Kate's deer was "normal," so to speak, in that, despite the mangled inspiration, it bent gently in a field of wheat or barley, directly through the canvas. It didn't have eyes yet.

She stripped her brush and hooked around to kiss him. That inevitable hour struck when sleep devoured her energy. Before too long she would be out on her feet. Jeff kissed her back, bade her goodnight, and she dragged her toes on the carpet back to bed, slopping left to right. Jeff joined her most nights to ride out the gnawing dark and quiet until his dreams took him, and if not, he stayed up reading a book on how to play specific scenarios in Texas Hold'em (those hadn't come to fruition yet; all in time) or following more instructional drawing videos online.

But tonight, he had a meeting with Gilbert Finnegan.

The email came a few days before. Gilbert only stipulated they meet at Jeff's house this time, lest he see another college student and have a depressive break and waste his trip out to the Pacific Northwest. Again. Jeff agreed, even brewed a pot of coffee for his arrival.

Gilbert knocked at the door, greeted him with a sweaty handshake, and dropped into the creaking wooden chair. His hair still leeched over his shining scalp, his face a weighted droop, the scar crawling up his lip like vines. He wore the same damn not-tan-not-yellow suit that jangled with each step and looked like it would finally fit him in about 20 years or once he stopped smoking.

Speaking of, "You smoke?" The tan and white package nestled in half-torn plastic wrap gaped out at Jeff.

"Haven't picked it up, Gilbert, no."

"Ehh." He tipped one out and struck it with a cheap lighter from his jacket pocket. His drag slurped with habit but flashed his comfort. Gilbert had been a smoker for a very, very long time. He leaned far back in the chair and crossed his legs on Jeff's kitchen table. "How you been, buddy?" His buffoon's smile shattered the quiet air.

"Doing well, Gilbert, thank you."

"Yeah, so did you get all your business sorted out or whatever? Don't want you getting spooked again."

"I'm working on it. Kate and I are doing much better," he said. Gilbert's smile faded to a smirk, sideways.

"You know you haven't talked too much about the wife. Maybe we should start there."

"The dreams, Gilbert. You're here for the dreams. Leave my wife out of it."

"Hey," he threw both hands up, tipping the chair back on precarious legs and shooting ashes behind him, "you're the boss, buddy, ha!" He laughed around the room, locking eyes with the corners and knife block and the coffee pot and empty chairs. "But really," he snapped forward, "what can I do for you, Jeff?"

"I don't like sleeping, Gilbert. I slept without a thought for 50-some-odd years and now I'm like a child needing a night light." Gilbert dragged long and through the filter.

"So these dreams are disruptive, not inspiring?"

What an implication. "The only thing they inspire me to do is drink more coffee. They inspire me to worry and panic all day. These dreams have to mean something."

"Like I said before," he settled around and yanked another cigarette from the pack. He snared it between his teeth and spoke, "they do." He flicked his lighter on, "You just need to work at it a bit," he puffed fire through the paper—and snapped his black eyes to Jeff—"and not lie," with a biting grin.

The old sin, Gilbert's trickery. Inevitable. *A lie for a lie, a truth for a truth.*

"Do we need to do the practice runs again?"

"Heh," he puked smoke out behind him, craning his neck like an upside-down V, "that's up to you. Yes, Jeff, I'm giving you the choice." Big grin. "I'll tell you, whatever you tell me will affect what we can do for you. Which also brings me to my other point—what do you want to get from these little meetings, Jeff?"

"Do you think I can learn to not dream again?"

Gilbert drank from his coffee cup and took quiet puffs of his cigarette. "I can make it so you don't dream, you know that." Jeff nodded. "But," he leaned back again, crossed his legs again, on the table again again again, "that's kind of at odds with my interests, don't you think?" He leaned forward, like he took pleasure flexing his hip muscles repeatedly, reclining and relenting. "I want you to dream, Jeff. It's good for me."

"Only for you. I'm not such a fan."

"Well you say your life is going so swell now, isn't it? Would that have happened without the *somnolent visions*?" he emphasized with hand movements. Jeff wondered this, and unfortunately, he didn't think so. It's possible he would have had an epiphany about his life and his relationship without a life-rattling occurrence such as the complete and total fear of closing his eyes at night, without second-guessing his actions, his subliminal realizations, the fear of impalement by pickup trucks—it's possible. But his life certainly spun wild since meeting Gilbert Finnegan.

"You said before, some of your other clients—not the Sharks, but the idiots—they can change actions in their life to impact their dreams, like they can do things to change them because they're afraid. If you act like I'm not a Shark, can we just change my dreams so they won't be so bad then?"

"That's not nearly as fun, Jeff. Think of the wasted potential."

That stung. "I don't know what potential I'm wasting because this doesn't make sense! My life is fine! My dreams are the disaster."

"Okay, with you, your 'gift,' let's say, your potential, with the proper research—my research—and your *honesty*," he lifted his greasy brow at Jeff, "this could change the world."

"That's not true, Gilbert." He tried his very best to calm himself through Gilbert's nonsense, thinking of Kate's pseudo-lectures on positivity. "This won't amount to anything other than headaches and wasted time for me. Either you can or you can't."

"Listen," another hinge forward, coat jingling, likely a sick twinge of pleasure in Gilbert, "I'm not gonna lie, I don't know exactly what could happen if we work together, but do you think anybody who did anything knew exactly how it would end? You know? Think of the first caveman who smashed two rocks together enough times that a leaf caught fire: that changed the world!" He settled back in the chair, but his legs stayed on the ground. His cigarette leaned with ash. "Or the first guy to go, 'hey, ya know, she looks softer than the log

I've been cuddling with, and I bet she smells nice, too': boom, world changed!"

Despite the crude nature of his examples, Jeff understood what he was getting at, and it even scratched an awful thought into his cerebrum.

"Do you, you know, d'you think Ben Franklin had any idea what would happen when he flew a damn kite in the sky with a key on it? This is science, Jeff. *You're smart.* You just have to try things. I'm a man with expertise, with experience, with an idea. And you're a man with a fucked-up head. Fly a kite, get Frankenstein's monster."

"No. I don't want to be your 'monster.' I just want to sleep. Just take the dreams away, take them all away."

"Alright, listen," and Gilbert stuffed the cigarette in his mouth and dug in his coat. Hooked around his hitchhiker's thumb was a bronze ring of keys; tiny silver keys for cash drawers or padlocks, dirty red keys that might start tractors, strange, pronged metals that could plug into manhole covers, stubby lumps of metal for roller skates, fake-looking simple keys like they sell in children's handcuff packages, garish, extended numbers that tickled tumblers in locks the likes Jeff had never seen before. There were probably hundreds sliding across each other sounding like the high register of a set of bells. "This is why it's helpful if you dream." Jeff's face was clearly bent and confused, because Gilbert continued, "Think of these things as questions. Maybe hunches."

"They're keys," said Jeff.

Gilbert looked around the room, not in his normal laughing, mocking kind of way. His eyes fell back to Jeff's. "Yes, they are. Correct." He took a breath and readjusted his cigarette. "Oneiromancy is a bit like charting your own map, Jeff. Not quite sure what everything means, need to go based off landmarks, you know. Symbols, even. Like your bull. That could be a symbol for something. Your deer." He held the keys closer to Jeff and the ring dipped into an oval from the weight. "Think of these keys, *symbolically*, as why I want you to dream. I have questions and hunches. Like I said, I'm a researcher. These are all keys that I've found in my life, walking the earth, so to speak. They're in junk drawers in plastic dishes or rusting in a puddle on the curbside, anything like that. I pick them up. But I don't know what they go to. I just have to try." Jeff hated where this speech was going and wondered if they could just jump to the end and tell him 'no.'

"Can I just tell you 'no' now?" said Jeff.

"Just a moment here, I'm building up to it." He lifted his shoulders and several pops and cracks sounded out. "Imagine if I just threw all these keys away? Right now? What if I just tossed 'em in your trash bin?"

Gilbert's eyes didn't move. He was waiting for a response. When it was too uncomfortable to bear, Jeff caved. "Then what, Gilbert?"

"Then we would never know what the hell they go to, exactly! Jeff, there are locks out there, all over, that these keys open—or close—you ever think about that? The keys go to something. Don't you want to know what could be behind all those locks?" Gilbert opened his jacket pocket up again and stuffed the key ring away. It sagged his already sagging jacket another inch or so. "There could be anything in these things—symbolically, of course, this is a symbol."

"Is my brain the lock or the key?"

"Well, it's," and Gilbert's face turned up, his brow smushed, "I guess it would be the lock. I have the keys. I think that's right, yeah."

"Then," and Jeff felt quite clever about this, "*symbolically*, I want to throw away the key to this lock. I don't want these dreams anymore, Gilbert. Truly."

Gilbert snubbed out his mostly-ashen cigarette. "If that's what you want."

"That's what I want."

He shook his head. He pushed his coffee aside and folded his hands. "Then, *Mr. Vickers*, you would be my client, not my associate. I'll send you a contract. $500 a week for vision therapy. You can pay daily if you'd prefer, but it's more expensive."

Jeff winced when he said the word *therapy*. "You said this was complementary—"

"This was complementary when we were going to be partners, Mr. Vickers, when we were going to work together to achieve a mutually beneficial end. Now I am working for you, because you'd rather squander your potential, and as such, I require payment. The Society of Divine Dreams isn't a charity, Mr. Vickers. We're researchers. If you want to utilize our research, then you pay. If you want to *do* research, then we party."

Jeff looked Gilbert in the eyes, but Gilbert wouldn't return the favor. He looked at his nails which he flexed oddly, he examined the pattern on the table, he looked out the smeared window, and he buttoned his not-tan jacket.

"And if you don't want to *pay* or *party* then please let me know so I can leave this icy hell."

The tonal shift jarred Jeff sideways. Gilbert was now a hovering, persistent wrench in his life. Things were finally going well with work and his wife, all except for these shocking dreams pouncing him, more garish each night.

"Don't you have other Sharks you can use for your research?"

"I'm not at liberty to discuss other associates."

"How long will this take?"

"That's up to you. Sometimes a couple weeks, sometimes months or longer. If you plan on lying to me about the process, then understand it's your nickel being nicked."

Jeff believed Gilbert was personally offended by his hesitance. All those times Gilbert stormed into his house, cackled aloud in the kitchen and helped himself to coffee; were all of these Gilbert's acts of friendship? Gilbert seemed to be the type to have very few friends, but not the type to seem lonely. Maybe he was sincere and only wanted to further his research? Jeff didn't sign up for that. He didn't sign up for anything. Not yet.

"Send me the contract."

"We'll reconvene after you sign and discuss a meeting place for sessions since I'm mobile."

"My kitchen's not good enough?"

"It wouldn't be appropriate to work in a client's home."

"How do I know you won't just manipulate my dreams however you please? You've done it before."

Gilbert, at long last, snapped his eyes—black and seething—at Jeff. His upper lip lit up like lightning from the scar darting across it. "I'm a professional."

Night Thirty-Nine

Jeff woke, drenched. Kate ground gravel in her mouth. He swiveled from bed and sat at the writing desk with his yellow legal pad and shaking pen, figuring that if he was about to pay for *professional* help then he should write these stupid things down.

I'm ~~swimming~~ floundering in deep orange water in a bath robe (it looks blue) (it's not mine). A massive squid (it looks purple) comes up under me and wraps around each leg, pulling me closer. It jams a tentacle into my mouth and down my throat. When I try to pull it out, it latches around each wrist and spreads them apart. I look like a choking Vitruvian Man. I suffocate.

Despite the irksome gurgle in his brain, the last images of the dream flickering on a gossamer loop, he was at least pleased he knew the term *Vitruvian Man* after watching one of his drawing videos.

Jeff saw an email from the Society of Divine Dreams containing a contract, just like he agreed to. A simple one-pager; had the same header as their website followed by a couple brief paragraphs explaining that he was entering into a contract with Oneiromancer Gilbert Finnegan for the purposes of *Somnolent Vision Negation, Dampening, and Deafening*. Just like Gilbert said, the fee was listed at $500 per week, starting that day, to be terminated at the client's will. He read it multiple times and didn't notice any funny Gilbert-isms—no trick language, misleading circumstances—honestly, aside from the completely absurd purpose of the contract, it appeared in all reality to be completely, as Gilbert put it the previous night, professional. He jabbed his screen and dragged his finger in his swirly signature and sent off the contract as well as the payment for one week. He only hoped this would end in just a few weeks so Kate wouldn't notice much money was missing from their account. Jeff and Kate weren't hurting financially, but with Jeff's secret ambition to retire as soon as possible always flickering behind his cranial nerves, this expense bothered him. He couldn't begin to explain this to Kate. "*Hey honey, you know when you sleep for twelve hours a day, I have nightmares that keep me from sleeping at all, so I paid a greasy man to absolve me of the ability to dream.*" Like a lead zeppelin.

Kate emerged to the hall and greeted him with a squealing yawn, grinding sleep from her eyes, and his mind thought of actually telling her the whole thing, right there. If their relationship was on the mend, and it was (a "good morning!"), then perhaps being open and honest was a new priority. Maybe it wasn't out of the question, admitting failure, even idiocy, if it meant clearer communication between the pair. Would it be so terrible to discuss his struggle? To tell his wife, his life partner, that he had fears? Was it worse to hide it from her and seek a form of therapy behind her back, or to admit he drank coffee late at night to ward off the boogeyman clawing behind his eyelids? Jeff's mind fell to Hank and their brief conversation outside the house, and how close he was to the horns on the front of the truck.

FATHER SLEEP

If everything went right with Gilbert, he could have the best of both worlds. The dreams would subside, or at least *dampen*, per the contract wording, and Kate would be none the wiser. She wouldn't have to coddle him, to wipe invisible tears from his unred eyes. She wouldn't have to know her husband, her rock, was having a bit of the scaries.

At work Jeff waited on pins for any response from Gilbert and the Society. Given the long stretch between meetings, Jeff racked up a worrying amount of sleep debt. His mustache bulged, flanked by a salt and pepper beard; his eyes drooped great bags under them like dead sea life; his focus blurred from blinks and headshakes. Colson, despite his friendlier demeanor, lost some of the sweetness to his salt. He called Jeff into the office the other day to ask why his quarterly reports showed errors in the tens of thousands.

The sleep office in Seattle called to remind him about his appointment for the study. Jeff hated traveling, and already knew he hated Seattle with its procession of homeless beggars, trash-laden street corners, and traffic which only relented at midnight. It once took him 45 minutes to drive five city blocks. Jeff hoped his pincer approach to the dream problem was correct. Relying solely on Gilbert Finnegan couldn't be more stupid.

Kate and her coworkers visited Claudia. The doctors started rehab as soon as she could hold herself up and she struggled through the painful burden, re-learning to use muscles and bones that were sliced and smashed just weeks ago. But she could go home and eventually return to work. Jeff wondered if an "accidental" car wreck wouldn't do something positive for his work life.

Just as well, Gilbert responded, very coldly, they could meet that evening at Shelley's Café, just like before. Jeff didn't feel this was the most "professional" place to meet, but it beat a therapist's couch where he was likely to doze into more terror dreams. It also seemed Gilbert hoped Jeff would, at the sight of some college student, call the whole thing off, so he could leave the Pacific Northwest for good.

Gilbert stood to meet him when Jeff walked through the neon-rich door, wiping his boots on the door mat. He shook his hand. "Welcome, Mr. Vickers."

Gilbert committed to his "professional" bit. His coat was buttoned, but it was still the same not-tan not-yellow. He sat up straight in his seat rather than slouched at a frightening angle, or even with his feet draped and crossed over the table.

"Thank you for your quick return of the contract; the Society is greatly appreciative."

"Enough with this, Gilbert, we don't have to do these formalities."

"I'm afraid we do, Mr. Vickers. We wouldn't want there to be any question of our efficacy and professionalism. We like to be as formal and up front as possible. It gives our clients the best experience and lets them know they're in good hands, that they can count on the Society to handle any of their somnolent issues."

"You're being formal and that's why we're meeting in a coffee shop?"

"As I am in a mobile capacity, we don't have access to standard facilities, and common, mutual ground is the best option. Unless you'd like to meet in the van."

"No thank you."

Gilbert's black eyes sheened like Jeff was a nagging splinter on his ass, but he pushed through it. "Are you sure you wouldn't like to step into my van, Mr. Vickers?"

"Coffee shop's fine, Gilbert."

"So tell me," and Gilbert plucked a leather-bound folder from the bench seat next to him and clicked a pen out, "what did you dream of last night?" He sat upright, waiting at attention for Jeff to begin.

"Last night? Last night a squid dragged me underwater and shoved a tentacle in my mouth and I suffocated." As soon as the first word left Jeff's lips, Gilbert's pen meandered around some surface Jeff couldn't see. It looked like drawing more than writing.

"I'm sorry to hear that, Mr. Vickers. That must be very troubling." Jeff took a massive and slow breath in through his nose. His jaw instinctively snapped. "Some specifics. Are you sure it was a squid or was it an octopus?" He looked up and slapped him in the face with his eyes.

"I'm not sure. What's the difference?"

"Well, Mr. Vickers, octopi have eight legs while squid have eight legs *and* two arms, or tentacles, that they use to catch prey. Octopi have rounder heads while squid feature more triangular heads. They do both belong to the cephalopod family so I can understand why you would be confused." Gilbert's hand tornadoed around the page. "Have you figured it out or should I continue on about marine life?"

Unconfident, "Then it was an octopus, Gilbert."

"Good, thank you. And did you truly suffocate, or did you drown?" Again, the ocular smack.

"Aren't they the same thing?"

"Certainly not!" Jeff understood that Gilbert prepped for one of his around-the-world laughs, but he managed to rein in the impulse and sat up straight, clicking his pen like a drumroll. "No. To suffocate is for the lungs to lose access to air for a long enough time that the brain dies. To drown is to inhale water into the lungs *instead* of air, thus overloading the respiratory system, disallowing oxygen to enter the lungs, and therefore removing oxygen supply to the brain. Which was it?"

"They still sound the same to me, Gilbert."

"Not true, Mr. Vickers. When one drowns one is much less thirsty."

"I don't know if I was thirsty or not," and Jeff realized the idiocy of that statement.

"Mr. Vickers, in order to provide the best service to you and help with dampening your somnolent visions, I will require specific and accurate information from you regarding said visions. It's very important."

"Okay Gilbert, I understand you're upset I didn't want to be your guinea pig. I just want to sleep. Can't you see?" Jeff felt his throat bob and his tongue felt dry and sticky. "Look at my face, Gilbert! I've barely slept in weeks with these damn dreams!" Jeff noticed his volume as shouts echoed back from coffee mugs and pastry cabinets. The usual college crowd glanced over. "I'm sorry," he said, hushed, "I just need them to stop."

"I don't know what you're talking about Mr. Vickers, but I will do my very best to help. As I mentioned, we need specifics." He spiraled his hand in alarming circles in the folder. "Is there anything else you can tell me about the vision?"

"Yeah, the water was orange."

Gilbert looked up. "Orange or pink?"

Jeff clutched his entire face in his hands and rubbed up and down, up and down. "It was orange, Gilbert."

"Oh good, at least there's that."

Gilbert's mockery behind his leather-bound folder shook Jeff's patience to rare lows. He should have seen this coming. He knew how petty Gilbert could be, from the trick questions about the toad vs the frog and the change of the rippling background, the repeated questioning of his nicotine usage. Everything seemed to be a trick or a test, some way of ruining Jeff's self-esteem or exposing him as a fraud or a liar. This entire thing was probably a ruse to steal Jeff's money. But Gilbert didn't seem like he needed money. And Jeff paid the Society directly, at least, that was the implication. Jeff wanted to quit, wanted to snatch the greasy man by the collar and pound his knuckles right over his stupid face. That's probably where he got his scar from, some other Shark slugging him good, and another for the road. But the sleep study was an even bigger question mark than Gilbert Finnegan. Jeff had dozens of nightmares so far and they only worsened, despite him growing a bit accustomed to them.

"Oh?" Gilbert looked up from his probably-drawing. "Well, now that we've noted what you saw last night, there's a few ways we can start. I instructed you some weeks ago to write your dreams down. You can start wherever you feel best." He readied his pen.

"You need to know all the dreams since we talked last?"

"*Need* isn't exactly the case, but it would certainly save time, Mr. Vickers, yes. Go on."

Truthfully, Jeff hadn't written them down, and they all faded from memory like ripples in a pink/orange pond. "So what can be done if I didn't write any of them down and can't remember?"

Gilbert *tsk*'d a couple of times and continued his insidious marking in the folder, scrambling every which way with pen held to paper. "Well that just means we need more data. Mr. Vickers, we are on your time now, not mine. But time is a factor here, and because your payment to the Society is based on time, it would behoove you to be cooperative and vigilant. You must write all your visions down. And more than that, I need you to document your emotions as well."

"It's mostly fear."

"Yes, fear is a common motivator for looking online to help with one's disturbing dreams." Gilbert never looked up, just darted his pen about, scratching. "Mr. Vickers, the level of *help* I can provide to you will depend on many things, including luck. Oneiromancy is not an exact science, as I've mentioned before. I am also not a doctor. I don't have access to blood panels, radiographs, urine strips, needles, or any similar implements. What I can do is guide you. If you want to dampen your nightmares, you need to understand what an acceptable change really means."

"Off would be nice, since you've done it to me before."

"Off is unlikely, Mr. Vickers."

"Why not? Can't you just teach me what you did?"

"To be an oneiromancer?" Gilbert looked up again. His jaw whirled around, knocking teeth together. "Mr. Vickers, oneiromancy takes time. An incredible amount of time. Also trust, patience, ethics, insight. It is a mental exercise, one of the subconscious, the unwaking, the wavering dance of the subliminal, liminal, and superliminal. Yes, I could teach you oneiromancy—"

"Then it's settled!"

"—but it wouldn't work." Jeff's face stared forward, incredulous, coaxing Gilbert to continue. "I can alter dreams to an extent, Mr. Vickers. Your dreams. The barista's dreams, the dreams of those girls you won't keep your eyes off. I can't change my *own* dreams. Can you tell me why?"

The answer, Jeff presumed, was buried right in front of him beneath a fresh spray of dirt. "No, Gilbert."

Gilbert smiled for the first time this evening, that slanted grin, burned by his scar. "Because I can't do anything subconsciously to myself. All my actions are manifestations of a conscious individual, a thinking mind, that is aware of what it's doing. I can't trick myself subconsciously any more than I could *suffocate* myself. Another person would have to choke me to death, just like another oneiromancer would need to alter my dreams for me, without me knowing. Otherwise, I would know I did it and there would be no change."

Gilbert's machine-gunning explanation made perfect sense, and for the first time Jeff started to consider Gilbert's life outside their interactions, having partners, coworkers, a nighttime hygiene ritual, having favorite sleepwear. What did an oneiromancer's dreams look like? "And you won't just," Jeff snapped his fingers, drawing the attention of the blonde barista, "black out my dreams, then?"

"Well, Mr. Vickers, like any noble pursuit, say boxing, painting, or drawing," Gilbert snapped his black eyes to Jeff's, "it's a daily practice. I *could*, technically, unless, of course, you caught on to whatever it is I do that sends signals to your brain, to do what I want with it." He got sour with this last bit, like the cartoon sound of a cartoon bomb falling, spiraling, to a cartoon earth, slowly. "But that would become quite expensive. Current rates are $500 a week, times 52 weeks a year, for however many years you choose to sleep tight. Most clients aren't that well off financially. Dampening, however, we can work on, and it will hopefully only run you a couple thousand dollars by the time we're finished, assuming you *cooperate* and are *honest*."

Gilbert had him at every corner. If he was being *honest*, that is, which Jeff couldn't say he was, but his choices were limited. He didn't want to tell Gilbert to go away because he might never come back after another spurn, and he still needed information from the sleep study. Jeff felt snared. Sometimes in a snare, you have to bite your own leg off to get out. Jeff was rather comfortable walking on two legs. The only thing he could muster was, "Sure."

"So, as I mentioned, you need to write all your dreams down. You need to find some method of documenting an emotional factor, perhaps on a scale from one to ten. Physical reactions would be an effective manner of calculating change as well, for instance, do you wake up sweating, screaming, fighting, naked, somewhere other than your bed, covered in blood, etcetera. And, because we will need some time to collect more data from you, there's not much else I can offer you until we have that. Let's meet up in seven days to assess the findings, and we can come up with a plan then."

"Sure."

"Good then, Mr. Vickers. It's been a pleasure." Gilbert stuffed his open palm toward Jeff's face. His hitchhiker's thumb stabbed out at an extreme angle. Jeff shook it. "Same time next week."

Gilbert gathered his folder, stuffed it under his armpit, and stepped, overstuffed keyring jingling around, out the door, clanging the bell as it shut. Jeff waited in battered frustration. For a brief, fantastical frame, he imagined himself following Gilbert's greasy scalp into the chilled air and getting in his car. He'd trail him, several car lengths behind to remain unnoticed. He would find his hotel or wherever he was staying at—motel was best—and wait until all the lights died away. He'd spray paint one side of his windshield pink, the other orange, and piss in his gas tank for good measure. He'd take unnerving photos of him through the slatted blinds in the bedroom. When Gilbert would question him, he'd respond, "Just go to sleep, Mr. Finnegan," and punch him right through the window.

Instead, he sat, listless, wondering which stupid decision was the best one.

It always seemed so simple, hearing others define their dreams and nightmares. Something unsettling that leads them to tell the story of it to someone or him or anyone who will listen in. As a child, they'd wrangle stuffed animals and sleep with nightlights on, or share a bed with their parents, keep the door open, drift off to a lullaby. He pictured Hank at his current age, bony in tight faded jeans, leaning over to calm a terrified Kate who flickered between herself now and the wiry, pink-shirted girl he saw in family photos, and Jeff knew full on in his heart that Hank would be the one she called to help her soothe a bad dream, not him.

The same couldn't be said for his own parents, so lucky they never had to cradle him asleep. The dreams were never there. The boogeyman never lurked in the closet. Now Jeff's boogeyman wore an oversized suit and jingled when he walked.

And still he sat, listening to the searing cackles of the college-age girls looming in the darkened corners of the café, wondering, even knowing, that it was too late for him.

He fell into bed without following his hygiene routine, so groggy he still had most of his clothes on. Kate's tiny body almost shot airborne from the Newtonesque surge of his crash, but it had little effect on her snores. Sleep took him, if briefly.

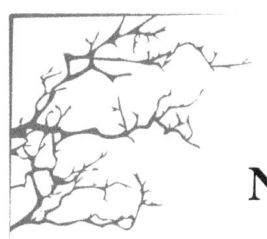

Night Forty

Jeff sweltered in his clothing, insulated like a burrito in the blankets, and he gasped, fought, and flailed away from the pillow and swallowed air, heavy. Kate slept on. In the legal pad, withered from forearm sweat, he wrote:

I was pregnant in the forest, running from a bear. I saw a white-tailed doe in the distance and ran towards it. It was faster than me. The bear was faster than me. It started with my stomach. Then I woke up.

Such upside-down logic penetrated his mind as his thoughts from the café jerked and spasmed from the dream. Then he remembered the new elements Gilbert required; emotion, physical effects. Gilbert recommended a scale of one to ten for emotion, and this one was a doozy, but he didn't have any other dreams scored to compare it with. He felt safe with an eight. And physical effects. Sweat, heavy breathing, not covered in blood as far as he could tell. Fully clothed, but he went to bed that way, save his shoes.

The recurrence of the deer bothered him. Hell, the entire affair would be most people's undoing, he encouraged himself, but the deer especially wrenched his brain around. It was the first recurrence he could remember, outside of the frog/toad dripped into his dreams by Gilbert. But this one, as far as he knew, was all him. The dream, for being a dream, made sense. He thought of both bears and bearing children (so to speak) earlier at the café, but what did the deer mean? He was chasing it. In his previous dream, the deer was running to him, seemingly, for safety. The reverse happened in the bear dream, where he ran toward the deer for his own safety, but the deer, once again, like from the jaguars, fled. And the fact that his belly was bloated (more than it actually was) and stretchmarked sent an awful weight and disorienting worm slithering through his guts.

Jeff felt perverted, corrupted, even more powerless than usual. Was it so literal? That him "bear"ing children would be his death? Many things were his death in these visions, and, as far as he knew, the one with the deer was the only manifestation in his real life. But here it was again, the deer, darting to and fro away from him, dooming him.

The early day battered his sunken eyes. The time finally came to make the trek to Seattle. He told Kate, "It'll be harder to lie to you, so I'll just tell you it's a surprise and leave it at that."

"Oh really?" She spun to him, excitement beaming from her face.

"Hopefully, if all goes well, yes." He spent the first several hours of his drive thinking of what in the world he could surprise her with that required a trip to Seattle. Perhaps, he thought, it would be best to truth his way out of his lie—tomorrow.

The drive to Seattle droned on, worsened only by the strict instructions to abstain from caffeine, the road splitting to multiple lanes with smoking semi-trucks, veering imports and funneling construction lanes. Jeff would wake, likely following some garish death-dream, and come home tomorrow morning. He packed his legal pad just in case.

The trip allowed him unfortunate time to ponder. What would Gilbert's reaction be if he found out about the sleep study? He'd probably mock him somehow, do his circular laugh around the room. "Professional" Gilbert who may remain indifferent, scribbling circles behind his folder. Kate was the one who should really be under the microscope.

Seattle, to Jeff, was packed with smelling hippies, useless diversity hires, rainbow-patterned umbrellas, all at a density that made him nauseous. The dizzying number of people banging shoulders in the graffiti-scabbed city only worsened with the quality of them: underside of the rock-bottom. He locked and re-locked his doors every time he saw pedestrians, fearing the button would soon break.

After a stressful elevator ride, a man and woman in white coats greeted him with unrelenting boredom and carried matching plastic coffee cups, he felt, in an effort to mock him.

"Which one of you is Dr. Kuttar?"

"Neither," said the woman, a brunette. "She'll look over your results when we're all finished."

"We're going to set you up tonight and you'll have results in a few days," said the man. Just like a doctor, Jeff thought. The more money you make, the less you do.

After checking in and overly disclosing personal information on their forms, the brunette, who had chocolate eyes similar to Kate's, but were glossed over by thick-rimmed glasses, showed him to his barren room. Beige paint, no pictures or paintings on the walls, and a bathroom so small Jeff had to climb around the cheap brown door to use it. The other technician glued cables to his head, chest, and legs with an adhesive sure to tear out hair when undone. The tech's pierced nose reminded him of a bull ring, silver, rounded and dangling. It was impossible to ignore that one tech had doe-eyes and the other may sprout horns to gore him through while he slept.

The bed crunched at each breath. The blankets scraped along his skin and tugged at the glued wires. It was never comfortable sleeping in a bed that wasn't your own. With the lights out, dark as the room was, the domed camera in the corner of the room distracted him. This pleasant vacation came with visual monitoring, too, just to make sure he wasn't sleepwalking or kicking his legs about at night. He supposed, as heavy a sleeper Kate was, it was possible he could have been kneecapping her all these years, but she'd likely have more of a limp.

His mind bubbled over with thoughts of the bull-ringed assistant and the restraint, however mild, of the machines he was strapped to, beeping, beeping. *Go to sleep, go to sleep,* he told himself, and the thought was a gentle drip of caffeine on his tongue dissolving each second.

Night Forty-One

But it happened. He slept, however brief, and scrambled for his legal pad, yanking wires along, catching his pen on them, and wrote:

I'm at home, sleeping. Everything is normal except I am lying next to a tiger who is also sleeping. I roll over and I poke my eye on one of its teeth. I scream. My screaming wakes the tiger. I am mauled to pieces. Emotion: 6. Physical: sweating, shaking, glued to machines.

Dreaming of a dream, huh? Or dreaming of sleep in general. He recalled the number of times he rolled over in the night and caught Kate's elbow right in his eye, picturing it smashing like a grape. For the first time in a long time, Jeff slept in a bed that wasn't his own, and the irony plummeted through his skull like a falling bowling ball that he dreamed of being at home.

However, unlike at home, he was supposed to continue sleeping for the study. Normally, or at least, what he would consider 'normal' over the last month or so, he'd wake, stymied, and stay awake after jotting notes at his writing desk, or second-guessing if he *should* be jotting notes. The glued cords pinched him, like tentacles dragging him back to their beeping boxes on wheels. He could try drawing, shading in shapes in the hopes they amassed into more coherent shapes. Or he could give it an honest go.

The absence of Kate's serrated wailing haunted him. He had learned, not necessarily to ignore it, but to accept it. Like a mole that hasn't grown in size over several years, it becomes less of a concern and it's simply there. Until it's not. And, if his dreams could mean anything at all, there was an implication that Kate, in big cat form, may render him to bits, possibly even in their bed. The only consolation was that not once in their decades-long marriage had Kate ever—ever ever—woken in the middle of the night or before he did, such a magnificent sleeper she was. Too bad the assistants will never know.

Jeff closed his eyes and breathed. He pictured Kate's bony frame, shadowed by the snowlight. He wondered how her painting was coming along, if the deer was taking shape by more than shaded ovals, and if she ever managed to finish that monstrous eye-having form he mucked up (still, potentially, without her knowledge). Outside, stories and stories below, traffic blared in cruelty, even still, in this cursed, ugly city. Damned, obliterable city. The saving grace was that, as Seattle was coastal, it was more rain and mud than snow, which only teased itself to the ground like spittle.

The domed camera cover snarled in red every few seconds. He pictured the poker game, Howard scraping up nickels from the yellowed tabletop and singing them into his tin can. He'd play more brazenly without Jeff there, keeping him in check, literally and figuratively, with safe bets and occasional howling bluffs. He might have even uncovered his motorcycle again to show it was polished up once more, eager for a more permanent melt of the snow.

Jeff imagined Colson, pressured, unsure of who to yell at, but still missing a friendly greeting from him. Thoughts of Hank, alone in bed now, presumably, since his wife's passing. Wondered if he'd gotten used to it, or, though no one would dare admit, prefer it. Jeff thought of the young women giggling around the coffee shop, enjoying a night with friends ignoring their studies, and how, maybe, there was some alternate reality that existed where he was a father to a freshman, dropping her off with her stuffed animals and a hot plate.

That side-stuck thorn, Gilbert Finnegan. Would Jeff tell him of this venture? Would Gilbert even care? Would he be curious of the data since he wanted him for dream-like experiments in the first place? Maybe he would think this sleep study was the "key" to something. Did Gilbert Finnegan even sleep at all...?

Night Forty-One (Again)

And then he woke, cool and bright, to sunbeams falling through the blinds. Indeed, he had fallen asleep a second round and found that it was miraculous, godly, and blank. The assistants, only a hair disheveled, beeped into the room to greet him. The brunette helped him unstick the cords (he noticed her fingernails, long, stamped with figures like whales and fish skeletons, mostly green) and, as he had predicted, ugly stickings of hair snapped off with them. The man with the bull ring helped him gather his things and even handed him his legal pad. Jeff felt a surge of unease, that these two things should not connect or be brought together like oil paddling away from water.

Jeff took it and thanked him.

Driving away from the city, Jeff smushed his head again and again on the headrest, an effort to push traffic forward. Like a coughing accordion it spit and wrenched and scrunched together in reckless tides. And then there was freedom, trees, hills, straight and beautiful stretches of grey highway. A superb mellow blessed him about 40 minutes outside Seattle, where he felt, *I made it,* though he knew full well it would be hours and hours before home.

And hours later, he remembered he promised Kate something. The obfuscation of his visit was pre-empted by some "surprise." But he knew it was ridiculous the moment it left his lips. Still, she would be expectant, and he should figure it out. On a slow, winding road near a turnoff for Mount Rainier National Park, Jeff slowed at a pull-off to piss. He hid behind his open car door, back turned to traffic from behind, and saw white on green in triangle form off the side of the road.

Curious. He'd never seen such a plant, though didn't spend much time looking over them. His yard was strictly grass with an empty garden bed lining the front of the house. Not even weeds grew there, and flowers never came because he never planted them. *Perhaps that should change*, he thought. He had tried over the last few weeks to give Kate flowers, though each attempt was thwarted by her impeding sleep schedule or friends compacted in twisted metal. If the identifier on his phone was to be trusted, the flower was called trillium, with massive leaves mid-stem, then in offset triangular formations of three long leaves, a green base and a white top. It looked like a strange cult symbol and his only thought when digging down and tugging its forking roots from the dirt was the hope it hadn't been peed on. He stuffed it on the floorboard of the passenger side and motored home.

Jeff remembered last night's sleep, likely funneling through some somnologists computer; the first sleep was ravaged as always, and the second was peace and air and pleasantness. Perhaps he should return to sleep more often and just knock the first one out.

After stopping at a store to swoop up a fake-crystal vase and patting excess dirt from the roots of the trillium, now wilted a bit, he groaned through the front door and hollered down the halls, announcing his return. Kate's echo bounced from her painting room. Jeff ditched his coat, clomped back, and walked through the doorway where she crunched over the drop cloth and had a comically bulbous wine glass perched on a stool next to her. The deer was coming around. The nightmarish figure still leaned on the far wall. Her greying hair swung back into a ponytail, and she had brownish-green fingertips under purple nail polish. She greeted him with a side smile and a "Hey" and asked how the trip was.

"It was okay. Couldn't nail down that surprise for you."

"Yeesh. All that way for nothing, then?"

"I tried to make the most of it." And from behind his back, passing it between upside down fingers, the fake crystal vase swung out and he held it out with both arms like a hug. "Got you these, at least."

Her head cocked. She set her brush down near the palette. "Thanks, Jeff." She took a sip of her wine, and then another.

"Do you like them?" *Of course not*, he told himself, *they're road weeds that someone definitely pissed on, and you failed.*

Another full swig and she washed it around her teeth before gulping down. "I can't believe, all this time, you forgot I hate flowers."

Somehow the miracle weed backfired. "Really? Are you sure?"

"I think I'd know, Jeff."

"Everyone likes flowers."

"Do *you* like flowers?"

"Sure."

"Very good for you. *I* think they are doomed to die. Because it's true. And the roots they're taken from will die, too."

"That's a bit cynical but I think I get it."

"But," her chocolate eyes throwing punches at his, "because you got them for me, I will try to care for them. Even though they'll die regardless."

"I think it's called 'trillium.'"

"Never heard of it."

"Neither have I. I think it looks nice though, and maybe you can paint it?" He stepped closer to her, standing for some form of forgiveness. "That way it won't ever die. We can hang it next to the deer." Smile, Jeff.

Kate laughed, stepped forward, and kissed him. "Thank you. They *are* pretty. They just won't be."

"Better paint fast."

Night Forty-Two

That night, or next morning, rather, after scribbling down a six on the emotion scale, logging that he was sweating and not washed head to toe in blood, nor was he fastened to monitoring devices (Gilbert's lie/truth mantra dinged around his head), and that he had been crushed by a great black rhinoceros while napping in the savannah, Jeff snuck back to the bedroom. He creaked open the door. Kate's grinding lightened. Her shoulders lifted beneath the white, layered sheets, gushing unconsciously. Jeff slid back under the covers like cash into an envelope and draped his hairy arm over Kate's slim frame. Somewhere up in his head, his memory already stuffed the rhino away like too many clothes in a cupboard and forced the door shut. He fell away, off into a valley of pure nothingness, with nothing for ground, nothing for water, negative air, and non-existent thought.

Night Forty-Two (Again)

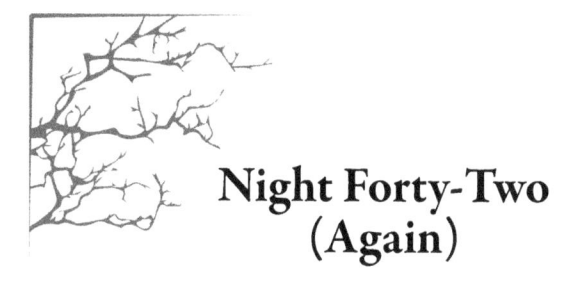

They woke, together. Kate stirred like a worm. They found each other. They gurgled and grunted and gave small simple kisses to shoulders and necks, the morning glowed over the windowsill in a wash of yellow.

Colson seemed pleased to have him back after two days gone and visited rather often to check in on his reports.

That evening, the trillium's triangled leaves withered down a few centimeters, just enough to give the feeling that they were unhappy with the current state of things. Kate cursed, a rarity. She scrambled, still in her scrubs, tipping over sloshes of water and ripping open packets of plant food. The hollow grey water inside the vase had a whispy film on the surface.

"Did you look up this 'trillium' when you killed it for me?" said Kate.

Jeff felt the air darken and wondered if the flickering of lights was all in his head like so many things these days were. "No, just thought it looked nice." He tried to church up a jar of pre-bought spaghetti sauce into something a little more homemade by introducing dried herbs and keeping the heat a bubbling low.

"The internet says they're not meant to be kept in homes. Says they'll die, and so will the roots you took it from." Jeff recalled some of the more harrowing searches he'd done himself, like when he asked the internet why his snot was black.

"That sounds familiar, now that you mention it."

Kate tossed the torn paper wrappings of the plant food. She squinted at her phone. "And trillium is also the official flower of Ontario, Canada, and their government, and is considered endangered in some parts of the world, making them illegal to pick, and also known as birthwort from its historical use as a uterine stimulant." She stabbed his eyes with her own. "Why did you go to Seattle, Jeff?"

He wondered, pausing, what the night would hold if he had decided against the flowers, or even if he had pulled into any other rest stop to relieve himself and perhaps seen some quaint lilies or marigolds to snatch up.

"Be honest with me," Kate added. Her lips sucked tight to her teeth, caught in their own crevices under the pressure of her jaw.

What would the hurt be, really, to tell her? Maybe she'd see it as a positive thing, that he cared for his own wellbeing or something of the sort.

"I went for a sleep study." She encouraged him to continue, wordlessly. "Not all of us are gifted like you, Kate. I don't sleep much these days."

"Why couldn't you just tell me?" She stepped in front of the flower, blocking it from view. "Is everything okay, are you fine, do they have the results yet, what's going on?"

A surprising amount of concern and panic from his typically cool wife. "I don't know yet, I haven't heard. And I've just been sleeping poorly, that's all."

"You're lying to me."

Jeff wondered, if the roles were reversed, and Kate was off visiting the big city overnight for shady reasons, if he would be as upset or be able to pick apart the truth.

"I have bad dreams, Kate." It spilled out of him like too much water in a vase, or too many flowers in water, or too little vase for the flowers. Without words, once more, she prodded him on. "I've been having bad dreams. Really, really bad ones. And I can't sleep, so I went to the doctor—"

"For bad dreams?!"

"What else was I supposed to do?"

Kate didn't answer, and instead crossed her arms tight over her ribs. "You usually play online doctor. That might make more sense this time."

"I've never had dreams like this before—not at *all* before. And they're... I was so scared, Kate." The admission was like standing naked in front of his entire middle school. A grown man, scared of his nightmares. Next he'd be wetting the bed.

"You should have told me." She looked away. Jeff sensed a guilt in her, that she was washing herself in what he said, trying to scrub off her own frustration and support him. "I'm your wife." It was a simple fact, but hearing it, Jeff's breath slowed. "You can talk to me."

And the guilt was his own now. He knew communication was important. Especially in a marriage tugging against a current threatening to hurl it over a waterfall. Jeff didn't want to admit that communication was more than "good morning"s and "I love you"s, of complimenting each other's artwork, but about sharing feelings. He feared, not just his dreams, but what expressing these feelings meant, would bring about. Somehow, acknowledging them threatened to make them real, give them a body and bones and rancid flesh.

"I was just embarrassed, I guess. I'm old, Kate. I'm having nightmares. Kids are supposed to have nightmares."

Her eyes fired when he said "kids." "It's okay, Jeff. Really. But we aren't meant to keep secrets. These things must be said. They'll eat you alive if not."

He nodded his head, near tears, but unwilling to let them win. Maybe that was the problem. "Yeah," he said, sniffling.

"How bad are these dreams that you went to the doctor?"

"Dreams where I die." Kate seemed unimpressed. "Dreams where I'm mauled, or gored, or trampled, suffocated, dropped from massive heights, dreams where animals die asking me for help. These dreams aren't normal.... Did I tell you I never had a dream before a month ago? Ever, in my life, ever, until then?"

"I don't think so, no."

"And now this. Every night, basically. I wake up yelling and sweating and shaking. I started writing them down just in case someone could help or discern some meaning or interpret them. You'd be able to tell, but you're so damn good at sleeping it never wakes you up."

She laughed, both at the accusation and the accuracy.

"You never dreamed?" Her hair fell along her ears. "What was that like?"

"I guess I never thought anything of it at all, not one bit. But now I can say it was the greatest thing, feeling nothing until morning. It wasn't even black, or white. It was nothing."

"That sounds like death."

"I've been dying a lot in these dreams Kate. I wish I'd go back to nothingness, while I sleep, that is. I guess I don't want to look forward to nothingness forever."

"I think that's what it's like. Nothing. But you wouldn't know it's nothing. You wouldn't know anything. It wouldn't be black. It'll be nothing. It won't be."

"Doesn't give you a lot to look forward to, does it?"

Kate's lips slanted and she gnawed her cheek. "No."

"No," Jeff said.

"Can I see them? Your dreams? You said you wrote them down."

The test was here, in stapled, double-sided paper, smack on his desk and pen was in hand. He could share, communicate openly, and expose himself, make himself vulnerable, or he could close up and deny her the only curiosity she's shown toward him in years. He already told her most of it, the general idea. This would be just like suturing up a wound after already digging the gravel out. Most of the damage was already done.

He pulled her to the writing desk and fished out his legal pad, folded over and over, battered by sweaty forearms and palms and pen scratches. Kate's chocolate eyes swam over the pages, squinting at scribbled words and flashing high eyebrows. "You get very specific in here. The colors you describe, the detail, when it's important, you put it in here. I wouldn't have thought."

"Yeah," he began, and decided that the Society *wasn't* something to be shared. Kate was a smart, intellectual professional in the medical field. Jeff felt if she knew about Gilbert and his oneiromancy, that he was slinking behind his doctor's back, that she wouldn't react as positively as she had thus far.

"It's no surprise then. Your interest in my paintings. Your drawings." Her smile split atoms in the air. "I think this is great, Jeff." Could it be this easy? The power of communication? He thanked her and scratched an itch that didn't exist on the back of his neck. "Would you mind if I tried, too?" Kate asked. He encouraged her to continue. "What if I wrote down my dreams?" Unexpected, Jeff thought. "We're married," sighing, "we make art together. We fight coyotes together. Sleep together. I just assumed we've always dreamed together. Now you're taking things a step further. Let me catch up."

She's coming around, he thought.

The years of seething about work, of wasting away in front of the news and simmering in its salinity, of wishing himself back to pugilistic youth, all of that had driven Kate away. But sudden things, shattering things, flipped a switch in Jeff's brain. All it took was a few bad dreams, a dead parent, and a near-fatal car crash. Simple cares worked their sweet charms.

Night Forty-Three

Jeff, forearms sogging the pages, wrote in slipping pen on the legal pad at his nightstand (he moved it after the discussion with Kate) of a mermaid swimming deep in the salty sea, an iron hook dug into her tail. The hook was an extension of his arm, rubbery twisted flesh tying through the eyelet.

He slept again in beautiful, clean silence, an empty blankscape until reality summoned him back. Kate's snoring ceased. Jeff, out of curiosity more than sharing an experience, reminded Kate of her resolution. She gouged sleep from her eyelids and sat, unsure of where to start.

"Better move quick. The longer you wait, the less you remember."

"It's just shapes, mostly. Shapes, colors, lines, all moving, crossing into the next."

She said that it wasn't anything like what Jeff wrote down, nothing so concrete and vivid. She took his cue, however, and listed *emotion: 2, physical: scratchy throat*.

That night, Jeff came home at an appropriate time and found Kate in the painting room, swimming in artificial light, greying hair glinting in a soft ponytail, wine mostly gone. She placed the deer painting off to the side, and the previous painting, the dark, bendy painting, the dragging and drooping painting with voids for what most would consider eyes, rested on the easel.

"Hey."

"Hey."

She sloshed her brush around, jagged and loose. Jeff couldn't see where he had smudged a finger on it weeks before. He clasped his hands behind his back just to be safe.

"I didn't think of it at the time, but with the painting I was already writing my dreams down. Sometimes."

"That's right, you said you saw this thing in a dream once."

"I did. I think I did. Painting it is more sensible than writing about them. 'Shapes and colors.' Do these look like any shapes or colors you've seen before?" She said it with an air of honesty and criticism.

"I think those things are eyes."

"These swirls, or tunnels?"

"I guess so, yeah."

"I never saw this as a living thing. But maybe that's what painting is for."

Jeff didn't have a good response. Quiet, he told himself, could be just as impactful as a verbal response. It could be the perfect response in the right situation.

"I thought my dreams were normal," she continued. "Now I'm not sure. I read what you wrote. Are mine the strange ones or yours?"

"I think mine are certainly the odd ones. It can't be healthy to see what I see every night. Dying with such surprising variety."

"But you see something, Jeff. I hadn't considered it. Is this always what I dream? Does it ever change?"

"I think you're reading too much into this."

"How so? You're seeing a doctor because of your dreams."

"I think mine are more a problem because of my reaction. I don't sleep, Kate. The dreams shake me alive, and I scream. It happens every night. And it was nothing before that—"

"—A sudden shift in the brain." Jeff noticed her stiff tone. She wasn't the type to worry so. He knew she was scared by her mother's unfair death (when is it ever a good time to bring that up?), and Claudia's faultless car wreck damaged her in vague, peripheral ways. She must have seen, similarly to the empty chair at her father's dinner table, what's left after tragedy reminds you it doesn't care for feelings.

"I think you're fine, Kate. You sleep enough for the both of us. Remember, 'emotion: 2'?"

"And a scratchy throat."

Introspection didn't suit her. He wasn't sure it suited himself, either, but it was all he had for a while, there. Her eyes, often a bubbling brown, collapsed matte and small. She moved her arm and brush along the canvas in wicked ways. "Are you gonna be okay, Kate?"

She turned to him. "Yes, of course." She drank.

He went off to draw. Jeff's (almost) daily practice improved. Tonight's sample was a lily, draping its petals over lush stems and a flowing, rounded vase. It sat on a windowsill, and he scraped at the shadows, focusing on the angles the light traveled in. The sound of a forest being sawed down told him Kate fell asleep without him. Jeff stripped and slipped into bed beside her. He worried, strangely, about her worry, and how his own problems seemed to erode onto her. And it wouldn't have happened if he hadn't shared his foolish fears. She would have continued to sleep, intensely, and dream of shapes and colors and lines blurring over each other without thought, forever. But this is what helped in a marriage, right? Communication of fears. She, herself, had chastised him for the secrecy, and yet it stuck in her like a venomous wasp stinger. Perhaps he was overreacting, and perhaps, he hoped, that this was a one-day thing that would soon fade once there was a bad day at work or a funny joke distracted her mind. Perhaps she wouldn't continue writing about her dreams, though he wouldn't dare suggest she stop painting.

Night Forty-Four

The next morning, bed lamp smearing his tired eyes, Jeff describing a surprising dream in which he did *not* die, but was, however, tied to a wooden structure (he hesitated to write "cross"), dangling in the desert. Crows perched near his shoulders and along the horizontal plank, sometimes giving a sharp nip to his forearms, but mostly they spoke to him—cawed in his ear, a rasping, threatening raven. Jeff was compelled to give a nine to emotion, on the grounds that the dream seemed to extend far beyond the length of the others, like visiting a planet with 100-hour days. He was tired from rethinking it, tired from experiencing it, but also assumed it could get much worse, and he might prefer if the crow flew into his mouth to save time. Dream Jeff probably wasn't escaping that one. He made the daily note that he sweated enough to change his underwear, but also noted scrapes near his wrists where ropes were tied in his mind.

Jeff stole another blissful REM cycle before returning to life when Kate's alarm went off.

Night Forty-Four (Again)

He palmed along her ribs and upper arm and shoulder. She grasped his hand and kneaded their fingers together. Jeff kissed her good morning and didn't remind her to write down her dreams, and she didn't mention it.

Night Forty-Five

In the middle of his better-than-average workday (Colson was out sick), Dr. Kuttar called him regarding the results of the polysomnography. He hoped she discovered the key to keep him from seeing Gilbert Finnegan that night.

"Mr. Vickers, your results are unusual."

Oh?

"You had two distinct measurements of sleep, which can be explained by you waking up in the middle of the study. What's interesting is the first set shows massive activity for about ten minutes before you woke up—this data is fascinating. It's both good and bad for you, really. In essence, you are experiencing normal sleep—no apnea, no restless leg syndrome or dream enactment. You went to sleep and remained asleep as expected through two REM cycles, then the second one had this explosion of energy on the readings, like an exponential blooming. The waves were the widest we've ever seen by a tall margin.

"And the opposite of that—when you resumed sleep after interruption, the data suggests normal REM sleep *except* complete absence of dream function. Mr. Vickers, this was only one night. My bet is that something unplugged or malfunctioned during the second round, as it shows you got out of bed. The equipment is very sensitive, any disturbance outside of normal parameters can affect the results."

Jeff felt the results of the test were perfectly accurate. "So what are the next steps?"

Sighing, "Unfortunately, there aren't any."

Doctors. This should have been a google search. "Go on."

"This study was performed to see if you had any sleep disorders that would explain your negative experiences while dreaming. It seems your ability to sleep is just fine, even enviable to some of us. For some reason you have hyperactive dreams, but unfortunately there isn't a specialist I could refer you to."

"You are the specialist I was already referred to."

"We could repeat the test, under the assumption that the second set of data is due to equipment malfunction."

"I don't think that's necessary."

"I'll do some more research and let you know if I find something, but my best guess is that the problem is emotional."

"Yeah. I'm pretty upset about it."

"I mean that it involves your emotions rather than some body or brain malfunction."

There was a sting in the back of Jeff's mind, some nagging swamp splash that echoed in the sound of his father's voice, aghast at the implication that a man, a son born from his own seed, had emotional problems. "What does that mean?"

"Medically, this isn't anything I can help with. If you've got money to throw away, I suppose you could see a neurologist, but without other symptoms I think it's a waste of your time. Our equipment didn't detect seizures or involuntary movements, and you've never mentioned anything like that. If you're open to it, seeing a therapist might help with the dreams, if you've maybe got some issues that your brain is struggling to work through, it's possible they're manifesting as nightmares, and—" and Jeff hung up the phone.

Night Forty-Six

Jeff met Gilbert that night in Shelley's Café. They sat at the same table in the middle of the row alongside the far windows. Gilbert remained, as ever, in his oversized suit, unflattering combover, and a tearing scar across his lip that seemed to warp and shift every time Jeff saw it. Gilbert carried his leather folder with him. Jeff imagined it had lined paper inside that he scribbled on.

"Mr. Vickers, pleasure to see you again," extending a hand with yellow-stained nails. The "Mr. Vickers"ing slashed his nerves.

"Thanks, Gilbert, how are you?"

"Oh so kind of you to ask, but unfortunately I can't share my personal details with clients. It's in the contract you signed for the Society."

"Right."

"So how have the dreams been?" He undid the folder and hid behind it, clicking his pen open.

"About the same as ever. I've got my notes if you want me to read them."

Gilbert paused and looked up, his grey eyes flattened. "Yes, go right ahead."

Jeff flapped through pages of wilted legal pad. He recounted the past week's visions: the bear mauling, the mermaid towing, the borderline crucifixion, all of it. Jeff noticed that Gilbert's absent tracing went to legitimate notetaking after the first one. Jeff's tone shifted from arbitrary to attentive. He tried to figure out which aspects Gilbert sparked at, when his eyes warbled, when his lips sneered or his jaw rocked. Any crossings-out. They could be underlines.

"Is that it?" Gilbert asked, after Jeff paused when it was, indeed, "it."

"Yeah." Gilbert continued to write. And write. A good two minutes he wrote beyond when Jeff stopped. He murmured to himself and his eyes swept around their sockets, glaring at the ceiling and the window, calculating.

"Interesting." Was it? "Very interesting." Hmm. "Are you sure you don't want my help? My *real* help?"

A tease. What would Gilbert's *real* help look like, anyway? He talked of Jeff changing his life to change his dreams to change his life, like some winding ouroboros. And was it even possible? Gilbert had shown him what he could do, altering his dreams to a more favorable state, i.e., blank. But there was no indication whatsoever that this could alter his waking life. Then he remembered the deer crumpling against his patio door. Was the incident something drawn up by Gilbert? Or simple dumb luck? Deer lived wild in the area evidenced by the multitude of crossing signs riddling highways in the Pacific Northwest (more of a farce than anything, given the speed one travels on a highway). If Gilbert could manifest Jeff's dreams, he certainly picked the tamest one, and that dream also happened before he ever contacted the Society. The odds were low, but Jeff had anted-in by contacting an oneiromancer in the first place. Some part of him had to believe. And with the medical route coming up dry, Gilbert Finnegan's greasy scalp seemed to be his only option.

Jeff didn't *want* his dreams to manifest, not in their current state. But he supposed that was where much of Gilbert's help would come in—molding the dream to his liking and flipping the proverbial "go" switch. But no. It felt awful and manipulative, like removing free will, like brewing a love potion. Jeff would know it wasn't through his own means, would know whatever he wanted would be a fabrication of Gilbert Finnegan's strange skill. The focus needed to remain on "dampening" the dreams, so he could have a decent night's sleep and not panic anytime he encountered something sharp.

"Yes, I'm sure."

"Well then. That's fine. Based on what you've recounted to me, if your goal is to dampen the harsh effects of the visions, I have some lifestyle recommendations."

Oh boy. "Sure, go ahead."

"First is that you begin some sort of exercise regimen."

Surprising. Gilbert had secretly given him subconscious signals to alter his dreams and now told him the secret was a few sets of jumping jacks? "How, exactly?"

"The surgeon general of the United States recommends at least thirty minutes of moderate physical activity per day for a healthy cardiovascular system."

"Does the surgeon general have recommendations on reducing nightmares?"

"Mr. Vickers, intense exercise is proven to change your brain chemistry. When people dream, a slurry of chemicals zoom around their brains. Some are absorbed, or received, some inhibited. This reception-to-inhibition level, combined with your unique soup of chemicals and which receptors, re-uptake receptors, re-uptake inhibitors, etcetera you uniquely have, is likely your culprit."

Jeff couldn't understand much about the sentence beyond "chemical soup," but he encouraged him to continue.

"Exercise releases norepinephrine. Perhaps changing the levels of this chemical, versus your specific amount of norepinephrine receptors along with the rest of the soup, will dampen your dreams. It also has the potential to help with your sweating problem."

"Wow, are you going to recommend I go on a diet, too?"

"Not at the moment, Mr. Vickers. Science requires specific controlled and manipulated variables. We can tornado all the chemicals in your brain and body if we want. But if we change all of them at once and you improve, we won't know which one did the trick, or if there are multiple combinations that warranted a specific result, and so on. This will take time, Mr. Vickers. Time, and *commitment.*" He smiled that slanted Gilbert smile. Jeff expected him to throw his legs up on the table, but at this moment, he was being a *professional.*

"So, specifically, I should change as little about my life as possible so we can see if the exercise thing is working?"

"I doubt you would be able to alter all of them without serious intention. Again, daily practice, Mr. Vickers. Do what you please, it's your dime," he leaned forward, just like he would at the kitchen table, "as long as what you please includes *exercise.*"

Ever since the sucker punch and the doctor telling him his boxing days were over, Jeff's exercise regimen plummeted off a cliff. Besides, he was already married—who was he trying to bag? And it occurred to him then that perhaps he wasn't quite so attractive as Kate was. Kate, while skinny, was *bone*-skinny, not the kind of fitness encouraged on television. She, too, hated working out, but her body didn't seem to care, unlike Jeff's, which bloated exponentially at each glance at apple pie.

"Which do you recommend?"

"Anything should do. As long as it's done every day, for at least thirty minutes, just like the surgeon general recommends."

"Anything?"

"Sure, you can run or lift or ski, whatever you do here when you're this close to Canada. You can jog or box again if you're up for it. Sign up for martial arts or join a Zumba class, anything will be better than nothing."

"And how long will this take?"

"Again, to be very clear, I don't know that it will work. It's the first test, the easiest one, at least. And the one that will benefit your health the most. If it's working, you might see results in as little as a week, which is convenient as that's when you'll pay us next. Again, very important, you must be honest, you must be clear. If you fudge the numbers, so to speak, I won't know how to proceed and you, alone, will suffer. This is for your benefit. I'm just profiting from it."

Night Forty-Seven

The trillium, obviously ill, sank its triangular trimmings to the lip of the vase. Jeff noticed it dying on the kitchen counter just as he came in from a brisk walk around the block, ribs scraping against his weak lungs. He wasn't pouring sweat, really, he was more awash with it. It crawled into every crevice, his armpits, his belly folds, his ass and knees and toes.

Kate didn't hear him come in, and when Jeff pushed the door to the painting room open, she scattered back and sloshed just a smidge of wine over the top of her glass, yelling.

"Sorry, didn't realize I was so quiet."

Kate brought her hand to her dashing heartbeat. "That's fine, that's okay, just caught me is all."

The painting, the strange one, now laid on the easel. Any evidence that Jeff fouled with it was covered over. It pained him, in a distant way, to see her back at this piece. It was becoming a *thing*. It still bent, low and gaunt, yes, but its eye-voids now sunk in a polygonal head atop a wretched body. Blacks and blacks and deep blues.

Kate saw him ogle the piece. She licked up a streak of wine that fell down the glass. "I figured it out. Can you tell?"

"It's coming along, it seems."

"Do you know what it is?"

Jeff was sure this was a trap. A trick question, a green herring, and an upside-down elevator. "A ghoul?"

"That's funny." She slurped her red. "It's you."

It was a trap. He knew it, he smelled it, he felt it swimming through his pores. "I'm struggling to see myself in this one." A miracle save.

"You're right." She cocked her head and grinned with only her lips, deepening in color with wine. "It's an interpretive piece. Impressionist. EX-pressionist."

The words fell through his mouth before he could stop them up in his throat. "I thought you saw this in a dream?" He didn't want to talk to her about dreams anymore, but it was too late to take it back.

"I did. I'm just now making sense of it."

Bad. Kate had one experience analyzing her own dreams and now she was falling down a wonderland rabbit hole. This *thing* wasn't him. It was a monster, a ghoul, as he had guessed, that's all it could be, and she was wild.

"The shapes I saw, the lines and angles shifting. It makes sense. Until recently, you would come to me in my sleep. Until recently, I fell asleep alone. I woke up alone. You were there somewhere in the middle of it. You came in like a dream and I couldn't remember you being there when I woke up."

"Kate, I'm sorry I said you should write down your dreams, it was stupid—I don't think this is a good idea."

"Nonsense. This is fine, this is my artistic expression. I started painting this long before I asked—and it was I that asked *you*, not the inverse—and I can keep on if I want. But this is more 'me.' This makes more sense."

Jeff wasn't sure it did, looking at the warped creature on the canvas, the creature that was supposedly him. "If you say you're okay, then I believe you," which felt like a kind lie.

She held the brush and gawked at her palette, overrun with dark blacks, greys, blues, all sloshed together for certain shades. Unhappy, she dunked her brush into her wine glass perched on the stool next to her. The glass bled strange and concentrated. She spread the brush around the eye-voids and the top layer washed away in running purple-brown.

"Neat technique," Jeff said, squirming. "Not gonna drink that, are you?"

The ugliest side-eye plowed over him. "Of course not. Don't be ridiculous."

Night Fifty-Four

For seven days, Jeff noted his dreams. Some left him serene despite their bizarre terror. He walked the neighborhood, past the semi-unfrozen pond, past the new school at the dead end of a housing development, through a trail of cattails and wire fencing. Was the exercise working? Surely not. The dreams still stalked him vivid and horrible; his favorite this week was the great spider who plugged his ears, eyes, nose, and mouth with its legs. But after waking he didn't seem to care as much. Gilbert's assertion that exercise would also address his sweating wasn't quite true, as he still stuck like fly paper to the sheets when he woke.

Some days, instead of immediately going back to bed for the beautiful second rest, he tended the trillium. Kate wasn't trying like she said she would. She painted every night this week. With said painting came glass after rounded glass of sloshing red wine. It started rough, with almost no conversation coming from her after the revelation that the void-like bendy thing she painted was Jeff. As the days trickled on, her demeanor lightened, and she even visited Claudia when she passed a milestone in her PT. Jeff regretted ever mentioning his dreams to Kate, ever mentioning his problems. Perhaps she moved on, or maybe after coming to terms with her piece, perhaps she had new dreams that were less manic. She resumed painting the deer, and Jeff swore to feed himself to a massive snake before discussing dreams with Kate ever again.

Jeff met Gilbert at the café. Same table, same row near the windows. The other corners buzzed with college students, and Jeff found himself pulled away at times.

"Mr. Vickers."

"What?"

"Are you paying attention?"

"I'm sorry.

"I asked you to tell me how the exercise regimen has been working. Any change in visions?"

"I'm doing it, I'm walking around. And I guess I just don't care as much about them. They're still awful. I brought my notebook; I can tell you. I feel a little desensitized."

"Maybe the dampening is working?" Gilbert clarified.

"Maybe."

"A shame." Gilbert fiddled with his hands like he wanted a smoke. His eyes were sunken and his skin leaked translucence, his scar piercing white. "Well keep it up, I suppose."

"That's it? That's all you've got."

"I could recommend some other things to you, but if we got lucky and the first one is working, then there's no need."

"Would it hurt? If we already know the exercise is helping, then what's the harm in adding something else? Either it works or it doesn't, and I can still exercise."

"The other recommendations aren't nearly as fun, Mr. Vickers." Jeff hardly considered sweating through three layers of clothes on his daily walks through shin-deep slush to be "fun," but they did seem to help. Jeff encouraged Gilbert to continue. "Bloodletting."

"Excuse me?"

"An ancient practice, purging of perceived bad blood, Mr. Vickers. Losing, let's say, an amount of blood, and forcing your body to recoup that blood requires resources. Those are resources that could be used to generate neurotransmitters which give you your foul dreams. If they're used to make new, fresh blood, there might not be enough swimming upstairs to give you a bad dream."

"Is this the only option?"

"Granted, if you are hoping to do this by yourself you either need to be very determined or come across an eager store of leeches, and I swore I'd never track down a case of those again, no sir."

"We can move on from the bloodletting, Gilbert."

"And you would probably want to keep it secret from your wife. You'd want to have a good method. Assuming you don't have any bizarre kinks, a simple razorblade would work best. Sharp, sharp, sharp. You can buy a box cutter at one of the hardware stores here. But location is important, obviously, if you want to keep it a secret. You just need to choose a part—"

"Gilbert—"

"—that you don't frequently use, or use less. Your wife would never notice a series of slices along the bottom of your feet, but you have to walk on the darn things and that can only inhibit healing." Jeff decided to let him finish. "I feel like most middle-aged wives try to avoid looking at their husband's backsides as much as possible, so that's a decent one, too, but really getting at it is tricky. Human beings, generally speaking, have a tough time seeing their own keisters. Then we're talking mirrors and so on. You're likely to do severe damage. And then, the same problem with the feet, you likely want to sit down now and again. It's tricky. The bloodletting is tricky."

"What else can I try, Gilbert?"

"Wow, fascinating," and bounced off his theoretical tangent. "You can try staring at the color blue." Jeff encouraged him. "What you see with your eyes determines what your brain sees, obviously. Clearly."

Jeff noted that it was almost certainly a visual cue from Gilbert that caused him to lose his dreams. He hoped he'd get back there one day.

"Certain colors elicit different responses in us. Think of bulls and how matadors wave the color red at them, and they become infuriated." Jeff hadn't thought of a bull in days; the dampening could be working. "It's all horse sh—.... It's nonsense. Bulls can't see red. They're completely color-blind, you know. It's baloney. But humans can. Blue is effective at initiating a sense of calm across the body. You can try staring at blue before sleeping."

"How much blue, like a blue dot, a blue marker? How long?"

"The more the better. I think ideally you would buy a massive sheet of blue paper and tack it to your wall and stare at that for a good couple hours before bed." Jeff hated Gilbert, fully, completely, and maddeningly. He wanted to punch him and choke him and squeeze his dull eyes out.

"What else is there?"

"You could try staring at the color green."

Jeff would have thrown his coffee across the room if he'd ordered any. "Do you recommend I look at both blue and green simultaneously?"

"Seems difficult, but if you could make it work, then it might prove beneficial."

"And what about when I cut myself open, should I start with my ass or my feet?"

"Mr. Vickers, I'm sensing some hostility. Do you have any other questions for me, or can we adjourn until next week?"

"I told my wife about my dreams." It fell out of him like shit from a horse.

"Did you? How did that go?"

"She supported me. We had a real talk." Gilbert had joked weeks ago they would be starting "therapy," and it seemed he was finally right, along with every other professional he'd seen recently. "She volunteered to write her dreams down, too. That part wasn't good." Gilbert encouraged Jeff to continue. "She's a painter, and she had this sort of crazed episode where she painted her dream instead of writing it, and it was this awful, mangled shape. She said it was me."

"But it wasn't you."

"No, it was just shapes and shadows that all flexed together. Blacks, lots of black."

"Your wife have trouble sleeping, too?"

It was all Jeff could do to keep from howling in the busy café. "Of course not, no."

"So the opposite?" Gilbert's shoulders stiffened like he was bracing for a punch. "Does she sleep too much?"

Jeff tried to act as natural as possible. Totally calm. He didn't want to let his eyes dilate or his brows bend or give any signs he was about to tell a lie. He tapped into poker to give a check, not a raise. "Not that she's told me, no."

"Well," he marked some lines in his leather folder, "we might just have ourselves a weirdo here, Jeff—Mr. Vickers."

"You know anything about trillium?"

"Birthwort?" Gilbert said. "Not a thing, why?"

"Just thought you might."

Jeff felt certain Gilbert was pulling his leg. Dragging it, in fact, toward where he wanted Jeff to go. The notion was absurd. It was ridiculous to think that staring at a color or, God forbid, cutting himself to bleed would fix anything. In fact, it was so ridiculous, it might warrant stopping the exercise, too. The brain that suggested he slice his feet open could not be the same one that warranted a moderate regimen of exercise. But his dream that night was middling.

Night Fifty-Five

A walrus rolled over him. Big deal. He wrote the petty details in his legal pad (now moved back to the writing desk, away from Kate's eyes), marked down a four for emotion and noted he did not sweat.

Ridiculous.

Jeff climbed back into bed and wrapped his dry arm over Kate's bobbing ribcage. She was warm and loud and smelled of mild winterberry. Her breath snarled like a warmed-up diesel engine. No unusual sleeping habits here.

Colson continued his trend of civility, provided Jeff appeared to take an interest in his wellbeing by asking him menial things about his wife or his kids or complimenting his polished shoes. Jeff even noticed he was lighter on the others in his department, too. None of them would thank him, though.

Poker met that night. Howard dragged out a new display of manliness: a bile-yellow box of "premium" cigars. *Joy*, Jeff thought, *more smoke*. He finally achieved respite now that he met with Gilbert in a public building, just to get washed in fumes here in Howard's garage. The seven or eight partakers, Howard included, Jeff excluded, thumbed their cigars. Some of them smoked too fast and, perhaps buzzing off the novelty, made foolish raises, their nickels clanking to Jeff's pile. Howard smoked his much too slowly and relit it more than he swore he ever had to before. Howard relished telling the table that each of these cigars individually was worth more than each person bet with that night.

His motorcycle was hidden under the black cover. Jeff was pretty sure he hated Howard. Hated his crude, gruff voice, hated how he bet obnoxious sums on meaningless hands (as long as Jeff bowed out), and hated how he needed to prove to the guys that he was "a guy." None of the others seemed to like him much either, but here they were. Jeff decided, at that moment, that he would make this his last poker game. Besides, he'd be smelling the overpowered smoke stuck in his nose hairs for weeks after this. Better run 'em up.

He played patient, yet present. He folded on nothing. Every hand was a check and a raise, atypical behavior for Jeff, who often bet on nothing unless the flop held promise. Jeff realized perhaps this caused Howard's need to keep relighting his cigar, as he was so baffled by Jeff's unusual patterns he forgot to smoke.

Going all-in, however, would actually require a good hand. Bluffing needed to be strategic, but a lie only worked when the other player wasn't confident in their own hand. So what kind of man was Howard? Jeff thought he had a good read after all these years. He displayed valuables to people, like his polished motorcycle in the dead of winter, and his box of cigars he passed out to guests, but what did that actually do? Show wealth? Manliness? He had games at his house, exclusively, the place for all the guys to gather up. He also played wild. That night especially, he threw coins to the table on any hand that came up, but bowed out when Jeff bet. If he was going to take

Howard's money, Howard had to put it on the line first. Jeff needed to ease up a little, give Howard some confidence.

Jeff played loose now, anteing on the opening hand before any card flipped. This frustrated some of the guys who played with more modest piles of nickels. And Howard, too, folded. After a few rounds, however, Howard got so frustrated, nostrils gaping wide, because he wasn't playing the game that he just placed a bet on the next deal, and it was a perfect time, too. Jeff only had the two of clubs and nine of diamonds in his hand. Nothing could come of that at all. He kept raising and betting and Howard clashed with him and the river came down and Jeff lost his ass. Intentionally.

Howard guffawed and blasted crude smoke through his nose. Jeff sucked up the loss and raised again with a shiny stack of nickels to start the next hand. One guy squirmed. Howard danced with him now, a flailing idiot with a cigar dangling from the side of his mouth, confident, just as Jeff planned.

The flop had potential for a king high straight, and Jeff had the king and queen in his hand. He needed the ace. He and Howard upped the ante and most of the others folded off. The river dropped, of all things, a nine. No ace, but the king high was still good. And he committed. All-in. And Howard bit.

Jeff's cookie tin threatened to buckle under the weight of Howard's nickels jingling inside.

On the drive home, Jeff felt little satisfaction. He didn't announce his withdrawal from the games per se, but the implication was in the air as he stood after the last hand. The victory felt hollow. Jeff set Howard up and knocked him down, but he figured he'd get more from it, some crude and bawdy testosterone high from besting a fellow competitor. Instead, he just plowed home in the dark rain with his wipers at max.

As he entered the house, Jeff heard Kate's megaphone snore from the bedroom. In the kitchen, Jeff's eye caught the trillium again. Its leaves sagged pathetic and sinking, and it melted its greens into browns. Kate didn't care if this thing died, but why did he? Maybe something about Kate's promise to watch over it and her disregard for its care. The fake crystal vase held foul, milky water. Jeff dumped it out, added new water, and added a quick bit of fertilizer. A move to the windowsill meant little at this hour, but in the morning, the winter sun would show it some love. But Jeff didn't think that would be enough to save it, not as far gone as the flower was.

He whirled his coat back on and stepped to the front garden, recently thawed of glassed snow, and, through squinting, rain-battered eyes, smashed some thick, mismatched kitchen spoons into the wet dirt. He dug a modest hole and placed the trillium roots in first, dribbling bits of dirt over the top of them. He filled the rest and tied it upright to a stabbed-in chopstick with twine. In the sideways rain, he emptied the rest of the plant food into the soil. *It's hopeless*, he thought. But even without hope, he wouldn't allow it to die. This flower would be no more than compost in a week, if that. But it stood a better chance in the dirt, where he stole it from, than soaking inside pretty plastic on a scratched countertop. The trillium's triangular offset leaves sulked, strung up to stand.

Night Fifty-Six

Jeff noted a five for emotion in his journal from the pathetic dream involving penguins smothering him in the arctic. It would have been comical if he didn't die at the end. No sweat.

Kate was coming around again and kissed him good morning. He felt the pressing urge to tell her about the itch in the back of his mind. Part of him hoped she'd notice the trillium missing and say something, then he could say he made a hollow attempt at saving it, and she would thank him and say how wonderful he was for caring for her gift even though she said she would do it herself. Instead, she brushed her teeth and cooked her toast and stomped off to work in her scrubs and didn't say goodbye.

Kate called him into the painting room that night, the only invite he'd received. The deer painting was finished; a profile view of the body with the head cocked toward the viewer and slashing, smudged brushes, bushes, and trees lining either side of it, dark, hunter green (enough to dampen dreams, Gilbert?). Obviously, Jeff said he adored it. Internally, he was pleased that she painted something real and not another misshapen demon she claimed to be him. She seemed lighter, carefree, the way she spun around, displaying the finished piece, toes sliding in pink socks. The trillium incident seemed behind them (or her at least), and the dream journal seemed behind them as well.

"Where do you wanna hang this thing?" Jeff asked.

Smiling, an unusual, almost forgotten smile, "I was thinking in the kitchen. Right by the patio door."

They put it up.

It was terrible.

It clashed with everything in the kitchen and was smashed in awkwardly between the frame of the door and the perpendicular wall.

"Amazing," Jeff said.

Kate laughed and laughed and took a photo to send to her friends.

Jeff found himself drawing late into the evening; a flower tucked behind an ear, similar to the trillium, but Jeff couldn't shade triangles properly. He tried to form a full face, but the jaw was in quotations, "a jaw," and the same for all the other features, too. The nose, the eyes, everything looked glued on like a serial killer's note chopped up from magazine letters. The ear looked okay. Many curves. Jeff was better at shading curves.

Night Fifty-Seven

Jeff hoisted up from bed with Kate, grinding gravel in her face, oblivious next to him. Sweat jagged him like on his brisk walks, which he still refused to take on account of Gilbert's idiocy. The crinkled legal pad nestled in the writing desk was close to full. He wrote, in shaky script:

I rode bareback on a chestnut horse with a black mane through a tall grassy field. The horse's foot caught on something in the ground, a hole maybe, and tumbled forward, and I with it. The horse landed on top of me and I woke up. Emotion: 6.

The dream was exhilarating at first, a speed shock. He hadn't ridden a horse since he was a boy. Kate rode occasionally on her father's farm where he, under some hick law, had his obligatory horses roaming a sparse pasture. She rode when times were terrible, like shortly after her mother passed. Hank told him, not Kate, that she spent many a high school evening galloping in circles in a wide, starry pen. Dust scampered over her jeans and her hips were wedged in from sitting, then her calves lit up to stand and haunch forward. Jeff didn't have quite the same access as Kate and was simply shown by a friend's father when he stayed with them over a long weekend. He was so young he had to be lifted into the stirrups and the man rode with him, managing the reins. Jeff only got to experience the tall sway and clomp of a bare gravel road.

Kate still snored in a way that hoisted her chest and neck to double their size, and Jeff slipped in beside her. Something was missing. He knew it, and he thought he knew what it was, but it was impossible. Fully impossible.

Night Fifty-Seven (Again)

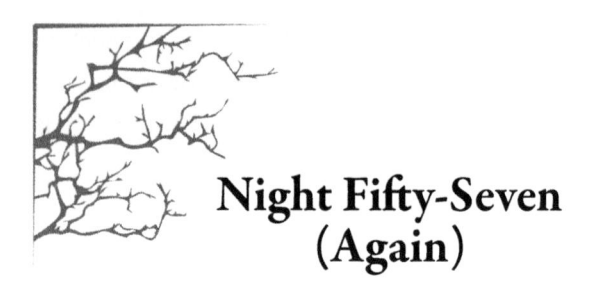

Colson, in a shocking turn, asked Jeff how he was doing that day, likely because of Jeff's lackluster greeting and low jaw. He spoke to his boss for the first time about something other than finance reports and quarterly earnings and shallow talk of his family and said, in full, blatant honesty, "I'm awful."

At home, the trillium in the front garden hung like a prisoner from a noose. Its petals, discolored, gawked at the ground in a limp sway. The quick wind threatened to tear each of them loose, the stem a sickly yellow. Jeff's stomach twisted.

In the kitchen, Kate, in a remarkable detour from her typical evening, swirled rich red tomato sauce in a pan. She greeted Jeff with a warm smile when he folded his coat over itself. He stepped to her, slid an arm around her waist, and she kissed him.

"Wow, you're cooking dinner?" and then he realized that probably wasn't the correct way to phrase that.

"I wanted to do something for you." Her sauce spoon sung along the pan. "I saw the flower. I'm sorry, Jeff. I said I would. Thank you."

She saw it. Perhaps on her way in, maybe when she got home, but she saw it. It told him she at least paid the slightest attention to it, that the trillium had taken up a centimeter of storage in her brain, and that could only mean good things. But was something still missing? Something here, with them?

"I appreciate that. You're welcome. I'm sorry I got you a flower," he said with a laugh. "I promise I won't give you anything to keep alive again."

"Thanks for that," chuckling through it and grinding pepper into the pan. They ate pasta from the same plate and Jeff had the flowery vision of the dogs in cartoons slurping on the same spaghetti noodle to a kiss. Instead, Kate poured herself a generous glass of wine and set to painting, while Jeff scratched pencil onto a new attempt at a face. Before long, Kate found him, purple and green blotches on her fingers, to see if he would come to bed. He followed, like he was on a road that led down the cardinal direction he needed to go but he knew, perhaps from a meandering Sunday drive years before, that this road had no outlet.

Night Fifty-Eight

This was a ten if there ever was one.

He thrashed and smashed and wished Kate woke up so she could tell him it was okay and rub his shoulder and kiss him on the forehead. Jeff gasped and gurgled, a shiny wet mess, swollen red scratches up his arms and chest. He imagined her voice playing in his head like a skipping record, *just a dream, just a dream, hey, hey, just a dream, just a dream, hey, hey*. He sat down and scrambled for a pen and wrote:

Some demon or devil, horns, dark eyes, hooves hacksawed through me, thin like deli meat, starting with my feet.

There wasn't anything more to write. Simply a fierce and violent dream, blaring and dim at the same time. He couldn't find any other details and didn't want to. He knew Gilbert would be interested in this one, but Jeff couldn't picture it anymore. Perhaps writing it down solidified it more than the others he had neglected.

He didn't go back to bed. He did as many pushups as he could before his shoulders screamed in heat. He switched to sit ups, squashing his round gut with each lift. *Not enough*, he thought. Jumping jacks, huffing and almost hurling, thighs and groin cramping under the sudden unfamiliar movement. Jeff dressed in a blue shirt and green socks.

Colson brought him a coffee that morning, cooled enough to drink, from Shelley's Café. Jeff plastered his desk and cubicle with as many blue and green post-it notes as he could find. On his lunch break, he walked, arms swinging, in the swooping wind, four blocks to the dollar store and bought every last package of blue and green tissue paper. When he made it back to work, his blue shirt clung to his fat torso, damp and mottled.

Jeff left work precisely on time to jog around the neighborhood. He passed the pond, fully thawed now, geese returned to the warmer water. Brittle vines sprawled between holes in the chain fence, slatted in with green plastic. Jeff didn't take his eyes off the slats as he passed, and he wished that pond water was blue like in cartoons.

Kate questioned him when he wheezed through the door near dusk.

"It'll make the dreams better," Jeff said, blasting breath out. He didn't stop to think he shouldn't mention dreams to her, lest she twist away again. He felt like crawling into the mouth of a snake with its jaw unhinged.

"Did you hear back from the sleep study?"

Jeff crashed through the cupboards and dumped water from the tap into a clear glass (he looked for a blue or green one but, alas). "They said I'm fine." He gulped as fast as his lungs would allow, dribbling on the outside of his cheeks. She encouraged him to continue. He hesitated, breathing, breathing, drinking, breathing. "The doctor said I should go to therapy."

"Sure."

Sure?

"Sure?"

"Yes, you should."

"Why do you say that?"

"Jeff, you clearly aren't happy." Oh? Jeff knew he wasn't happy, but he didn't know Kate knew it, too. He tried to be strong for her, didn't want her to know anything was wrong. But he feared some missing thing. "It's okay to need help. Therapy should probably be required in the modern age. I think you hate your job and it seeps over everything else. You don't have any friends except your poker buddies. And now you can't sleep, and these dreams are affecting you. It makes sense. You're doing it, right? That's where this exercise is coming from?"

"I already am," he blurted out, not elaborating further.

"You are? That's fantastic," she said, without a hint of pleasure, simply stating an appositive. "Any progress?" She honeyed a teacup, glancing over at him, heaving, every few seconds. "You don't have to share if you don't want to. I know that's private. You don't have to say anything." Jeff was sideswiped by this entire conversation. Kate, of the two of them, should be in therapy more than he should. He didn't have a parent die. He had lived more or less the same life for decades, changed only by Kate's shifts and rattles. Her mother passed and she never stepped foot in a doctor's office or a therapist's chair or even a massage parlor. She did paint more. The garbage cans shattered with more wine bottles.

"Okay," he started. "It's hard to say." It really was. "I don't know what started the dreams. I don't think anything new happened. And you," he stammered, unsure about the water he was about to dive into, "Your mom...." Kate didn't blink. "It would make sense for you. My dreams appeared out of the blue. They just came on and I didn't do anything."

"I bet that's the problem."

Later, Jeff taped tissue paper on and around his writing desk, sheer blue and green, on the left and right, respectively. It smothered the table and lined the walls. He intended to stare at blue and green simultaneously. Jeff drew in a blue pen, which did give a stylistic difference, but wasn't as subtle or malleable as a pencil, at least with his novice, crackling hand. He gritted through more pushups and his chest screamed in protest. He pushed until his hands puffed and his neck strained, like tapping into the potential of every muscle connected to his pecs. The ten couldn't happen again. *Five is boring now, give me a five*, he thought. Never again ten. He stared at the colored paper right before bed as much as he could without blinking. A white glaze drew over his eyes and billowed out around the edges in blue and green.

Night Fifty-Nine

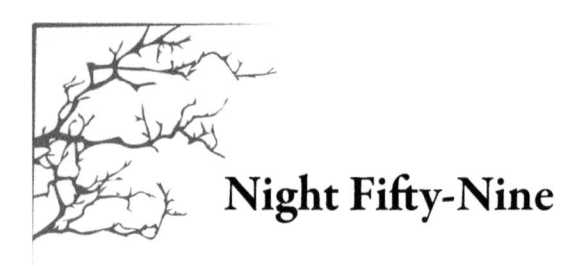

It wasn't a ten, but maybe a nine and a half. Kate, again, didn't wake, would never wake, to comfort him, her superpower winning out over Jeff's shouts. His chest muscles growled as he drew a pen from the cup and scratched on his legal pad about the slithering gorgon that froze him in place and fed him, limb by limb, toe by toe, to her young, alive but unable to squirm.

He emailed Gilbert, apparently his therapist now, and requested an emergency meeting before next week.

The entire day, while wearing blue and green, he jogged in place, crackling and jutting his knees whenever he wasn't on the phone or taking a break. Jeff shadowboxed in the car at traffic lights and flexed his thigh and calf and ass muscles when driving.

They met that night at Shelley's Café, per the contract agreement. Gilbert slithered into his seat and cupped a mug between his two pale hands. His black eyes bloomed electric. He looked very pleased with himself, and Jeff felt his spine slouch in the chair.

"Mr. Vickers!" he said, as if greeting an unexpected friend at a department store. Gilbert, in typical fashion, wore the same outfit, swimming in his oversized not-yellow, not-tan suit. It sagged off him like an old robe. "I'm so glad you felt comfortable enough to reach out in a time of crisis like this. Tell me, what can I help you with this evening?" His mouth sprung up at the side opposite his scar.

"I had a ten dream."

"Oh my."

"It was terrible."

"Yes."

"Can you make it stop?"

"I can, yes. But, as I mentioned previously, it will come back if appropriate treatment and dampening techniques aren't utilized. How much bloodletting did you do, in fluid ounces?"

Jeff, inhaling a breath as deeply as his wrecked lungs could muster, wondered why he continually found himself opposite tables with Gilbert Finnegan. He seemed only to enjoy torturing and taunting Jeff. But, unfortunately, he was often correct with his wicked assertions. The extent to which he was correct was variably, frightening, and sometimes hard to trust, as his interactions bordered on taunting. But time and time again, Gilbert told Jeff what would happen, and time and time after, it eventually did.

"I opted for the exercise and color therapy."

"And the dreams still worsened? Shame. Might be time to consider bloodletting."

"Gilbert, I might have stopped doing them for a couple of days."

"I see. And because of that you experienced a significant jump, or at least what you would consider to be your worst vision to date?"

"Yes."

"And you tried to exercise a whole bunch to make up for it and it was still bad?"

"Yes."

"Shocker." He dragged the mug to his mouth and slurped his coffee. He made a loud, obnoxious exhale, clearing his airway after drinking. "And you'd like me to silence the dreams until you do enough exercise and color therapy to have a more regular effect?"

Jeff hadn't considered that, but it was a good idea, so, "Yes, please."

"Sure."

Sure? Gilbert often denied Jeff the easy answer. Always on about the daily practice, which, admittedly, Jeff ignored. "Sure?"

"Sure! You don't need to suffer." This was wholly unexpected. "You go ahead and enjoy your evening, Mr. Vickers," and he extended his hand, red from the heat of the mug. Jeff didn't shake it.

"My wife says I need therapy."

"Yeah."

Yeah?

"And I remember you mentioning therapy a few weeks ago...."

"It's likely something like talk therapy, or psychotherapy, could help you through some things that may assist with your visions, yes."

"But you're not a therapist."

"I'm an oneiromancer."

"And still, I called you."

"Funny."

Jeff didn't know what to do or say. They seemed at a stalemate. He didn't like bringing up their old arrangement, as it seemed to kick up Gilbert's malicious side, but it might help.

"What did you have planned before, when you were using me as a Shark?"

His eyes dimmed, as expected.

"That therapy is different than psychotherapy. As I said, I'm an oneiromancer. My therapy makes things happen. With psychotherapy, *you* make things happen."

As ever, Gilbert remained impossible. Gilbert said he could change things, and Jeff couldn't ever believe him. Yet... he inevitably was right, one way or another, and he hated him even more, hated that white, flaring scar and greasy combover.

"And what if I wanted to talk to someone?"

"Get a psychotherapist."

Hmm. "Would you say both are effective?"

Gilbert made a movement like he was sucking on an invisible cigarette and realized the pointlessness of it, and, annoyed, continued, "They're both effective, Mr. Vickers, yes. It mostly depends on the client's decisions, their willpower, and their situation, obviously. There are certain things psychotherapy just won't do, no matter how determined you are. With me, and you, your potential—there's probably nothing you can't do. Most people aren't so lucky."

"Lucky? To need a therapist?"

"To have the ability to change things. Most people aren't Sharks—that's why they have a name, Mr. Vickers. Otherwise you'd just be 'Jeff the white guy.' People see therapists for years and never get anywhere because they're weak." Harsh. Was Jeff weak?

"That doesn't seem nice."

"I'm not always nice, Mr. Vickers. And seeing a therapist doesn't make you weak. But seeing a therapist and complaining about the same damn thing every time, like your job, or your wife, or husband, or whatever, and not learning anything, not taking advantage of the help and bettering your situation," and he gulped a huge glug from his cup, then forced a dramatic exhale out with a leaning smile, "weakness."

"Do you think I'm weak, Gilbert?"

Gilbert took a long pause. He shuffled his blazer around and it billowed along his side, keys jangling in his pocket. He eyed his coffee mug which didn't seem like it could have anything else left in it. "It doesn't matter, Mr. Vickers."

That was a yes.

"That sounds like a yes."

Gilbert's eyelids lifted for a second. Mocking. "Do you want to find out?"

Intriguing. Terrifying. "Okay."

"Typical." What did that mean? "What do you want, Mr. Vickers?"

"I want the dreams to stop."

"No, no, that's what you're coming to me for. Pretend I'm a psychotherapist—which I'm not—what are you here for? Your wife says you need therapy. I'm not surprised. What's the deal?"

The scraping, the itching at the back of his head wiggled awake. He maybe had an answer, but maybe it was simpler than that. "I'm not happy."

"Ding ding! You're not happy, exactly, welcome to America. Do you know why?"

Jeff could almost hear his lungs expand with fragile air.

"I can tell you," Gilbert said.

"You can?"

"Of course, it's obvious."

Was it so? "Okay."

"Every time we come in here you can't keep your eyes off these college girls, Jeff—Mr. Vickers. It doesn't surprise me that a man your age is just a little worn out with dinner at home. And hey, not for nothing, but whatever old lady you got tucked away back there probably ain't enamored with you either. It happens."

"You're wrong."

"This is what I was talking about, this weakness. Say I was a psychotherapist—which I'm not, I'm an oneiromancer—and I got to the root of your problem based on evidence I've witnessed with my own very observant eyes over the course of several weeks, you're going to sit here and tell me everything is fine and that I don't know what I'm talking about—which I don't, I'm an oneiromancer—but you see what I'm getting at?"

The hate built up again. Gilbert was a worm. Jeff had the sudden vision of smashing him underfoot into separate pieces that kept wriggling post-heel. Jeff closed his eyes and nodded and tried not to bite his teeth to cracking.

"The difference with you," and Jeff perked up, eyes locked on Gilbert, "is that you really *can* change something. You just need to utilize my services. It'll all be better once you do."

Impossible. Maybe things weren't right at home, but it wasn't that Jeff didn't love Kate. Not exactly, anyway. Gilbert did see him correctly, that he was eyeing the college girls, but he didn't understand the full extent. A surface-level judgement probably based on bad television and smut magazines, a lifetime of cynicism. Gilbert thought he knew Jeff, but he didn't have a clue. Yes, he could tap into his mind, but he didn't know what was really going on, had never lived his life, never met his wife, never seen her smile and chocolate eyes, her greying hair and prominent hip bones.

"Just make the dreams go away tonight."

"Done. Same time next week?"

Out front, on the way inside the house, the trillium glared at him. Jeff didn't think it looked much worse than when he put it in the dirt. It sagged a bit, leaves warbling between green and gross and white and wilted. But not looking worse wasn't the goal; restoration, rehabilitation, and eventual renaissance was. The trillium wasn't dead. Not yet.

He brushed his teeth and stripped and slid into bed next to Kate, whose howls babbled cavernous. She radiated warmth. His knees melted against her thighs. His hand slid over to her belly, and each of his fingerprints buckled down into place.

Sleep blessed him in the blankest unfelt form, cradling him back and forth like a child on a sweet, swinging bough. His mind, though he didn't know it until his eyes wept awake, was the deadest nothing, not even black, and he nearly cried when he woke quietly to Kate slipping around under the covers.

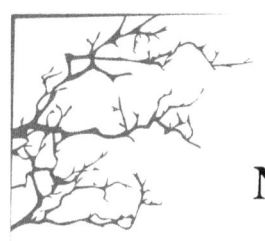

Night Sixty

"Good morning," she said.

"Good morning." They kissed with patient lips. "You home tonight?"

"Should be."

"Perfect. We'll do dinner."

Colson was sick today, which meant the office lulled. Quiet along the halls and the stalls and cubicles, gentle clacking and flapping of paper, sporadic coughs and sneezes. Jeff left early, because not a soul would stop him.

He swung by the store, did *not* get more flowers for Kate, and came home with ingredients for dinner. By the time Kate spilled through the door hauling more things than she left with, he was dumping ladles of chili into bowls glazed blue-green, and Jeff hoped the combination would be effective.

"The flower is looking nice out front," Kate said.

"I think so, too." He slid cheddar cheese down the sides of a grater, careful to keep his knuckles back. "It just might make it."

Jeff ate light. "I'm going for a run after this."

"If you're not careful you might extend your life. Did you do anything different with the chili?"

"I added cumin."

Kate licked up her bowl and sidled out from the table to grab more. They concluded that, while cumin felt like the right move, it never seemed to change the taste of the chili. All the ingredients mushed together to make what they make, and Jeff's chili tasted like Jeff's chili. Jeff wondered if Kate's red wine might change the experience.

Kate settled in the painting room while Jeff jumped in a pair of shorts and set off on a painful jog. The pond splashed with white birds gliding around splintered branches. His knees ached. His feet twinged at the edges and threatened blisters. Even his hands jabbed like they had splinters buried in the bones as he bounced from foot to foot. Gilbert had given him one night of pure peace and he needed to continue his dampening techniques, to settle his dreams down to fives, maybe lower.

Home, sticky, Jeff passed by Kate in her painting room. She started a new canvas and washed the background a cloudy blue and dappled it with spring green. A good sign.

He showered and dressed, then stalked behind Kate and clasped around her waist and sunk his face into her neck and swayed with her.

"I think I'm going to try to paint the garden."

Jeff laughed and breathed in the sweet scent of her hair. "We don't have a garden."

"We've got the start of one."

"And where will you hang it?"

"We'll see if it's any good, first."

"I bet it's fantastic." He pressed his lips in small intervals in her neck. "Where will you hang it?"

Laughing, Kate said, "I'm not sure, there's space all around."

"Plenty." He rested his hand on her right forearm, not guiding, but following her movements and strokes while she swathed the canvas in tremendous emeralds.

They brushed their teeth and flossed and lit candles and fell into each other. They kissed and tumbled and hummed, throaty, echoing hums, eyes closed, eyes open. Jeff prayed to himself, to God, to Kate, that this would be it.

Before Kate could collapse into sleep, he clutched her hand and wrapped over her. "I want a kid, Kate," he said. "I want a family with you." It was like loosing a crater from his mouth, and the crater melted and shifted through space and burned through the atmosphere and tumbled through ozone and clouds and sizzled in rain. It baffled scientists and children with telescopes and anyone foolish enough to be outdoors on a night like this, simmering, glowing hot, red and terrorizing the earth.

"What?" She turned.

"We should have a kid."

Kate shifted around again. The moonlight behind her blew out her shoulders and hair and hip. "You're serious?" Jeff assured her he was. "We've talked about this. I don't want kids, Jeff."

"But I do, I think it would make me happy."

"What about me?"

"I think it would make you happy, too."

"I'm already happy." Jeff resisted pushing back that he did not, in fact, think she was happy.

"You said I should try to make myself happy. This is what I want. I've thought about it a lot. I saw my therapist."

"Your therapist told you to do this? To do this to me?"

"No, but," his tongue dragged like sandpaper, "you and the therapist encouraged me to do what will make me happy."

Jeff often heard Kate breathe in the night, rough and pulsing in the dark, but this was a clear and quiet breath, not calm, but steady. "You need to make yourself happy, Jeff." Her eyes glowed like remnants of a burned down house. "Do it in a way that doesn't ruin me."

"It won't—"

"You don't know that!" Her mouth was mauled and battered by sharp teeth and crackling muscles. Her chocolate eyes went black.

"People have kids all the time." His breath, unlike Kate's, was not steady. He felt a tense twist around his chest and smelt burning inside his nostrils.

"Some people want kids, Jeff. I don't."

"I do."

"Then we have a *problem*." She left the bed. It might have been the first time it ever happened. She waddled over to the bathroom door and snagged her white robe from the hook and tied it on. She crossed her arms in front of her stomach like a shield. Jeff followed and threw his own robe on. Kate walked to the kitchen without turning any lights on. Jeff followed still. The mess of dinner cluttered the counters.

They stood, Kate still with her arms crossed, her hair a wavy tangle. She yelled in frustration and turned. "How many times have we talked about this?" Jeff didn't have an answer. It had come up before, he supposed. "How many times, tell me?"

"Things change, Kate. We're older now."

"How is that better?!"

"We're more secure, we aren't the same people we used to be, we have different goals. Different means."

"Jeff, this is not going to change with time. It hasn't for me, and it never will. In fact, it will only get worse."

"How can you know that? You haven't even thought about it."

"Says who? I have thought about it. I thought about how I'm old enough now that any child we have, even if they make it nine months, will have problems. They don't mention that anywhere, but it just happens. *You* are probably fine, but *I* am not."

"That's just a risk—"

"A risk I'm not willing to take! A risk I don't *want* to take. It takes two to tango, Jeff, but one of us is going to tango harder than the other. I don't want it."

He hated the way she said "it" about their potential child. "Please—" but Kate was a fortress.

"I will not do it. I will not. I don't want children. You knew this. You knew this and married me. You knew this and stayed with me. You knew this and kept wanting it, thinking that I didn't *really* know, right? Thinking that I'd fall in line, or that I'd get dumb and complacent, that I'd come around? I don't want kids, Jeff. Period."

"So I just let you decide—" again, pointless.

"On this one? Yes! You want to debate dinner, or where to hang a stupid painting, I'll take your insight, but if you want me to be pregnant and give birth to a child then it damn well concerns me and it's going to be my decision. The answer is no."

The air between them shattered and fell all around and bounced in tiny shards along the floor. When it seemed like all was silent another bit of air-glass tinkled along and shocked them to death.

"You said I wasn't happy."

"You aren't."

"I don't know what to do."

"I can't make you happy, Jeff. *You* need to do that. You need to be happy without my permission, without my say-so. Without ruining my life. I cannot make you happy."

Neither of them moved. Jeff glanced around, at the walls, the fridge, the curtains, the door, the terrible painting of the deer gawking back at him. Kate pierced him directly in the eyes, or where his eyes would be if he dared to look back at her.

He repeated, "I don't know what to do."

She repeated, "I cannot make you happy. If you want a kid, go get one. I can't make you happy, but I can ask you to leave."

No.

"Please," shaking, "go."

Jeff dressed himself like he was dragging his limbs through a swamp. He was cold, shaking, heavy. His pants shuffled up a bit more carefully than before, his shirt slipped across his skin with a kiss of kindness. He noticed his socks were crooked, patterned just off from the natural shape of his heel and arch and ball of his foot.

Kate escaped to the bathroom and closed the door and ran the tap and turned the fan on. Blaring light shoved itself out from under the door and the cracks on the sides.

What would he do? It was nearly midnight and below freezing in the northwest Fool's Spring. Kate asked him to go.

She was angry enough, he knew, that if he didn't go that *she* would, and he didn't want to put that on her. He had put children on her, time and time again, and this was one time too far. He would go, but hopefully not for good.

It seemed to him, after he snatched up his keys and wallet, that he would get into his car, and if he was getting into his car to go somewhere he may as well stay in his car. He drove out, anywhere, away from town and away from Kate and the trillium and the semi-frozen pond in his neighborhood. It wasn't the main highway he took, but one of the side roads he always drove straight by, wondering who lived out that far in storied houses with large yards, rotting wooden fences, southern sentimentality.

What had he expected? Surely, he knew, that Kate wasn't about to bend on this. Surely, he knew, she would stand her ground. It wasn't that he didn't consider she would be putting her own body under strain, or what her feelings were, but more that he felt a calling and in her laid a potential answer.

Could he live without children? Seemingly, he had done it for decades. But what would life be if he didn't approach it, address it, and try, like she encouraged, to be happy? It seemed, to him, in his upside-down, nightmarish and color-strained state, that achieving one thing would be a tipped domino to drop everything into place, like ridges on a key knocking a tumble-lock over and swinging the door open where happiness greeted him on the other side, bathing and loving him, cheering him on and hugging him like a mother after an extended absence.

Jeff pulled into a rest stop near a cement bridge, as good a spot as any. He killed the engine and settled down. He wasn't sure if he should leave his seatbelt buckled or not. Unlatched, the stub hitched up into his hip. Latched, the belt bit into his belly and nipped at his neck. It seemed there wasn't anything to do but sleep. Except, of course, for sending an email. He wrote Gilbert Finnegan, again, asking for a meeting tomorrow night (Jeff figured Gilbert was quite awake at this hour, but Jeff couldn't stomach seeing his stupid face, not right now). The glaze took over his eyes. Kate's grinding breath was missing. He remained fully clothed, but sleep stalked him with its claws drawn and shining.

Night Sixty-One

The muffled echo of his shouts rumbled in his ears and pinged there while soundwaves died down, and he breathed and heaved and willed his jaw to settle. It occurred to him, quiet, in the bleary morning, that he didn't grab his legal pad. He pulled out his phone and emailed himself:

I'm curled up inside an egg, but it's translucent and I can see I'm in a high nest on a desert cliff. A bird-woman, a harpy, kicks me in the egg and I tumble off the sheer cliff. The egg never shifts or spins but points straight downward and the ground approaches and I explode.

Jeff noted an eight for emotion and that he was screaming and sweating through his only change of clothes.

This dream wasn't a mystery. Jeff hadn't analyzed his own dreams much lately, merely swimming through them like he was on a trolley cart going through a haunted house; the things that were going to jump out to scare him were going to jump out to scare him when they meant to, and he was buckled into the trolley, much like he was buckled into his seat. But this one, the nest dream, the egg dream, was quite pointed. The nest could symbolize both his home he had just left, or been kicked out of, as well as a nest that didn't have children in it. Did his mind see Kate as a "harpy," though? Perhaps the dream was just another innocuous and charnel vision that seemed to have no real purpose like most of the others, like the gasping Shark or the snake that ate him alive, like the bull, goring him through.

Night Sixty-One (Again)

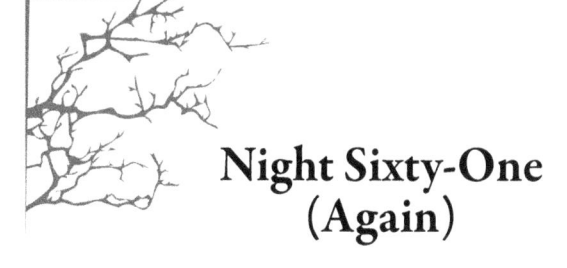

At first, when he woke up from his now-regular second sleep, peaceful, he figured he wasn't going to work today. Eviction from one's wife seemed a decent reason to call out. However, after he made the decision and found himself with nothing to do for fifteen minutes or so, he rumbled the engine alive and spun back into town through the morning fog shuffling along his grille. While Colson showed concern that Jeff was in rumpled jeans and a faded t-shirt, and initially suggested he leave, when Jeff insisted that he stay, Colson was supportive and left him appropriately alone, if with an encouragement of time.

Jeff made it to Shelley's Café with armfuls of time to spare. He ordered some pastries for dinner, a bacon-wrapped croissant stuffed with garlic and gouda cheese, and a chocolate donut. It was too early for the college kids to be there. In fact, he'd never seen the shop so empty. The two baristas behind the counter (was one of them Shelley?) counted leaning stacks of cups for inventory. Jeff drew the blind down over his window and shade warped the layout of the room, darkening the table scratches.

Gilbert woke him with a slammed fist and a sneer, and Jeff bounced and shook in the bench seat.

"Mr. Vickers, another rough night, then?" Gilbert slid into the bench seat opposite him, bloated ring of keys clinking in his jacket pocket. "What did you dream of?"

"Why don't I dream sometimes?" Gilbert didn't seem to care that Jeff stole the sway of conversation.

"Sure. You're a Shark, as we've discussed. It's part of the deal. You get one good crack at it each day. I'm still trying to find the reason why—probably something to do with lunar cycles, I think, time isn't just made for you to get to work at 8:30, you know."

"I used to be afraid to go back to sleep because I didn't want another awful dream, but that's when I sleep like I used to." His face squirmed, "Not dreaming."

"I see. Yes, the other Sharks I've worked with had similar issues. Sleep avoidance, excessive caffeine intake—they'd do all sorts of things to keep themselves from sleeping so they wouldn't have the dreams—exercising, sexual activity, loud music. One person even tried gravity boots, and they just fell asleep upside down—just ain't how it works. It's gonna come. And you can't hide."

"Unless you or some other oneiromancer stops it."

Gilbert emptied the table sugar by heaping spoonfuls into his cup. "Yes, unless I or someone like me stops it." He gulped from the steaming mug. "So, what's the emergency?"

Gilbert had told Jeff weeks ago they were going to start therapy. Jeff didn't want therapy. He wanted to sort his own problems out, make Kate love him again through his own hand, get her to understand and agree to have kids, but that effort splattered all over the ground like a hurled egg and was dripping down the wall, yolk and all. "Kate asked me to leave."

As he spoke the words into the air his lungs loosened like undoing the top button of his pants.

The face across from him twisted, just so, and Gilbert clenched to prevent his true reaction painting itself on his skin. "I see. Does that mean you're getting a divorce?"

Jeff sincerely hoped not. "I hope not."

Jeff, through everything, had a murky vision of what his life could be, if only he could put the pieces where they needed to go. In the forefront of his mind he felt Kate could possibly love him, could have possibly loved him had he not brought up children, *again*. Their relationship had been stagnant for so long, and Jeff's misguided efforts over the last few weeks hadn't earned him enough good grace to keep her from slamming the door on his affections.

In his mind, they couldn't simply be together, no. He had that, and the gurgle in his stomach sent a telegram to his brain that "together" wasn't good enough. In his mind, they had two happy and healthy girls. Adventurous and fearless, creative, kind, respectful. They baked cookies with Kate, scooping raw dough out of a mixing bowl and slurping it off their fingers. They sat in fully-inflated puffer vests in the backseat of the car, buckled in with their shoes dangling, going to the pond in the spring to catch trout.

If Gilbert was right, and he was pretty damn right thus far, then this new dream could be real eventually. Time didn't matter. He had the eyes for it and the heart for it, just not the ability.

"Let's play ball, Gilbert."

"Really?"

"Really."

Gilbert gawked around the room as if looking for a camera crew and a host with a microphone to come wailing around the corner blowing confetti.

"*Really?*" he pushed again.

Jeff nodded, "Really, Gilbert."

Gilbert's fingers danced along the sheen of the table, drumming, tapping, spread palm down. "So we're no longer dampening, we're *doing*?"

"Yes, Gilbert." The breath gushed out of him and puffed out his chubby cheeks. "We can get to getting."

"Well god damn, son!" Gilbert pounded the table and shot his body up, his combover catching air, betraying most of his shiny scalp. "God damn that's what I'm talking about!" He scrambled through his baggy jacket. Out came the classic white and red, plastic-wrapped smokes, and he beat the bottom of the box with his palm, and one jumped out and he snatched it up and as soon as he clamped his scarred lips down on it the flicker flame of a translucent green lighter seared the paper to whisps, and he dragged the burn back along the white body. "God damn I almost lost faith there for a minute."

"You can't smoke in here, Gilbert. Not for, you know, decades now."

He blasted a surge of smoke from his rounded, jutting mouth, "Been living in blue hell this whole time, holding out." Most of the college students scattered, save for a pair of blondes in the corner who seemed to be searching for their own cigarettes, smacking their jacket pockets and unzipping brown, ragged purses.

Despite Gilbert's claims, the barista behind the counter glared at them and never flinched. Jeff offered a smirk. His mustache tickled inside his nose.

"So!" Gilbert settled in. He loosened his shoulders and slid his tongue across the corners of his mouth. "What the hell are we gonna do?" under jagged eyes.

Jeff felt the familiar, but still uncomfortable, crawl of sitting across the table from the madman version of Gilbert, the version he knew from the kitchen table in his home—old home—and the slaps of bewilderment that would fly up and skew his posture. The politically-correct version of Gilbert was an obnoxious know-it-all that mocked him no matter what he said. The wild version of Gilbert, the pseudo-scientifically-untethered version, always appeared to him like some stunted version of Frankenstein that clacked together the clamps from a car battery to make a spark.

But he was usually right.

"You tell me, Gilbert. What the hell are we gonna do?"

"Well I'll tell you," he said, dragging so hard on his cigarette that he had to pause and re-breathe through his nose to continue, "we're gonna have some fun."

Jeff a month ago would have said "no." *Did* say "no." But that only wasted time. Perhaps if he had listened to Gilbert in the first place, went along with his wild schemes, he never would have lost Kate. Perhaps if he had never reached out to the Society at all, he never would have lost Kate. But what did "having her" even do for him if it meant not having a real family?

"Okay, so what's the first step?"

Gilbert's shoulders relaxed. He leaned sideways in the booth and his eyelids shuddered just a hair. "You don't have anywhere to go, right?" Gilbert was, once again, spot on. "Fear not."

"We're not sharing a room, are we?"

"Oh hell no." He finished his cigarette, stabbed the butt down on the bare table, then leaned way back against the seat, "You'll have your own room," he dragged the next cigarette out and stuck it to his bottom lip, "I'm staying just down the way," it bounced as he spoke through the side of his mouth, "No charge."

"I don't have to pay?"

He lit the end and tossed the lighter to a sliding stop against the wall. "Benefits of research, Jeff. The study pays! Not you, of course, the study won't pay you directly, to be very clear." He was re-hunched again, hands clasped and covering his mouth, smoke wedged near his knuckles. "Your payment will be in the form of," and he waved his hand over and under, as if crackling his wrist around activated neural ways in his brain, "say, immense, encompassing satisfaction—we'll get your life back on track." The classic Gilbert smile, equal parts diagonal and bent.

Just go with it, Jeff told himself, eyes closed, wedging his ribs out with every whisp of breath he could suck in. "Okay," he shoved all the air out. His coffee ebbed like the unfrozen pond around his neighborhood—old neighborhood. "Then what?"

"Then, I'm gonna give you a freebie night." Jeff encouraged him to continue. "Y'know, the location change and all, I need to do some measuring, need to do some scouting of the area. That affects the visions, it's important. Not worth you getting all worked up over something trying to kill ya in your sleep if it's not gonna lead to anything. So you get the night off!"

"That's very nice of you Gilbert."

"Thank you, yes it is. And then: daily meetings! And we don't have to come back here." He cracked his knuckles. "Of course, we can't go back to your place, and I really don't want you in my room, and I don't wanna be in your room." His cigarette dragged behind his hand motions like someone signing the air with a sparkler in a long-exposure photo. "I guess I'll figure that part out. But daily meetings, nightly meetings, really, unless you lose your job somehow, but you shouldn't unless that's something you want."

Jeff didn't know what to say. He felt like Gilbert still had air to get out.

"Yeah, probably for the best," Gilbert continued. You don't have to pay for housing for the time being, but we don't have any food or anything. You'll probably wanna drive around and whatnot. Plus, if you get back with your old lady you don't wanna have to explain the sudden career change. Might hinder things, a bit."

"*If* I get back with Kate?"

"*If*, yes."

"I thought this was going to work?"

"It will, Jeff, if you want it to. Hell, I don't know that's exactly what you want. Most Sharks don't fully understand the potential of their condition." The students in the corner fully committed to smoking in the café and the staff behind the counter just ignored it all. "It's so funny, people always think they want what people tell them they want."

"It is what I want," Jeff said. He meant it.

"Well good for you, Jeff, good. You've got to want it, got to have that picture in your mind. But you could have more, you know. I believe you can, at least. If you want it." Jeff encouraged him to continue. "Do you really want..." he did the hand-warbling again, ashes crumbling to the table, "the same thing? You could have a Lamborghini or something, or some other car that isn't even invented yet. Under very specific circumstances, which we aren't anywhere close to and unlikely to come across, you can make a car, Jeff, ever thought of that?"

Jeff had never thought about making his own car.

"Hell, I shouldn't mention it. Those are the keys talking. Okay, I'll clarify, *you* can't, but in a way, you can!"

Clarification, thought Jeff.

"You don't have to drive the car you already own. You can have that guy's car if you want. Isn't that better than the car that just tossed your ass to the curb?" Gilbert knocked back against the seat and it clunked in protest. "No imagination."

"Well if I want something you tell me I want, aren't I still just wanting what people tell me?"

"Fair. Good stuff, Jeff, good. I can tell you're starting to really listen. Good. I like it. But really. You can want what you want. And that's fine, I ain't you and you ain't me, alright? Just trying to," and he pushed his hands outward like he was measuring a fish that couldn't decide how big it wanted to be, "let you know you have options. Maybe one of them college girls you keep gawking at."

"Yeah, maybe."

Gilbert snarled in laughter, sucking air in that wasn't smoke. Then he dragged again and blew smoke out, looking over his shoulder at the lone table with the blondes at it who, definitely now, were adding liquor from a flask to their coffee. "I'm a bad influence."

"Anything I want then?"

"More or less."

"And what if I wanted something strange?"

Gilbert's head curled back around to face Jeff. He left his cigarette clamped between his fingers but picked up his cup of coffee and tossed back most of it in one big glug. "Like what?"

"Oh, nothing in particular. I'm just wondering. Like, what are the lines, really? You said I could make a car that doesn't exist—"

"—Can you imagine a car that doesn't exist?"

"I guess, it would be kind of like a space car or something, maybe a flying car."

"And what are you gonna do when you take your flying car out into the world, Jeff?"

Jeff didn't respond.

"That's right, correct answer, Jeff, the U.S. military will blow you the fuck outta the sky."

"But you said I could—"

"—You *can* Jeff, you *can*, if you understand what a single person can do in a society such as the one we're living in. *Can* implies potential, but not necessarily likelihood. If you have the connections, the means, the brains. You aren't a military general—though we could probably make that happen if you really want to, it would just take some time—so you can't *really* have access to some fancy flying object now, can you? Yes, you *can*... but not *really*. Besides, your power, I believe, as all the other Sharks have been before you, is more that of manipulation. Actual creation is something far, far beyond you and even me. Yeesh." He patted his pocket, and it clanged.

This made sense, in Gilbert's twisted way. But it did deflate Jeff's true ambitions enough to tuck doubt beneath a layer of soil. "What about a person?"

"There's people everywhere, Jeff. We can get you whatever person you like."

"What about the girl of my dreams?"

"Well technically, that's what she'd be, yeah. What's her name?"

"I don't know, yet."

"Is this a real person?" Gilbert asked, his cindered end painting symbols via his loose wrist. Jeff didn't respond. "You know a real person, like one of these college girls you keep staring at or an actress or something? One that already exists?"

"No, not yet."

Gilbert let out a squealy laugh like a horse mixed with a chipmunk. "Hell, if you want to help me track down a Nori then we'll get down to some real work creating the girl of your dreams. But remember, just like with your flying car, other people are gonna notice. You better dream up a convincing birth certificate and a working social security number, buddy. But then, I suppose if the republicans are right, then there's tons of undocumented people in this country doing whatever the hell they want anyway. And if the democrats are right then they'll roll out the red white and blue carpet for 'em give 'em an MRI for free, why the hell not," and horse-laughed again. "You want one with knockers out to *here* right?" and he gestured all the way across the table, almost tickling Jeff's shoulders.

Jeff shrugged them, embarrassed by Gilbert's comfortable tongue. "What's a *Nori*?"

"It's kinda like how you're a 'Shark' because of Charcot-Wilbrand syndrome, right? But you don't have Charcot-Wilbrand syndrome," his hand floundered and ash flew, "probably. Noris are the same. Really, 'Nori' is the Japanese word for seaweed. But don't go all pronouncing that 'r' like a 'd,' we're both far too white for that my friend, am I right?" Gilbert retreated and laughed in his circle, just like at the kitchen table.

"What does seaweed mean?"

"Heh, it means 'Nori.' But no, Nori comes from Norrie Disease, it's this really rare condition where boys, children, basically go blind. One of the side effects from this blindness is limited perception of the sun, thus throwing off their sleep cycles. These patients are known to sleep for extended periods of time, so... there ya go."

"I need to help you find a blind child?"

Gilbert smacked the table, palm down, palm down, brief pause, palm down. "No, no. I guess our naming conventions in oneiromancy are a little dated. Just like all these conditions named after the people that discovered them; doesn't really tell you what it is. *Hypersomnia* is a better name for the condition a Nori has. We in the business refer to them that way because one guy in South Africa actually did help treat a kid with Norrie Disease. But the Noris we're talking about are hypersomniacs."

Jeff tried not to move a muscle on his face. "That means they sleep a lot?"

"Ding ding. But here's something you don't have to imagine, Jeff: whatever car you want, whether it's *strange, sleepy,* or *buxom,* you're in the driver's seat; just know that I'm the one with the keys and the map." He jangled his keyring and they shimmered into his ears. "You don't go anywhere that I don't tell you to."

Jeff and Gilbert shook hands for the first time as they crawled from under the table. Gilbert led him to the parking lot where the rain blew sideways and dripped into his ear canal. Jeff climbed into his car and followed Gilbert's white van out of the lot and down away from his old home. It felt strange, taking an opposite route away from Shelley's Café, but much of his life was strange for weeks now and getting stranger every day. He'd just agreed to sleep "down the way" from Gilbert Finnegan for an unspecified amount of time and be a guinea pig for the Society of Divine Dreams. And if he wasn't mistaken, it seemed Gilbert would be very interested in Kate if he knew about her.

What constituted a hypersomniac? Kate was known to fall asleep without effort, occasionally still standing, and remain in place for half the day. Weekends were shot for her, her snores blaring and bouncing off the walls of their home until midday or later. A *Nori*? Gilbert made it sound like Jeff could find happiness alone without dragging another person into this, he just needed to be specific and sure of what he wanted: Kate. Clear as day. But could he convince Kate to want a child? Gilbert thought he wanted those college girls, not that he wanted to hug them and be the first person on their emergency contact list and fix their showerhead. Even still, Gilbert seemed confident, as long as Jeff was. But the nag of what this whole act was, a strange form of love potion in the end, stung Jeff.

Kate would take him back, yes, but was it really Kate? Perhaps Kate could even be convinced to have a child, but would knowing the truth—that she feared pregnancy, childbirth, what it does to the body, and even the potential aftermath of carrying a baby in a middle-aged womb—would Jeff be able to put all of that on her? When she didn't have a choice, possessed like a voodoo zombie?

Jeff pulled up to a brown building along a winding road on the scenic route out of town and parked next to Gilbert and heard his van door *chunk* over. The building had two stories with a flat roof and wooden slats shielding the outside. The railings to the second floor were made of metal painted black and chipped from neglect and northwest winters. It wasn't too large, five doors to the five rooms on each floor, all facing the parking lot, simple yellow lamps putting a foul light over them. There was an old, knotted log stood up on two stakes at the edge of the parking space and the yard that looked like a hitching post. If Jeff was driving by, he'd assume there were drug cooks and welfare cases inside.

Gilbert, burning the end of another cigarette dripping off his lip, coddling the flame inside cupped hands from the misting wind, beckoned Jeff to follow him. Careful not to trip over crooked chunks of broken cement, Gilbert led Jeff to room 103, smack in the middle of the floor, and pulled his "normal" keyring out. The door clicked open.

"You don't really have much shit, right?"

"Guess not."

"Good enough. There's no dresser in here, anyway." Gilbert flipped up the light switch just inside the door and it plinked on a floor lamp at the other side of the humble room, which seemed to shrink the more Jeff looked at it. A ten-by-five living room with a curl-around kitchenette, one door opened that exposed a toilet with the seat up, and another door closed that was probably a bedroom. The tarnished brown metalwork of baseboard heating gapped along the trim, hissing. Gilbert flicked his ash on the every-colored carpet.

"And you said I'm not paying for this?" Not that he'd want to pay given the state of it.

Gilbert clapped him on the shoulder with his non-ashen hand. "Through your service to the Society of Divine Dreams, Jeff. Researchers like to spoil their subjects, that way they want to continue to be subjects."

"You gonna make sure I don't dream, then?"

"Already been done." Jeff wondered if he closed his eyes hard enough that Gilbert would just vanish and he'd be back home and Kate would forgive him. Gilbert pulled deep on the cigarette and checked the time on his phone. "Hey I gotta get going. I'm just down the way in 101. Leave me alone, would you?"

"Sure." Jeff checked behind the closed door and was surprised at the bed. It wasn't a strict and tight army cot like he expected. The metal frame had small wheels at the bottom which dug well into the carpet. It had layers of quilts and blankets on top and two pillows, all white sheets, and bedposts at the top corners with rounded knobs. A black oscillating fan sat near the foot of the bed with its cord stretching way over through the air to the wall plug.

"I'm gonna leave you be. You enjoy your night off, get comfy and all that. Nothing in the fridge, sorry. Oh, almost forgot." Gilbert ran out the front door and left it open for the rain. Jeff pulled the fridge open with a rubberized suck and it was, indeed, empty. Not even ketchup.

His thoughts ran toward Kate. He wondered how she was doing. If she was crying. If she was drinking. If she was on the phone with her dad or at his place, if she was with Claudia planning her anniversary party, or even with another man. He wondered if Gilbert's coworker Jericho Dillinger ever brought clients to buildings like this for dream therapy, if the situation would be different if Jericho was assigned to Jeff instead of Gibert. Jeff doubted Kate would seek a rebound but, like many thoughts these days, they hooked on a fold in his brain like a pocket catches a doorknob, and he couldn't silence it.

Gilbert darted back through the door, his shoes slicking over the small linoleum entry. "Here ya go." He tossed him a silver key attached to a white dongle in a rounded diamond shape that had grimy edges. Smack in the center in chipped and faded black ink was written "103." "You sleep tight, now."

The sheets felt grainy against his legs, his shoulders. He shivered in the chill and the unfamiliarity and the worry. Sleep fled him like a deer from a crunch in the forest. A healthy mind, he told himself, all in the cramped caverns of his head, would look at the positives. Similarly to many religious factions on earth, Jeff had plunged into the act of belief; he, with little evidence, chose to trust Gilbert. Thus far, Gilbert had shown him more evidence of power than God ever had, through his uncanny gift of blackening his somnolent visions, less than black, completely empty.

Gilbert gave him the gift of palatable dreams, like the toad over the pulsing background. Jeff believed now, perhaps, if only because there was so little to lose, that Gilbert would help him. He and Kate would be back together. And if Jeff could bring himself to wish his own will on Kate, they would have a child.

A girl, he thought. A girl he could carry around on his shoulders while she steered him by the ears, a girl he would make mud pies with, pocked with gravel and worms, a girl named Mariah, or Cecilia, or Brie, or Sarah. He pictured a small girl with blonde hair, despite how genetics were likely to treat her, with dirt wiped on her cheek and crackling eyes. He chose to believe, just like he did with Gilbert, that Kate would forgive him after absorbing the joy of their daughter, after seeing that her body wasn't ravaged, that she was healthy and had soft arms and wet giggles. And if she didn't... there was always oneiromancy.

Night Sixty-Two

He woke early, he supposed, based on the pale bleed of light around the curtains. It was never comfortable sleeping in a bed other than your own, but he figured he should get used to it. For a little while at least. Jeff didn't know what to do. He had hours before work and the room was empty except for the insects. And now he'd considered it, he didn't have any clothes for work either. Colson made such an effort to console him yesterday, despite not admitting that anything was wrong, that he'd surely worry if Jeff arrived in the same wrinkled shirt and jeans from the day before.

Jeff didn't know how long this dream stuff would take. Would he be here a few days, weeks, months? He shuddered at the thought of spending months in this empty room, reluctantly stocking more things in the meek fridge and having to get a separate toothbrush and toothpaste and deodorant.

Jeff snatched the 103 key from the kitchenette counter and sucked the featherlight door behind him to a click. A drive through the window of sunrise uncaged butterflies in his belly. Something about seeing the new day begin always threw off his rhythm, his mentality, made him think he'd squandered the night and the sleep that came with it. It was warm enough, out of Fool's Spring—Kate always hated what Jeff called it, what it really is—mud season—everything was caked and dripping with the stuff, from the grass to the gutters, it clung to cars and streaked across the calves of pant legs. His car tires gurgled in a puddle before spitting free.

Jeff didn't know this part of town that well, but he knew driving south would take him to a familiar road and he'd follow it back home, to Kate's home. His old and future home. On the way, he stopped by a grocery store to grab a simple glazed donut and a coffee he could drown himself in if careless, and pulled up in front of his—Kate's—home. All lights out. It surprised him that Kate's dragon snores weren't pounding against the walls. Stopped dead in front of the door, his eye caught on the front garden bed, and he could see the lone plant strung up and dangling.

The trillium, white and triangular, somehow, lived. It was surviving, not thriving, but surviving was the first step. Jeff made a mental note to come check on it in the daylight. He and the neighbors weren't very acquainted, so it was unlikely Kate had explained the situation to them. They probably went weeks without seeing one another, usually; Jeff digging in the garden on a Tuesday would be just that: a Tuesday.

Jeff parked down the road, almost a full block away from the house, where Kate would never notice him. With nothing better to do, he ate and drank. In the waiting, he slumped into several micro-naps and was somehow grateful he kept his seatbelt buckled. The time came for Kate to leave the house, and he slunk down even though he was well out of sight. He breathed. He noticed his wobbling pulse yipping in his neck and forehead.

Kate crossed the yard in black scrubs and a ponytail hanging her long hair square down her back. If Jeff hadn't been there the other night, hadn't been the reason for the other night, he would have thought it was just another Tuesday. The unfamiliar neighbors probably would too if any of them were out here. She drove off.

Jeff waited longer just in case she realized she forgot something and had to zip back home. The waiting, after witnessing her walk with ease to the car and open the door and start the engine and pull away from the curb, wounded him slightly. He didn't know what to expect, coming back to the house. Perhaps the trillium gave him hope. Hope that Kate would be visibly upset or disheveled, unable to care for herself in her beloved husband's absence. He wanted her to be hurt like he was hurt, and hope for his forgiveness. He wanted her to call him, sobbing, asking where he was, asking him to come home, asking him why he ever left in the first place. But this Kate he saw was simply going to work on a Tuesday. Nothing more, nothing less. Jeff pulled in front of the house.

He felt his lungs twist and writhe as he keyed open the door and stepped into his own home. He was only gone one day, and it was exactly the same, but it glowed in a soft bloom from every corner as the gut-punch of sleeplessness hulked like a brick of sharp ice around his stomach. He snuck, in his own home, guts pressing in his throat, to the bedroom. The bed was perfectly made, not a sock on the ground, and the blinds, normally shut, were spread wide open inviting the day inside. Jeff snatched a few pairs of pants and shirts, only caring that they weren't blue or green.

Jeff stripped and felt like some sort of pervert, naked in a place he shouldn't be. He climbed into a pair of faded jeans and a crimson polo. He stuffed a few more changes of clothes in a plastic bag.

He stopped by Kate's painting room and opened the door like a bomb might go off on the other side. It was dim but he didn't dare touch a light. The easel was empty, the stool next to it void of its typical wine glass, and Jeff couldn't see his "portrait" anywhere in the room. *Maybe she burned it*, he thought. But then he corrected himself: she probably didn't care enough to waste a match.

Jeff stepped into the brisk air from the front door and locked it, then squished into the yard, soaked through from a season of scornful rain and sparing snow. He crouched in the garden, like a gargoyle over a city, and touched the triangular leaves of the trillium. The soil caved at his touch as he palmed a clump and packed it closer around the stem sticking up. Jeff hoped, to whatever spirit of flora might be invading his thoughts, that the flower understood how much he wanted it to survive, and that his hope, along with sun and soil and the grace of spring bees, would lift it to a second, prosperous life. He had snatched it, mindlessly, from its comfortable home and its new bed would take some getting used to, would need some work and love and a few peaceful evenings.

Colson greeted him as he came through the door. Said he was glad to see Jeff in better spirits. Jeff wanted Colson to go flush himself down the toilet. "Thank you, I finally got a good night's sleep." Colson insisted he take time if he needed it. Jeff thanked him again and began to wonder if he ever should have tried to change his relationship with Colson in the first place. A simple "hello" had bloomed into a daily curse that fed on affirmations of fineness, that Jeff had to assure Colson he was doing well in order to get peace. Perhaps, once things really were fine, and his relationship with Kate was welded back together, he could work with Gilbert on fixing this whole work situation. Maybe Colson could be convinced Jeff needed an unheard-of raise, needed to pull back to part time, or even remote work. Jeff could tend the trillium and keep the house clean and draw and paint; he and Kate could have a gallery of swirling and stark oils on canvas hung on twine, and in time, they could teach their daughters how to hold a brush and weed gardens and shade circles.

Jeff had to spin the car back around after habitually drifting towards the old house following work. He pulled in front of the horse hitch and unlocked room 103. The dim living room sprang up after he flipped up the light switch and the lonely floor lamp buzzed.

"Hey partner," came Gilbert's voice behind Jeff.

"Hey."

"You need a minute, or...." trailing off. Jeff said he didn't know what for. "We gotta talk tonight before that beautiful brain of yours gets to work." Jeff didn't care. He wasn't hungry, and stabbing thoughts of Kate pierced his concentration all day.

"We can talk, Gilbert. Can I change?"

Gilbert smiled, crooked, capped by his streaking white scar. "That depends on you, pal. Why don't you meet me in 102, right next door." He leaned around the door like a peeping Tom and smacked the jamb to announce his departure. In the bedroom, while he unbuttoned his hopeful spring jacket, Jeff saw a projector screen in the corner of the room, angled against either wall. On a small, battered end table, four feet in front of it, sat a squat grey projector, wrapped in a lunking chain and padlocked, its filthy cord snaking off to a crooked plug at the base of the wall. A semi-transparent dust cover, yellowing orange, plastic, topped the projector, and concealed a black carousel of slides. The heavy, rusting chain prevented the cover from being lifted without breaking it. It looked ancient and brittle, something Jeff didn't even see in school, but something his parents would have seen. He hit the "on" button. The bulb clattered alive and spat out a milky blue color onto the screen, which flickered at first, but grew more confident the longer it was kept on. Jeff pressed the forward button and the screen blackened, then purpled over, mangled and syrupy. Battered tangerines, gross greens, split lilacs, each separated by a stark emptiness as the slide changed, no light showing at all.

Jeff kept his work pants on but changed his shirt and threw his jacket back on. He looked almost the same but felt less itchy and cramped, and that mattered somehow.

He knocked on the door of 102.

"Come on in," Gilbert said. The inside of room 102 looked about as barren as his own in 103—every-colored carpet, hairpin kitchen, lurking bathroom and bedroom—but it had a ceiling light right above where Gilbert sat, at a scratched green card table, wobbly on every end and bookended by two metal folding chairs. "Come on, sit down, sit down." Gilbert was already on his second cigarette, the first smashed out in an uneven ceramic blue tray, its crimped end wet and bitten. He drank coffee, steaming into his nostrils. The scar on his face wasn't visible in the poor light and the fog of smoke that cut and stung Jeff's eyesight.

"So what are we talking about?" said Jeff, scraping the metal chair under his legs. It was cold against his back and ass, and he was glad he kept his coat on.

"The stuff, Jeff!" said Gilbert with wide arms, scattering ashes on the carpet. "It's finally time to get to it. We fix your life. And before you get cold feet on me again, yes, I stand to gain something from helping you—for free, and reverse-free, actually, for your stipend—I get to witness. I get to hone my craft, see? This is what I do. It's not a trap. It's what I care about. We can fix things."

Gilbert acting so forward, so friendly, uneased Jeff, like seeing a spider crawl from under his blanket. "Thanks, I guess."

"Hell yeah, thanks. And you're welcome. In advance, I suppose." Gilbert leaned against the chair, which crackled and groaned from the weight, and Jeff imagined Gilbert's back was bothering him in the way that he wrenched and bent and seized. "Smoke?" Gilbert snuck his hand into his tanned jacket pocket and presented the red and white, plastic-wrapped pack to Jeff.

"No, thank you."

Gilbert smiled. "Just checking." He stuffed the pack away. "Wanted to check for any change. This whole thing is about change, of course. I expect change. You should, too. An unexpected change, though, that can change everything—well, you know what I mean—we have changes we want and some we don't want, I suppose. We want to change the things we want and presumably *not* change the... you know."

"Unexpected change is bad?"

"Could be! I dunno, maybe, it all depends. I'll give you an example," and he shuffled in his uncomfortable chair. The cold metal pinched into his leg fat and Jeff did the same. "Say you wanna snag one of those college girls, alright? We may not know exactly what changes with her, aside from the fact that she's suddenly interested in you—that's a change we want, one we intended, alright? But, say, one of her friends goes, 'Oh, ya know, Missy,'" and he folded his wrist around in a corking shape, "'she was always afraid of needles and now she's decided to get her nose and nipples pierced'—that's maybe an unintended side effect that we might be cautious about. Not that there's a rock-solid way to know that *we* were responsible, but it's worth noting. Now," and Gilbert twisted a bit and metal jingled in his coat, singing, "what are we doing for you, Jeff?"

There were two things Gilbert could do for him, now that Jeff tumbled to the new low of his life. The first was to get Kate back. Easy enough if Gilbert was to be believed. The second was to have children with Kate. His conscience sparked and grinded especially about this one. He pictured her face, exhausted and jagged, the other night when she *again* explained her fears and concerns. Using Gilbert's abilities to bypass those fears didn't take away the knowledge that Jeff knew better. But Gilbert's confidence made Jeff believe there was another way.

"I want to get back together with my wife."

"Easy, done. Wait, what? Your *wife*? Why?"

"She's my wife, Gilbert. I love her." He was sure of it.

"Buddy, you just gotta say the word and we can turn a few knobs and whatnot and throw you on campus and we'll get you a youngin' instead if you want, you know that right?"

"Yes, Gilbert."

"Je-sus Christ." Gilbert dragged his breath along the cigarette pinched between his dry lips and plumed every huff of air in his lungs back out. "Any woman? And you choose her?"

"Yes." His face was rigid as stone.

"Boring, but it's your life."

"And I want kids."

Gilbert's face puckered and strained like he was playing internal tug-of-war with every knee-jerk insult flooding his tongue. "Hmm," he allowed out, seemingly under great duress. "Question—why don't you have kids already? No shame now, be honest, it matters."

"Kate didn't want them."

"So it was all her? Everything working down there, plumbing-wise and all?"

"As far as I know, yeah. She never wanted to try."

"Well good," Gilbert slumped back and flicked his cheap green lighter alive and burned the tip of another cigarette stolen from his coat pocket. He seemed to have forgotten his coffee and Jeff thought the surface of it looked chilled as it sloshed from Gilbert's wavy arm motions. "You and me, we can manipulate, you know? That's really where this goes. Lots of manipulation for sure, that should be good and dandy, provided..." and he spun his wrist again, sputtering ash to the table, missing the blue tray almost entirely. "If she's already had a hysterectomy or something I can't un-ectomy anything. But if she just needs a stern hand, figuratively speaking, then that's fine. Done, we can do that."

"But she's afraid, Gilbert."

"We can make her unafraid."

"But it will change her body, Gilbert."

"Pregnancy tends to do that."

"And she would hate me."

"We can make it so she won't, Jeff."

"But I will *know better*, Gilbert. It's not what she wanted."

Gilbert chuckled and scraped his smoking knuckle along his brow. "So that's where the moral compass stops spinning? Doesn't sound like she wants to be around you at all, but you're wanting to get back together and that's all fine? But a little pregnancy she didn't want is a bridge too far?"

"If I hadn't brought up kids again, she wouldn't have asked me to leave. It'll be like turning back time, right? We can just make her forgive me, or forget it, or whatever, right? Manipulate her so she doesn't care anymore."

"Basically."

"But I don't think I can make her go through with nine months of pregnancy if she didn't want it."

"Y'all ever fucking consider adoption?"

It was the dumbest and simplest thing. "Well, no," and suddenly his brain burbled and buzzed. Why hadn't they considered adoption? Jeff spit out the first rational thought that whipped by his mouth like it had a foul taste and couldn't be kept inside any longer—"I want it to be my kid." Perfect. Of course that's why.

"Oh hell. Every guy's got a complex don't they. Okay then how about this—suppose your wife takes you back and agrees to have kids and her eggs are all dried up, what then? She has this desire for a brimming babe and she can't make it happen. Or what if your little swimmers are feeling lazy. How are you gonna deal with that then? Is your sham marriage going to survive that? Or would you consider, maybe, perhaps, adoption? Even if it's not your kid? And we can get moving on the good stuff."

"We don't know that." Jeff's brain was a circus, lights lining the edge of a whirling ride that you needed to be *this tall* to hop on, and the lights blinked off and on as children howled. "Everything's probably fine, we aren't that old."

"Well maybe it is, Jeff. Maybe it is, and hell, we can convince your lady to go through with it and be happy as, I dunno, a happy clam or something, as long as you can stuff that guilt down your throat and bury it. And bury it good. But if it's *not* fine...." he clapped his hands in mock defeat, and ashes landed perfectly in the tray.

And now it was on the table; the idea Jeff had in his head, the one Gilbert would drool over. "What if we just make a kid without having her become pregnant? Can we do that?"

That smile Jeff spent too much of his time hating spilled over Gilbert's face. "You know, I like where your head's at. Really like where it's going." Jeff knew he had him, snared his silly ankle. "But no, already told you, we can manipulate things, can't create 'em. If we can't fix her potentially failing fallopian tubes, we sure as hell can't birth a human out of thin air."

"I think Kate's a seaweed."

"A what?"

"A Nori, or whatever you called it the other night. Is that it? I think Kate's a Nori."

Gilbert's eyes burned grey. "Why." It wasn't a question. It was a demand.

"She sleeps a lot."

"So do you, Shark."

"She sleeps *a lot* a lot, like a strange amount. Half the day or more if I let her." Jeff patted his thumbs together and split them and then back together again, a soft drumming that rattled the card table. Gilbert's bitten cheek told him to continue. "She falls asleep real fast and snores super loud and all, everything you were talking about the other night."

"She's also a woman, Jeff. *Women* sleep longer than men."

"You said they sleep a lot—Kate sleeps a lot, why can't she be a Nori? I'm a Shark."

Gilbert's chest bulged out and his throat splayed with strained neck muscles, and he forced himself to speak in a calm tone, likely to not dissuade his new guinea pig. "The statistical likelihood of that is absurd. Sharks are rare. Hypersomniacs are even more so, a testament to their potential," and as he said that he snarled and ground his teeth through the filter of his cigarette. His wispy hair billowed from his greasy scalp. "I believe the Society has noted their occurrence at half of a half of a half of a percent or some such miniscule number. What are the chances that in god damn Bigfoot country that a Shark and a Nori are living under the same roof?"

Jeff wasn't good at math, never was, even before the concussions. The number seemed small. Maybe Jeff put too much on this strange hunch. How would Gilbert know for sure?

"How can you know for sure?"

"Testing, obviously. But I still doubt it."

"Okay, humor me here, what kind of testing?"

Gilbert stabbed out his bitten cigarette and picked up his coffee cup and drank. A twitch behind his eyes told Jeff he was trying not to care that the coffee wasn't hot anymore. "Jeff," and Gilbert tossed his mug to the table, it clunked and slopped brown and thin over the brim, "I think we just need to focus on you. *You* are the one that matters now, not your wife." Gilbert stopped looking at Jeff and instead ogled the kitchen, the door, the every-colored carpet, the gaunt spiderwebs waving in the corner.

"I thought you'd be happy about this."

"Jeff, I just don't think it's true, okay, trust me. Your wife ain't nothin' special, no offense. Let's get you happy, get you back in the saddle, so to speak. That's the focus. And we can make your wife want to have kids and you'll just have to stomach that, okay?"

"I can't, Gilbert. I can't, it's not right."

"Right? Right now is a funny time to have a conscience about *right*."

"I've had a conscience about it the whole time, but you've been convincing me to work with you and do it anyway. You wanted the research." Jeff scratched his elbow, even though it didn't itch. "And now I think there's something more here and now *you're* the one backing down."

"Jeff," Gilbert breathed huge and heavy, deflating his smoking lungs and sucking in new air for arguing, "you need to understand that there are things you don't understand. Okay? Understand that you don't understand."

Admittedly, Jeff knew very well he didn't understand; about Noris and Sharks, about the Society of Divine Dreams, even about Gilbert, whom he had come to, in an obtuse and roundabout way over the last several weeks, trust. Trust, if not his motives, then his methods. Jeff didn't understand manipulation and creation and based his feeble hopes on offhand comments made by Gilbert Finnegan between slurps of hot coffee and long drags of smoke. "Alright," Jeff said.

"Alright. We'll focus on you." Gilbert's shoulders slunk and his nose reverted to its unflared state. "But I'll tell you something, because I like you, and because *you're smart*," and Jeff found this curious because moments ago Gilbert assured him he understood nothing. "Once we get you figured out, once you're back at home with the wife, I'll humor you." Jeff realized he was holding his breath and did his best to send a signal down the long wire of his brain telling his lungs to hop in gear. "You're right. I've twisted your arm enough. I'll look into it, okay?" Jeff's head bobbed up and down. "But promise me—and I mean *promise*—you say nothing. Do not utter a word of this to your wife. And understand that I am giving you these instructions *because* I'm humoring you. If you're wrong, it wouldn't matter. But if you're right, and you talk to her about this, it won't matter if you were right or not."

Jeff lost control of the motion of his neck, but his mind bursting in every direction led him to believe he probably nodded in understanding. "So what now?"

"Now," Gilbert stretched his arms out and curled his back like he was trying to push his whole spine through muscle and skin, "you sleep. You're gonna see a projector in your room."

"I saw it."

"Good, don't use it."

"I won't."

"Not tonight. We'll probably use it here soon depending on what you dream about, just like the blues and greens. But for now, sleep, dream, and write it down. Just like before. We're going to meet every night, just like this, right here. I'll come get you. We'll talk about what you dreamed about, and then what you did during the day, and we'll tweak from there, okay? Any questions?"

So many, Jeff thought. "Dream and tell you what I did that day. Seems fine. Anything I shouldn't do?"

"Well, don't turn that projector on, and don't tell your wife you think she's got fancy sleep powers."

"She hasn't called."

"Maybe that's for the best."

Jeff's right arm tingled from being curled under his head as he laid in bed searching the internet. He really *didn't* know anything about Gilbert. He searched, rather than specific symbolism of his dreams—the bull, the deer, the snake, the eagle—about the Society itself. Aside from their own bland, whitewashed website, information was scarce. Most hits led to small forums where people, probably searching for similar dream symbolism, asked what other's experiences were, if it was worth it, if things got better. Jeff wondered if any of these people were Sharks, like him, or if they were just regular fools who had a few bad dreams.

Has anyone contacted them?
Why don't you go to a professional?
Is this a cult?
I haven't heard back.
Dreams are dreams, nothing more.
My friend reached out to them and got amazing help.
They sound like the Parasomnolent Assessment Academy.
Of course it's a scam!
All my dreams got dimmer when I stopped smoking pot.

Real information on the Society was scarce. Jeff, in his hurry to fix the plague of sleeping, didn't do much to vet this group, but he wouldn't have found much if he did. He searched for Gilbert Finnegan and found nothing related to the man he spoke to almost daily for weeks. Yes, some poor fools throughout the U.S. shared his name, but none of them matched. None of them claimed to be oneiromancers, none of them knew anything about somnolent visions or Sharks or Noris.

But Gilbert *was* something, for sure. He changed Jeff's dreams, gave him blank ones, gave him toads on pink, toads on orange. Gilbert wasn't a complete sham, but he acted out of character in 102. Jeff understood Gilbert frothed over anything research related, the rarer the better, which was why he demanded to work with Jeff in the first place. But when presented with an opportunity to utilize Kate he took up arms, more or less, and refused any involvement. *I'll look into it*, he said. *I'm humoring you*, he said. What about Noris was so strange that wasn't also true of Sharks?

Night Sixty-Three

Heaving harsh air, Jeff groped for his legal pad and click pen, and jotted down that night's vision:

I'm a big monkey, or a gorilla, I can see my arms and my body. We're in the snow, in the mountains, and I'm chasing a deer. It has a tiny white tail. I leap and crush it. I kill it.

Jeff never dreamed inside another creature before. All his dreams were of him, human Jeff, and he oddly morphed between first and third person. This dream was truly first person, like virtual reality, and he raged along the mountainside as a hulking black gorilla, not quite King Kong, but nothing would stand a chance aside from a tank or King Kong itself. He was used to his dreams abusing him, not the opposite. Never the perpetrator until now, and he didn't have the heart to describe the horrible extent of the damage done. *Crush* and *kill* were descriptive enough, and he prayed that Gilbert felt the same.

It was 2 a.m., and moonlight shimmered through small peeks in the waving curtains, blown about by the oscillating fan. The thick chains and rusting padlock hugging the projector looked smeared out in the light, and Jeff, acknowledging a shift in his dreams, knew he had taken the next step, the first step, into getting Kate back.

Night Sixty-Three (Again)

He woke from his empty second sleep and jumped inside any clothes he dragged from home. Jeff squinted at the sun as it spread over mountaintops on the horizon. He opened his dew-drowned car door, then stopped at the drive-thru of Shelley's Café and got breakfast. He parked down the road from his home, near where he waited the other day, and thumbed his phone open. He hadn't received a call or text, or even a carrier pigeon with a small scroll strapped to its tiny leg, from Kate. At all. Their only contact was one-sided; when Jeff saw her strolling from the house, looking perfectly fine, looking like she was untroubled, looking as if she hadn't just asked her husband to leave, and heading, presumably, to work. He typed in a message to her: *Just checking in on you*, and hit send.

She came out just then, spun to lock the door, salt-and-pepper ponytail swaying as she stepped, and walked to her car. Kate pulled her phone from the pocket of her purple—maybe a fuchsia, a set Jeff couldn't remember seeing before—scrub top, glanced, and buried it again. He was far enough away, the windshield smeared with mist, that he couldn't see those micro-inflections; a scrunched nose, squinting eyes, a twitching hand. Even a heavy sigh was indiscernible. As far as Jeff could tell, she moved forward, unphased, and left in her car.

Jeff opened his car door and planted his shoes on the street, and he saw a van further down the block, white, plateless, pull away in the direction Kate went. *I'm humoring you*, Gilbert said. Jeff couldn't tell if this was good or bad. Could Gilbert tell if Kate was a Nori from a distance? Or would he approach her, sweating and greasy, oversized jacket and pants? Maybe he'd wear a hat to cover that shining scalp of his. Maybe he'd bathe. Maybe hide the smokes, spritz his coat down. Maybe he wouldn't shave to keep his white scar hidden. Maybe she'd be with him instead and Jeff would be chained to a projector in room 103 without any food or water or will to live until he expired.

Jeff crouched down by the trillium with a squirt bottle in his hand. The air's chill stung, though the frost had all but gone away. The soil was dark and steeped. The flower stood tall, somehow resilient to mother nature's attacks. Helpless, he sprayed some foam from the plant food bottle into the palmed dome of dirt near the base he packed the other day.

Room 102 echoed every word off the cracked and hard walls. The card table between Jeff and Gilbert rocked whenever a tired elbow found its way down. Jeff brought Chinese takeout, occasionally digging potstickers out like treasure from his box of white rice.

"Alrighty, pal, hit me with it." Gilbert dug in his fat jacket pocket and stole a white cigarette from the box. The flame from his cheap plastic green lighter—apple green—was set to fly higher than needed; Jeff imagined it zapping his eyebrows off. "What did your *somnolent visions* show you?" He leaned back in his creaking metal folding chair and tried to cross his legs on the table, but it screeched and almost spilled over. Gilbert settled for crossed legs sideways angling to the ground.

Jeff stabbed his plastic fork down into the pillows of rice, thinking. "I was a gorilla, I think. I could see my arms, all thick and hairy, like I was inside the eyes of the gorilla. It was snowing in the mountains, and I chased down a deer." Jeff didn't look up to see what Gilbert's face was doing as he spoke. "I jumped out and killed it." He snatched a dumpling from under a scattering of soy-sauced rice and shoved it into his mouth and the fork twinkled on his teeth.

"Interesting." Gilbert smoked. "How did that make you feel?"

Interesting, thought Jeff. This seemed like an extension of "therapy" from before. Kate's aloof response to his doctor recommending therapy shuttered out from a lobe in his brain: "*Clearly you aren't happy, Jeff,*" she had said. Like she knew all along or something.

"I dunno, it was weird. On the one hand I was happy to not feel death. I'm usually mauled or something in my dreams. But this time I was doing the mauling. I've been thinking about it."

The room fell to a ringing hum. Gilbert said nothing. His grey eyes looked dim, and he pulled the cigarette to his mouth and dragged some away. Time passed. "Been thinking about what?"

"The dream, how it was different."

"Sure, that's it? You wanna share that at all?"

Jeff tossed his food box to the card table and it rumbled and tipped. "Just that it was kind of reversed, like suddenly I was the bad guy."

"Suddenly, yeah," and he tongued his teeth like he was calling a horse. "Well, I think it's something we can work with if you want. Do you want to work with this one?"

Jeff didn't quite understand what "work with" was supposed to mean. He picked up his food again, stomach screaming for more. "What does 'work with' mean?"

"Yeah," Gilbert rocked up, "if you want to keep going with this one, the dream's gonna get a bit more vivid, things are going to adjust and shift and whatnot, but functionally it'll be the same. You're the gorilla or whatever. Maybe an orangutan if you want to look up the difference and try to judge by arm size, heh." He puffed down to the filter and hurled out a cloud of smoke so dense it overtook the room and stung Jeff's eyes. "Just make sure you're sure. And that you're honest."

"Should I hold out for something different?"

"It's up to you. In this phase of the process, it's all a dice roll. We could hope you have a comfier dream, but I doubt it. Sharks don't really work like that then do they?" Jeff knew the question was rhetorical, but he couldn't help but think, no, they probably don't. Not if they get in Gilbert's hands. "I figure the first night out we got something like this and I think it'll do just fine, might as well strike while the iron's hot as they say. But it's up to you."

"So I'll have the same dream over and over now? It won't be different?"

"It will be. Just not *so* different. It's part of the process. Your brain is working through things. You know what you want, you've got the goal, right? It's all in there." Gilbert reached toward his jacket pocket, the pocket with the bulky keyring, then pulled away, waving. "I come in and do my thing to kind of streamline that, okay? I imagine, unless the goals change, the dream won't change much. You might be in a Chevy instead of a Ford, but you're still driving a truck, you know? Your brain wants you in a truck."

Jeff recalled a prior conversation; "But I've got the keys?"

Gilbert hardened. "Metaphorically, maybe. I've got the keys," his thumb thumped the muffled metal inside his pocket, "but your brain has the map. It knows you want to get back with the wife and all that serotonin and soup is shaping your dreams into a sort of," and he gestured with his hands like he was juggling a mound of loose gelatin, "monolithic, you know, some art piece, I guess. That's part of the fun for me, at least."

Fun, thought Jeff. There was the Gilbert he knew, in it for the fun. "We can use the gorilla dream, sure."

"Excellent." Gilbert coughed. It was the first time Jeff saw him cough. "So the counterpoint to this is keeping track of how your real life is playing out. So what did you do today?"

"Woke up, got dressed, got breakfast at that café." Jeff dug in the box, hoping to find another potsticker, but it was only browned-over rice left. "I stopped by the house. Is this enough detail?"

"So far. Nothing interesting yet."

"I sent Kate a message. Said I was just checking in on her."

"You stopped by the house and didn't go in? You sent her a message instead of going in?"

"Yeah. She said she wanted me to go. I assume that means she doesn't want me to come back, and that's where you come in with all this stuff."

"What did she say?"

"Nothing. No response."

"Maybe it didn't go through?"

"I saw her get the message."

Gilbert looked up and bored through Jeff with his slate grey eyes. "You stopped by the house and didn't go in. You sent her a message. You watched her get the message." Gilbert lit another cigarette and dragged in. "Did you buy some binoculars at any point?"

"No. I was just watching down the block."

"Mmhm." Gilbert gave nothing away, not a jump in his eyebrows or cock of his scarred lip. "What else?"

Jeff scooped up puffy grains of rice, dyed brown in patches. He carried the scoop to his mouth, tiny grains of rice spilling into the box, to his shirt, to the floor. Snagged in his mustache. "Pretty sure I saw you there, too."

Gilbert grinned. His scar leaned to the side, glossy white like crooked lightning. "I was there, yes." He blew smoke hard into Jeff's face and it climbed through his mouth and nose.

"Humoring me?"

"Humoring you."

"What did you do?"

"I just followed her." He leaned back.

"Do any tests? Am I right?"

"Dunno yet." Gilbert took a few moments. Drummed out an odd beat with his finger. "You know you two are probably good together, she's about as damn boring as you are."

Jeff felt floaty, like he couldn't possibly care about what happened before, about Kate's anger, about Gilbert's strange stakeouts. He just wanted things to be back to "boring" normal. "I want to know what you were doing, but I also don't."

"Then forget about it. If I find something I'll tell ya. Keep going."

His day. Right. "I fed a plant in the front garden."

"You call that a garden?" Gilbert scoffed. "Birthwort is weird, a very strange, very," again, motioning with yellowed fingers, "very peculiar plant. Why is it there? It's big for this time of year."

"I brought it down for Kate from the mountains. I found it there and pulled it as a gift, but she didn't take care of it like she said she would."

"That's fucking weird man."

"Giving a flower to my wife?"

"No, just," and he leaned forward, hunched shoulders creaking, "I don't understand how it looks so good. It's basically still winter." Jeff agreed in silence and knew that Kate would disagree. "I don't know shit about plants, really," and Jeff silently disagreed, but figured Kate would be none the wiser, "but I'm pretty sure they don't grow that way this time of year."

"Guess I just took care of it right. It was dying in the house, so I put it outside."

Gilbert chortled under his smoke haze. Jeff didn't want to know why. "Okay, what else?" Gilbert asked.

"At work, Colson brought everyone donuts. I had a plain glazed." Gilbert snorted smoke out of his nose. "And I just did accounting stuff, reports, listened to the radio. Got off work and drove back around to the house."

"And she still never responded?"

"No." Gilbert made a face. "Then I ordered the takeout and came back to the room until you came and got me."

"That's a long day without taking a piss."

"Do you need to know that much detail?"

Gilbert waved him away. He nodded and stamped out his cigarette even though it was only half gone. "Alright then. We'll split for now and I'll come get you about the same time tomorrow. Same thing. Let me know what the dream is like, specifically how it changes, if any details are different, that sort of thing. You should probably look up if it was really a gorilla, at least as best as you can."

"How long is this gonna take?" Jeff realized he was holding an empty take out box.

"What, don't like the new bed? Heh." Jeff didn't laugh. "Anyway, we're going in the right direction since we're just using the first dream, alright? Give it a few days, a week, we'll get you right snuggled up there, pal." Gilbert stood up and motioned like he was dusting off his jacket and pants. "Oh, I've got a remote for that projector in there, but tonight you go ahead and turn it on and get it to a color you like. Doesn't matter to me which, just pick a color that makes you think, 'that's the right color,' and leave it there. All night, even while you sleep."

Jeff shuffled the projector through its slides, oozing greens, interstellar purples, rippling oranges, and settled on a cranberry-streaked red. The slide was warped at the edges and panning itself into a creamy pink. He, in turn, humored Gilbert, and googled "gorilla arms." As far as he could tell, he was right. Sleep felt cursed and blaring. Behind his lids he tried to relax, the projector whirled and bled over the skin, searing red over his closed eyes. He felt blown out and stretched, still unfamiliar in the bed which cramped his thigh, creaked with every turn. Kate's bear growls were absent in his ears like an old photo pulled from a dusty shelf. As he spun away from the direct line of the projector, the light bounced off the white of the walls and spilled red to his eyes regardless.

Night Sixty-Nine

Over several days, Jeff dreamt in curdled Technicolor from bounced summer blues and aged yellows. He met with Gilbert in 102 over bad pizza and deli sandwiches. He refused to stock the fridge or permit any accommodations allowing comfort in 103. He thought if he bought bread or peanut butter, got a fresher pillow or a laptop, those actions meant accepting failure, that Gilbert's experiment would take longer than necessary. Jeff plowed through a week's worth of number crunching with Colson bringing donuts twice. Gilbert's smoking plumed so egregious that Jeff grew used to the filmy air in 102 and his neck felt fuzzy on the surface. The gorilla dream morphed slowly each night; the snow faded away to snow-spat forests, then wet streets; the deer changed to a fawn, then warped to something between an antelope and a fox with a blazing tail. The violence never changed. It stayed wet and sticky and hot, then wouldn't steam on snow when spilled, but instead seeped down gum-clogged sewer drains. He woke shouting and sweating each night, and despite the repetition, it never stopped scraping ache into his brain.

And then the phone buzzed. Kate, five days late, sent a text back: *Thanks for checking on me.*

He took a breath. Then several more. Deep into his lungs, his chest heaved out and up and down again.

Was this the experiment? Or was Kate just being polite, at last?

I hope you're doing well, he thumped on the screen. And he thought, was now the time to strike? To ask to see her? Jeff couldn't possibly comprehend how anything with his dream, with the gorilla destroying the helpless deer-fox, could result in this. How was this manipulating anybody? But he trusted Gilbert to guide him through. And what else could prove trust than fulfilling the quest? *Let me know if you need anything*, he added, and pressed send. His heart throbbed in his throat. He kicked himself off the bed and pulled his clothes on, peering at his phone. He mashed the volume button up to make sure it was at maximum. Jeff walked to the entryway and checked the phone. He locked the door behind him and checked the phone. He settled in the driver's seat and checked his phone. He stopped at the red light three blocks down from the apartment and checked his phone. He ordered drip coffee with cream and checked his phone. He ate his scone and drenched it in his emptying cup and checked his phone. He pulled up the street from his house and checked his phone.

Then he checked for Gilbert. No sign of a white van. The ultimate prank, he thought, would be if Gilbert followed Jeff here, and he necked into his mirrors, left, right, center, and whipped his body behind on both sides to check. Gilbert couldn't be seen, unless, of course, he was in some other vehicle. Jeff never saw the van at the hotel following that first night, and never knew for sure if Gilbert was actually staying there aside from his word. The trillium seemed sturdy and bobbed in the wind, its triangular white and green leaves resembling a broken pinwheel.

Kate stepped out of the house in harsh white scrubs—he didn't know whites well enough, more research needed—and a long ponytail, locked the door, and stared left, right, left, all around the block. Jeff dumped himself low in his seat and gasped, grasping his knee as it banged the front console.

He was had.

It was over.

It was done.

Kate would leave him for good, and probably sock him one for being here.

And about a minute passed. His phone buzzed. *I'm doing well*, said the phone, and nothing more. Jeff hoisted his shoulders up and peered through the steering wheel. Kate was gone. Further up, her car was gone, too. Surely she recognized the car her husband drove for years. Unless she was looking for something else, like an unmarked white van. Did she know Gilbert had been following her?

The rest of the day, Jeff bumbled incoherent sentences from his thumbs to his phone screen, then erased them fully. The bait dangled in front of him. He wanted to bite and hopefully not get snared through the cheek and dragged up and clubbed. *I'd love to see you.* He pressed the send button and shivered.

"You really went for it, huh?" said Gilbert, leaning at a painful angle, cigarette wet in his fingers. Room 102 was dim as usual. Jeff sat with a crumpled fast food bag in his lap and plucked out crisp fries. "What did she say?"

"Nothing."

"Yet!" Gilbert jutted forward, grinning, his scar a smear of fat lightning on his lip. Jeff spent most of the afternoon making sure his feet weren't numb. He found his pulse bumping in his neck and panicked when his BPM clocked at over 150. The internet told him this measurement indicated a considerable state of panic. And then he felt foolish when he realized he was checking with his thumb which also had a pulse in it, distorting the value. "Hell, I think it's a good sign she messaged you at all. Means we're making progress."

"I guess so." Jeff wiped ketchup from his lip with a brown napkin.

"Tell me about the dream."

Jeff recounted the slight adjustments to last night's vision, which added up to a small scenery change of the street and the garbled amalgam of a small deer and a thrashing fox.

"Interesting." Gilbert never took notes, never buckled him up to machinery, never even weighed him. Exactly what did he do with this information?

"What are you doing with this information?"

"Careful observation," he said, lugging his full coffee cup, steaming, to his mouth. "Much of what I see with you is based on what I've seen in others. The further along you go, the more context I get for other, you know, other Sharks I've worked with before. Everything becomes clearer. And I'm sure the next one after you will be even more so."

Night Seventy

That night's dream (Jeff really needed to ask Gilbert about laundry due to all the sweat) was a similar steady progression of events. Further into the city now, a grosser blend of deer and fox, about 50/50, diagonally from the shoulder to the rump, where the head was a small deer's face with treeing antlers and it became Frankenfox, gradually bristling out into wild fur and a reckless, whipping tail. And then the shredding.

Night Seventy (Again)

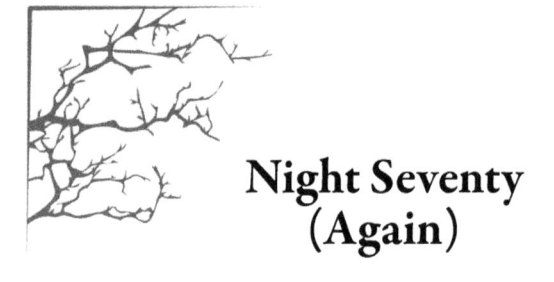

Sure, come by for dinner, blinked his phone when he woke from his empty second sleep. Somehow, it was working, he thought. Soon he would be back at home, back in bed, and then could figure out what to do next. He considered playing hooky from work, but instead gathered it would better occupy his brain if he just went in like usual. The day dragged like a blunt sled over wet snow. It felt like a full workday passed before lunch hour blessed him, and he sped to the store to buy a new flannel shirt. After work ended (Colson invited him to go with some of the other workers to the bar because he seemed "on edge") he blared back to 103 and took a quick shower, then dressed back up in the new flannel and drove, hopefully for good, back to his home. He pulled in the normal spot like he always did. Kate waited in the door, graceful, leaning, in capri pants and a simple overshirt with a high ponytail, letting her long, greying hair whisp in the wind.

He stepped up the curb, and for the first time he could remember, told himself *left, right, left, right* as each opposite foot fell. *Let her lead*, he thought. This moment had blurred through his brain in a thousand manic ways all day. Would they kiss? Hug? Shake hands? Would she pull out a concealed weapon and blast him away? Would her friends be waiting behind the side of the house to pummel him and drag him to the back and stomp him to death in the trees? "Hey," he said. Jeff didn't lift his hands or move his shoulders, anything to indicate any expectation.

"Hey Jeff," and there was a simple fall in her voice, like she was uncertain what he would do as well. Perhaps she had every reason to think he would come armed and make her a statistic on that night's news like so many dejected husbands did.

He placed his left foot in front of his right, again, and continued to her. She stood on the front steps, and it elevated her half a foot or so above his level. Kate's fingers tugged the long sleeves of her shirt into half-gloves over her knuckles. She clenched her shoulders, and extended her arms, signaling a hug. Careful not to trip, Jeff followed her lead and leaned into her chest and wrapped his arms around the small of her back, unimposing. They swayed there. Her arms fell over his shoulders and Jeff felt her breath blowing over his skin. "Come in," she said.

The house was clean. Cleaner than when she asked him to go, cleaner than when he snuck in to get clothes. A piney fresh smell seeped into his nostrils like mountain wind. It seemed Kate busied her own mind by tackling spring cleaning early. Then the allure of baked potatoes and boiling corn on the cob took over as they stepped into the kitchen, past the painting of the deer. Jeff slammed his eyes shut as images of him as a gorilla tearing hooves perpendicular in the snow flashed forward.

"Thanks for having me over," Jeff said.

"It's your house," she said. Not the reply he expected.

"Sure." He pulled out the wooden chair at the small table while Kate bothered seasoning red slabs of beef on a cutting board. "What have you been up to? The house looks great." He didn't mention the wide smack of a deer on the patio door. "You look great."

"I've been cleaning a lot, yeah. Helps keep the mind busy." She pinched a mound of salt from a bowl and sprinkled it over the board, then snatched another and hurled it into the corn pot.

"Anything I can help you with?"

"No, let me make dinner. You cooked for me a lot lately. Let me pay this back."

Despite the amusement he got from Kate volunteering to cook all on her own, Jeff didn't like the words "pay" and "back" being used so close to one another. Visions of a secret hazing spilled over where Claudia and Howard cupped chloroform over his nose and tied him by the ankles to the bumper of his car and put a brick on the gas pedal. Jeff stood anyway, creaking the legs of the chair along the laminate, and stepped to Kate, who turned her neck slightly toward him. He watched her swaying hair.

"I'm sorry Kate." She didn't speak, and instead pulled a long wooden spoon from the crowded drawer and did not whack him over the mouth with it, but dipped it in the boiling pot of corn and stirred it, not that corn on the cob needed the stirring. "It was wrong of me. It was inconsiderate of me."

"What was?"

Was this a joke? Or a test? "The other night. You know—"

"Oh that wasn't a big deal." Another surprise. "I overreacted." Jeff's guts felt snakey and slimy, like he put something expired in his mouth and was considering whether he should swallow it. Was this all Gilbert?

"You sure?" Idiot, he thought to himself. Now is not the time to poke the forgiving bear.

"Yeah, it was... no, I overreacted. Completely." She let go of the spoon and it sunk far into the salty water. Kate turned to face him, her hair whipping around and resting over her shoulder. "You should come back home. I was wrong."

"Say no more," Jeff said, and hugged her. He ran his hands along her back, and she leaned up and kissed him, careful at first, then full and freely, hands to his neck. After they slid down his shoulders and ribs, she dug them into his back pockets and sunk against him.

It was too easy, Jeff thought. Was this what he fought all along? He tried for over a month to really repair his relationship with Kate and it only served to drive them further apart than ever before. Less than a week with Gilbert the oneiromancer and she forgave his worst trespass already. But maybe that wasn't Gilbert at all? Maybe it wasn't the dreams or the projector screens, the gorilla and the deer. Maybe Kate just loved him? Maybe he could convince himself of that? Maybe she had done the same.

"We've got to get the steaks on." Plump and vermilion, impossible to ignore, impossible to stop drooling over, three steaks rested on the cutting board.

"Three?"

"Daddy's coming over for dinner."

"Is he coming to kill me?"

Kate laughed and undug her hands from his pockets. "No, no. I didn't tell him anything. Didn't tell anyone, actually. Like I said, I overreacted. I took so long to get back to you because I was embarrassed."

"Really?"

"Really. I just kept going. But Daddy wanted to come see us so I figured it would be a good time to suck it up and bring you back home."

Jeff heard Hank's truck chugging like a stampede down the street and into the driveway. Zipping visions of the bull goring him came fluttering up when Jeff saw the horns tied to the front grille. He rang the doorbell and Jeff answered, shoving his soft hand to Hank's, and he shook it with his own, calloused and thick knuckled, Jeff's joints stabbing like broken glass under his skin.

"Son," he said, his full greeting. Hank lurked in the entryway a moment and took his dirty white cowboy hat off, and Jeff invited him to sit at the table. The sound of searing muscle blared in the kitchen as Kate laid the steaks down on a hot iron pan. "Smells good, baby," he said, and he kissed her on the cheek as he took his seat. "How you been?"

"Just fine, just fine, thanks. Want a beer?"

"Nah, I don't need that stuff."

"How's the farm?"

"Lonely." He took a moment. "Maybe I'll have a beer." Jeff pulled one from the fridge and Hank popped the top with a fizzy *chh*.

"You know you can come here any time you want, it's not a problem." Jeff secretly hoped he would never take him up on that offer.

"Same to you, Jeff. Same to you, baby Katie."

"Thanks, Daddy, I'll come round sometime."

When her father was around, Kate's speech trickled to a lazy drawl. Vowels plumed in her throat and syllables dangled in the air like a balloon without a string.

"New painting?" Jeff tried his best not to give it a direct gaze.

"Yeah, I painted that one after we had a little incident here at the patio." Kate flipped the steaks, and the loud sizzle bounced off the kitchen walls. Rosemary and thyme and garlic and butter smoke hung, and Jeff's tongue twitched, yearning for a real meal after his week of take-out.

Shuffling sideways in his chair, Hank rested his faint blue eyes on the painting. Kate watched him from the stovetop. "I think it's lovely." He meant it. Kate's smile bloomed, then she clamped down with her teeth to stifle it.

"Thank you," and she turned away, and Jeff knew she was letting her full smile loose so the wall could witness it.

They sat through dinner, gnashing on corn dragged through a buckling slab of butter, snagging strings from their teeth. The steak seared into a lusty medium rare and mixed its juices with the mashed potatoes, which Kate left a touch lumpy for texture. Every bite was a velvety dive and pillowed chunks surprised Jeff at just the right intervals. The men thanked Kate for her meal, and she excused herself to the bathroom, leaving the two of them alone.

"You must be so proud of her," Hank said. Jeff turned his head and met his eyes, hazy blue. Hank's face looked tired, and a faint line from his cowboy hat rested light on his hair like a halo. "This painting. I'm glad she's doing something with, you know," and he lilted his head at slight angles, searching, pawing for a word, "with her emotions."

"I'm so proud," Jeff said. He never considered it. To him, pride wasn't the word. He thought Kate was talented in a backroom kind of way, and he appreciated the outlet, just like Hank mentioned. But *pride* was something reserved for a parent. "Can I ask you," he said, the opening line before just letting it rip anyways, "what's it like having a daughter?"

Hank's lips spread diagonally. His teeth were all there but yellowed from years. "Afraid you might have missed the boat, son?"

"Maybe. Just curious."

"Look," the opening line before saying something one isn't confident will land with grace. Hank shuffled in his chair and led his eyes down the hall where Kate was. "It's none of my business. It really isn't. I've learned that." His throat gulped, swallowing air or a drink that wasn't there. "I think, for me, it's one of the best things that ever happened to me." Hank's soft voice pulled a lightness from his chest, allowing his faint eyes to shimmer. "When Annie told me, when she said, 'Hank we're gonna have a baby,' I thought, 'shit.'" This time, he did pull a sip of beer from the can, wetting his throat. Building to something. "I thought of myself. I thought of my brothers and sisters and my mama. I was a hellion when I was younger. My poor mama always trying to wrangle us kids up and make sure we had clean clothes, ironed, all that. Gosh." Another sip. He stared down the hall again, looking for a sign of his daughter. "And bless Annie and what she gave me." He shook his head. "Jeff, if she was still here with me, I think I'd have to get down on my knees and," Jeff examined this pause. Hank's lip curled up beneath his teeth. "And pray to her, I guess."

Jeff nodded his head, unsure of when was the appropriate time to speak, and what he might possibly say in response. After a few more beats, he went with, "That's amazing."

The sound of the tap blasting in the sink dragged from down the hall. "Katie! Baby." Kate stepped into the kitchen with shining hands. "I love you, baby."

She laughed, leaned down, hugged him, kissed him on his thin cheek, "I love you too, Daddy."

Hank left just before the spring dusk dampened the eyes of drivers with maybe one too many in them. His words sunk into Jeff's skin like a tattoo. The ease of Gilbert's methods was alluring, and he wondered, truly, how far he could go. Kate accepted him back like nothing happened, even assured him nothing happened.

Jeff's phone buzzed with an email from Gilbert around the usual time, jokingly asking if Jeff was still alive. He let Gilbert know he was back at home with Kate and thanked him for his help, and that he wouldn't need the room. Gilbert sent another congratulating him, and said he'd be in touch tomorrow. More research?

It didn't matter. Tonight he was back inside his own home, cleaner than he had seen it in years, and Kate looked at him that way he had been wanting her to look at him, the way he wished he could dream of, if it weren't for the horrible things his brain came up with.

Kate grabbed his hand and pulled him down the hall and opened the door to the bedroom. It, too, was fresh and smelled like clean laundry. "I've been thinking about everything," she said. They were standing in the doorway. "Maybe we can give it a shot, Jeff."

He almost couldn't believe it. "You mean...." Standing in the door to the bedroom, Jeff was reminded of the knotted wooden arch they were married under next to a rustling, peaceful creek decades ago.

Kate nodded her head.

"You want to try?"

Kate nodded her head. They closed the door.

Night Seventy-One

The dream shocked him awake. Somehow, he had been fully happy, complete, and the thought of his brain betraying him had wandered off like the curious child of a distracted parent. In his dream, a crocodile snapped its fierce jaws over his whole torso and thrashed about, whipping and rolling, crumpling Jeff's skeleton into twigs. And then, even though gasping was a mere suggestion, the beast dragged him into the green bog, somehow squeezing tighter with each second that passed, tighter, sharper, tighter.

His legal pad was still in 103, so he drafted an email to himself and sent it and brushed the new message notification away. Kate's nose roared in hyperdrive, and the image of cartoon characters huffing curtains off the rods washed over his mind.

Night Seventy-One (Again)

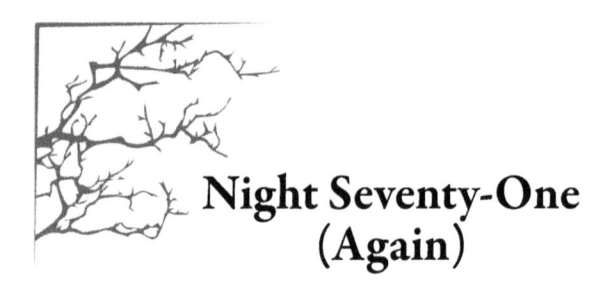

In the morning, light pierced tiny slits in the blinds. Kate shut off her alarm without snoozing it and curled over to kiss Jeff's mushy face. She dressed for work and brushed her teeth.

Impossible, he thought. Something about his conscience could stay clean. Yes, he had used oneiromancy to worm his way back into Kate's good graces, but that was almost like hitting the undo key on a word document; he never would have been *on* her bad side had he not brought up his desire for children, again, despite knowing Kate's feelings. But now, she seemed open and willing to try. Perhaps he didn't understand Kate's love for him after all. Maybe it was real. Maybe more than just contentment, age, years, convenience. And that was her decision, not Gilbert's talents. It must be.

Gilbert insisted they meet that night. He said he didn't want to go back to Jeff's house or the café because he wanted to smoke. "Tell me what happened," Gilbert said, puffing as promised. He clanked the cheap apple green lighter down on the card table.

"She started replying to my texts. And then I said I missed her and she invited me over for dinner and said everything was fine. She said she overreacted."

"No shit?" said Gilbert with a smile. The scar darting across his lip looked greasy and wrinkled. "Now I just want to point out that none of this would have happened without yours truly," and he gave a small bow, biting his cigarette and dipping his balding head towards Jeff.

"I guess you're right," Jeff said. He fiddled with his hands as he didn't bring any takeout. "Thank you."

"Yep," he groaned, deep in his throat, and belched out a bolt of smoke. "Now," he slurped hard on his cigarette and pre-emptively stole another from his oversized jacket pocket, "what about this whole kid thing?" Gilbert stamped the nub out and lit the next smoke.

"Probably no need Gilbert," said Jeff, and Gilbert's eyes squinted overdramatic, "Kate said she wanted to try for real."

"No shit?" Both of his elbows clomped to the table, and it shook and threatened to collapse. "Hmm!" and smoke bolted from his nose.

Gilbert seemed genuinely surprised. "You seem surprised."

His head nodded, beams of light blaring off his greasy scalp. "I must say, Jeff, I am quite surprised indeed." He didn't smoke, only blinked, then formed a strange, shifting face and puffed again. "Interesting."

Jeff's familiar annoyance with Gilbert crept up. His vagueness, his pomp, his pretense. He would not bite on this one.

"You know we can keep working together." Gilbert leaned back and locked into Jeff's eyes. "Your brain's fun."

"I'm not a toy, Gilbert."

"Oh."

"Besides, we did it. I'm back home. And it's gonna be better because Kate is willing to try for kids. We don't have to do any of that other stuff. You don't have to 'humor' me anymore."

Gilbert rubbed his chin. "And what if you humored *me*, just for a little bit, yeah?" He wasn't smoking, instead lurched forward, looming. "What else do you want, Jeff?"

"What do you mean?"

"You know, therapy doesn't stop just 'cause you figure one thing out. No. Hell, people have a whole lifetime of shit they're working through under the surface, just lurking there, waiting for it to get sorted out. And why go to therapy when you got me here?" He grinned, like posing for a painful picture. Jeff mummed his lips. "Oh come on, you've got so much potential up there. Just think, we could make your job better, make your sex better, make your bank account fat and plump like you want your wife to be."

All the times Gilbert had prompted him, just like this, to try bettering his life, Jeff turned him away. And just yesterday, Kate brought him back home, loving, better than ever, and it was oh so easy. Perhaps it was time to stop being a wet blanket. Perhaps Gilbert should have his fun.

"And what does this do for you, Gilbert? Seems like a whole lot of benefit for me and work for you."

"As I've always said, I am a humble student of research. That's all. I have the questions. So, so, so many questions. Your silly brain brings me the answers." He wiped his hands in a clapping sort of fashion and raised his eyebrows. "But there's a new little problem." Jeff encouraged him to continue. Gilbert crumpled his cigarette into the tray and didn't grab another. "You aren't gonna be staying in 103 now that you're cozied up and gushing with your wife now, huh?" Gilbert didn't wait for a response. "Exactly, the projector, glad you made it there with me."

"Is it completely necessary?"

"Maybe not completely. Encouraged, certainly. It can do a lot to help catalyze these things, these developments. You think the old lady would mind?"

"I don't know, Gilbert." Jeff wasn't sure she'd even notice the projector there if he could just slip it in while she slept, droning on in her unflinching slumber. He usually dreamt until he spooked awake and gave it another crack, all peaceful-like. "I might not have to tell her, honestly. Like I said before, she's a real heavy sleeper."

"Perfect," he grinned. "But you be careful, she's an antique, heh." Jeff wasn't sure if Gilbert was still talking about the projector.

Night Seventy-Two

Without Gilbert's help, the death dreams continued. A pelican swooped from afar, closer, closer, closer, and gobbled Jeff's whole head up, clean.

It was a rare sight to see Gilbert in the daytime. His skin was sallow and semi-transparent, like he'd done his best to evade the sun for decades, nicotine sick. Spring light bounced erratic from his combed-over scalp. "Hey, wait right there!" he shouted, peering around the side of the van. Jeff waited on the curb. The open van door left Gilbert's shoes, unpolished and scuffed, swimming around dark long socks, about the only thing in sight. A shuffling, bumbling dance of only two left feet, and gurgling groans of Gilbert's strains as he dragged, hauled, and unloaded the projector onto a wheeled cart. Gilbert walked back and shut the van door, and Jeff observed the sweat gushing over his greasy face, the mixture of the two components like oil and water, slick and scattering. "Alright," he said, huffing, the smokes bearing down over him.

"Do I need a screen?"

"Nah, hell," a wide breath, knuckles to hips, "you got walls. Long as they're pretty much white, we're pretty much good."

"They're pretty much white, Gilbert."

"Well. Turn this thing on then, just like you would."

Jeff said his goodbyes and clunked the cart up the pocked walkway to the front door. The chain trembled and scraped along the carousel holding the colored slides, and the padlock rhythmically *thunked* the bleached teal of the cart. After some rotating and shuffling, Jeff jumbled the projector through the front door, then shoved it squeaking down the hallway to rest near his writing desk just outside the bedroom. It's a good thing that when Kate slept it was like she was jailed to slumber, as the wheels at the base of the cart could use a proper greasing. Gilbert produced enough, Jeff thought, that maybe sliding his forehead along the tracks would help. The lens, a warped, black iris, stared at Jeff, judging him. He covered the projector and cart with a crimson and black blanket from the closet and hoped it wouldn't draw Kate's eye.

As Jeff stomped out to the refrigerator, he noticed the wheel marks dug into the carpet from the cart like the heels of a dragged corpse.

Kate opened the door just as Jeff wound the cord on the vacuum cleaner. "You vacuumed?"

"Thought I'd do my best to keep it nice in here, like you had it, since you worked so hard."

Kate said it was sweet, thanked him, kissed him, and unloaded her things to the kitchen table. They ate spaghetti with extra meatballs. Jeff joined Kate in her painting room with permission and drew in a fresh spiral notebook behind her. The well-worn brush in Kate's right hand left behind vermilion streaks and bruise purple pools. Jeff arced his wrist left to right, left to right, over and over again, hashing in shading on the shape of Kate from behind.

They tried again that night. Jeff wasn't sure he believed in God, but each night he felt like he might be praying. He thought, to someone that could only be God, *Please. Please. Please.* When Kate's face sounded like a wet sawmill, Jeff crawled from bed and squeaked the projector into the room, slow, one small squeak at a time. He plugged it in and flicked over the "on" switch. A sickly pink slide clicked on and blasted bright to the wall on Jeff's side of the bed. Looking behind him, the whole room was garbled and washed over like melted cotton candy. Kate's gentle chest rose and fell, completely undisturbed.

Night Seventy-Three

Gilbert must have given him one of his subconscious signals. The gorilla dream returned. A glance around the room revealed the projector had shifted from Pepto pink to pond-scum green. The slide looked burnt in the corner like it had rested on a radiator or got caught in just the right angle from a magnified sunray. Jeff spun from bed, making sure that Kate was asleep. It was a foolish waste of energy to spin his neck around; his ears gave it all away. Jeff croaked the door open, unplugged the projector, and squeaked it, inch by carpeted inch, out of the bedroom, and closed the door again. Kate sounded another snore and he let out his breath, then wheeled a little faster to the desk.

Jeff marked down the changes on his reclaimed legal pad. *Attacked outside of a bar with a neon sign that said "Candy Jack's." Deer-fox is smaller and has one and a half tails.* He climbed back under the covers in the normal darkness of the room and slept until morning, at peace, and still pleading.

Night Seventy-Three (Again)

Another uneventful day passed, and the projector glared red once Kate started snoring, and was back to the gunky green when Jeff woke, stuck to the sheets in his own cold sweat. He noted the deer-fox was now just a fox and had six (!) tails, and in the first-person view of the gorilla stomping mad he had ripped each of them off and tossed them into different lawns on the suburban road.

Colson called Jeff into his office, gifted him a donut from a box he purchased fresh in a dozen from the grocery store (plain glazed, of course), and offered Jeff a raise.

He could almost hear Gilbert cackling in the recesses of his skull. Jeff and Kate did fine for themselves, they truly didn't need more money. But more money was more money, and seemingly more money for the same work. Win-win.

102 that night was dense with smoke which swirled by the pale wallpaper like fog kicked by eager feet, floor lamp light blaring through it. Jeff snacked on french fries that weren't quite cooked enough.

"That fast, huh?" Gilbert asked, elbows planted on the card table.

Jeff nodded and ate another fry.

"Interesting," said Gilbert. "Two days is fast." He didn't look at Jeff, but instead stared with stony eyes to the faded card table, like trying to make out a face in the cracks. "What's next?"

"You tell me."

"What do you want, Jeff?"

"I mean...." he considered this. What did he want, aside from Kate and some kids? "I didn't really need the raise, but I guess it's worth having. But I'm good." Was he? "Can't think of anything I'd want or need aside from having a family, being a dad," and speaking the word "dad" out loud caused his throat to gurgle, his belly to tremble, and he hoped Gilbert didn't pick up on it. "I think I'd really like that."

"We can move the needle that way, Jeff."

"I told you, we don't need to. Kate and I are..." he shifted and shuffled his hands, "we're already trying, okay, she wants this now, too. For real."

Gilbert fell back to his chair and exhaled loud and premeditated. "Ahh, Jeff." It sounded like Gilbert had loaded this sigh up and was finally unleashing it, gunpowder and all. "I'm telling you this because—well, for three reasons, one of which is because I know you're going to ask 'why are you doing this for me blah blah blah' and the answer is because I do research, and I like doing it with you, okay? So there's that. I'm also telling you this because I consider you a friend, and I don't want to see you in a bad spot."

"No you don't," Jeff said, without a thought, and he knew it was true.

Gilbert waited. He stared straight at Jeff, straight through him, really. He allowed the cigarette in his fingers to smolder.

"Alright, no, I'm not your friend, but still, you're sort of like a partner to me in this, and if you keep going on thinking what you think, then that won't work well for me."

The exhausting side of Gilbert revved its engine up. "What is it, Gilbert?"

"Yep. You know I was following your old lady, right?" He leaned forward, the Gilbert Finnegan classic. "Wanna know what she was doing?" His eyebrows danced and his teeth shined.

"You said she was boring just like me."

"You got that right." He took a drag. "Except one day, right at the start." Gilbert paused, waiting for Jeff's retort, but he sat, not blinking, not eating, breathing very loudly. "Alright. She went to work, okay? Every day she went to work. Except that first day. She didn't go to work Jeff, you follow me?" Another period passed where Jeff didn't respond. "She went to Our Lady of Hope. Recognize it?"

"Is that a church or something?"

"It's a god damn abortion clinic, Jeff."

"Fuck you."

"Hey, fuck you, I'm right." Gilbert didn't smile.

The door to 102 flew open and a skinny man with floppy grey hair and a patchy grey mustache strolled in, stuttering, "Oh hey, sorry."

"God damn it, Tony."

The man named Tony waddled uncomfortably in the hallway. He had a large glass of bubbling brown soda in his hand, and it bobbed with each awkward shuffle. Gilbert closed his eyes and took a deep, smokeless breath in through his nose. "Hey mister, sorry about this. Wait, you're... you're him." The man named Tony stomped forward in his waving, oversized clothes with his arm stuck outward like he was being pulled by it. "Tony—Tony Glasicola."

As is polite, Jeff shook the hand in front of him and a river of questions broke the dam in his brain, pouring over everything. "Who am I, Tony?"

"You're him, you're the Shark, Jeff Vickers, right?"

"Hey, Tony, it's not a great time," said Gilbert.

"Sorry, I—I—I'll be leaving ya. Sorry Mr. Vickers, hope you're gettin' everythin' you want, now." His head bowed as he backed away, hair flopping over his ears.

"Hey Tony, why don't you come sit down with us here, come on over," Jeff invited.

"Tony, we'll meet later, okay?"

"Nah Ton', come on over, have a seat. I don't know where a chair is but park it."

Tony, eyes bright and youthful, despite his age, hustled over to the card table. Jeff offered Tony his seat and stood to the side. Tony set his glass down after gulping a huge mouthful and expelling an exaggerated "Ahhh".

"How is it that you know me and I don't know you?"

"Well Gil told me about you, about your talents." Jeff encouraged him to continue. Gilbert put out his cigarette straight into the table and balled his fists white and red.

"And what did he say I do?"

He swallowed another huge pull of soda, "Well that you can make anything you want happen, that you were able to get back with your wife. I'd like that myself."

"And did he say that you were a Shark, too?"

Gilbert interjected here, "You know why he's called 'Tony Glasicola?'"

"Why's that?"

"He's always got a glass o' cola." Gilbert didn't smile.

"It's true," said Tony Glasicola.

"So what's your last name?"

"Glasicola."

"I'll be."

"Tony here contacted me after he started having some pretty crazy dreams, isn't that right, Ton'?"

"That's right, Gil. He flew me right out of Tennessee, all expenses paid."

"A red state. Could probably smoke anywhere I want."

"You can't, Gil."

"Christ." Gilbert puffed out a plume towards Tony. "And to let him know that I could help him, I told him a little bit of your story, Jeff. Nothing crazy."

"What sort of dreams do you have, Tony Glasicola?"

"They're so strange." He gripped his glass of cola with both hands and fog swam up behind his fingertips. "It's always my wife murdering me with stuff from around the house: kitchen knives, fire pokers, blenders—that was the worst one, I looked up Gil after that one, found the Divine Society thing after that one—"

"Society of Divine Dreams," said Jeff.

"—yeah sure, and Gil's been helping me since. For a bit I was dreaming of that frog."

"Ahh, the frog, yes."

"You seen that one, huh? What a doozy. And now—"

"Why don't you get out of here, Tony?" said Gilbert, cutting him off.

"Yeah," said Jeff, though he was curious about where Tony's head was at now, "I'll finish up here with 'Gil' and then you can get your reps in, okay?" Understanding the sign, Tony Glasicola grabbed his glass and left the seat, waving to Gilbert and Jeff as he shut the door. Jeff sat back down.

"You're making me rich, Jeff. See? Told you this would pay off. Now you know what I'm in it for."

"I don't believe you—Gil." He didn't. "Why did you say my wife was at an abortion clinic?"

"Because she was."

"And what was my wife doing at an abortion clinic?"

Gilbert smushed his lips together and his scar bloomed like lightning. "Have you ever heard of the concept the liberals call 'pro-choice?'"

"My wife wasn't pregnant, Gilbert, or whatever your fucking name is." Jeff wanted to jump over the table and strangle Gilbert's pale neck. His hands stung from the thought.

"Look, I didn't go inside with her, I just followed her there. But I imagine she wasn't buying flowers." Gilbert chuckled at the intended depth of his joke.

"You know what she was doing, don't you?"

Gilbert bobbed his head around, wondering what he should say, and the action of this let Jeff know that he did, in fact, know, and Gilbert realized it too late. "Okay. So yeah, that van I got is pretty fancy, alright? I can find things out. Your old lady didn't have an abortion so just calm it on down." Jeff knew this had to be true, but he was still relieved. "She did get an IUD put in, though."

Jeff shook his head. "That doesn't make sense, she said we're going to try for kids, she was probably, I dunno, getting... getting tested or something."

"For what, an STD? You think that's better? Who's she gonna get an STD from?"

"Gilbert, Jesus," and he slapped his hands over his face. It didn't make sense that Kate would get an IUD. But if she hadn't changed her mind at all, if this was a lie, and for some reason she just wanted him back.... "How long does it take for an IUD to become effective?"

"'Bout a week."

"Jesus."

"Look man, *you're smart*, just think—this means she really does love you, okay?"

"Enough to lie to me? Deceive me?"

"Yeah, you make a brilliant couple."

Jeff rocketed out of his seat and his legs shook like an overstuffed washing machine. "We're done." It wasn't often that Gilbert refused to look Jeff in the eye, but this was one of those occasions. Jeff went to the door. "Come get your projector tomorrow. And hope I don't trash it tonight."

"Just think about it Jeff." Gilbert struck another cigarette, leaned back in his chair, and finally met Jeff in the eyes. Jeff strained his jaw, lips taut. "That thing's an antique. And this can all be fine." He stuffed his lighter into his breast pocket. "Just think about it."

Jeff fell into the dark and threw his car door open and slammed it shut and pounded the steering wheel like Gilbert's face was the horn. He breathed in. A flash caught his eye at the apartment—203, the blind flickered. Jeff suspected Tony

Glasicola was behind the blinds in the window and hid when he saw Jeff's eyes turn up.

The car ride home cooked him slow, simmering, stewing. Gilbert said Kate lied to him and had an IUD placed, and that he was using Jeff's story to bait new recruits into his research games. If Gilbert was right, then maybe Jeff didn't have any abilities at all. Either Jeff really had willed Kate to take him back and the incident at Our Lady of Hope is a lie or a cruel misunderstanding, or Kate simply loved him, but was lying to him about trying for kids, knowing she won't get pregnant.

Jeff couldn't decide which idea was worse, and cursed himself for instigating in the first place, for having an opinion, and for being a hypocritical ass.

He pushed through the front door like a bomb would blast if he went too fast.

"I'm back here," shouted Kate from her painting room. He walked to the back of the house and into the painting room when skinny Kate slid her brush along a streaked canvas leaning on a marred easel. She greeted him and he felt comforted when she said his name, and his eyes fell shut and he leaned on her, smelling her neck and her hair, and kissing them.

"What's this?" Jeff asked. He could see a pale rose sky with cobalt cloud shapes smattered all over it, and indigo and scarlet lines gashed about, seemingly at random.

She chuckled that small way that makes air dash out of your nose, and admitted, "I don't know." She reached next to her on the stool to her stemless wine glass, sloshing with red, and slurped. "It's just what I'm painting. Maybe I dream all these up." She chuckled again, "Maybe that's why I sleep so long, because I'm trying to figure them out, or I'm trying to memorize them enough to paint them later."

Jeff didn't want to think about what Kate's dreams could be doing to her. This could be another form of journaling and perhaps she had her own secret Gilbert she met with to decipher her *somnolent visions*, or maybe it was Gilbert himself. It seemed Gilbert or whoever he really was had woven his way into every thought in Jeff's brain like a wretched thread that caught and unspooled the whole arrangement when pulled.

"Do you think it's okay for you to be drinking? Just in case?" She dragged, very intently, the glass back to her stained lips, and drank deep.

"I don't know," she said, her teeth brimming still with wine and her tongue slopped around, trying to contain it all in her mouth, and another to wash it down. "Doesn't that only matter if I get pregnant?"

"*When* you get pregnant."

She spun around and faced him. Her chocolate eyes tinged with cherry. "And what if I don't?" Jeff's only thought was to not move a single muscle in his face. "What if I can't?" He felt it was okay to let his face move now. He molded it into something he hoped resembled concern. "What if I'm too old, Jeff? What do you do then?" She refused to unlock her eyes from his, though his fell on the carpet, on her hair, on her forehead, her shirt sleeves. "Go?"

"No."

"No?"

"No."

She breathed again, loud and only through her nose, but she wasn't laughing this time. "How do I know?"

"I love you for trying. For listening to me and giving this a chance." Kate's head nodded in response, and she finally unstuck her eyes from his and they wandered to the carpet, her bare toes, his shoulders. "I believe in you. This will work. And if it doesn't, then... there are other things we could try if you wanted."

"Okay." Kate squirmed a little bit and her hands squeaked on the glass. "I don't know how those women do it. Adoptive mothers or mothers that use surrogates. Imagine waking up one day and you're just a mom. Or a dad. I wonder if I would," and she shook her head, embarrassed, "I wonder if I could ever love a kid like that, you know? One that wasn't really mine, one that I didn't carry?" She gnawed on her lip until the red from the wine bloomed from the pressure of her teeth.

"Hey, we don't have to worry about that, okay? And look, fathers do it all the time. I wouldn't ever be carrying the kid, but I'd still love her as much as I love you."

"You think we'll have a girl?"

"I think I'd like a girl." He thought of the college students at Shelley's Café, looking lost and adventurous at the same time, and thought, yes, a girl would be the way. "But beggars can't be choosers."

"I think I'd like a boy."

"And why's that?" The pair started to sway. Kate's arms circled Jeff's neck like a slow dance.

"I don't know," she said again, for the however-many-th time that conversation. "Just feels right."

"Well," Jeff cleared his throat. "We'll just see then," he smirked, rubbing the small of her back, "won't we?"

They flossed and brushed their teeth and crawled into bed and Jeff just held her, her back to his chest and their legs crossed together, quietly, until Kate's loud snoring blared up. He let her go and spun to his back and studied the speckle pattern on the ceiling. Jeff's mind kept lurking, tugging back to Gilbert and his accusations, his deceptions. The house clunked—adjustments from the HVAC system, spurts from the dishwasher, some cracking that could have been squirrels darting outside the window. Sleep became elusive and luring. Jeff hobbled out from the covers and opened the window blinds, allowing the moon to wash into the room like a projector to the silver screen.

He remembered the first time he saw Gilbert, out in the trees, attempting to hide behind a whitebark pine while flashing his camera toward the room. Something was missing. Jeff felt eased by the light, bright, and how when he closed his eyes it left a film over the lids where they blushed a veined rose. Something told him this was a good idea, and then Jeff squeaked the projector into the room and plugged it into the wall and switched it on and a corn-husk blue painted the crooked square where the lens pointed. Jeff heard the subtle hum of the internal fan whirring away and could, perhaps, maybe, feel his heart rate slow by just a beat or two each second. It was a good idea, he thought. And he washed away to sleep.

Night Seventy-Four

The dream forced him upright in bed, elbow in his pillow, forearm to his forehead, sloughing sweat. Kate purred in time like music. The projector shining on the wall bloomed an ugly white, or former white, like parchment rolling at the edges. It bounced light all around the room, even outside its beamed rounded square, and the aged white reflected on the sheets, the blinds, through the window, fighting the moon. Jeff clicked the projector off, and the fans died down. He squeaked it through the door, down the hallway to the writing desk and tossed the crimson and black blanket over it. He thought about it. A force of habit at this point, he slumped in the chair and the writing desk and flattened his legal pad to the next page:

I'm in the head of a gorilla ripping through a deer, fully grown, in the front lawn of my house.

Returning to bed, he detoured through the bathroom, and he couldn't help but check in the trash can, toeing up the lid, to see if there were any tube-like wrappers from a tampon or paper strips from pads. It was all discarded (white) tissue, toothpaste boxes, and floss, some stuck to the back hinges of the can and most kinking down from a snag on the bag. He molded to Kate's body when he climbed back in bed and warmed himself to her temperature, then collapsed into the peaceful second sleep he'd come to count on.

Night Seventy-Four (Again)

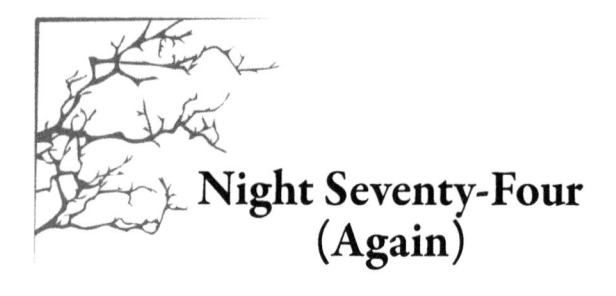

Kate clambered out of bed, stretched in the sunshine of the open blinds, and dragged herself to the dresser to pick out a scrub color. Jeff shuffled around, wishing he were second-sleeping again.

"Do you want to go out to dinner tonight?" Kate asked.

"Fuskies?"

"There may come a time in a few months where I'm craving bottomless fries, but right now, I think I'd prefer a more delicate meal. We should go to Audette's." Kate cinched down a pair of mint green scrubs.

"You got it." Charlie Fuskies *did* serve the best fries in the Pacific Northwest, in Jeff's expert opinion. But the comment... in a few months... Kate was either hopeful in their endeavor or planting a seed, one that would grow in his head instead of a child in a womb. Jeff hated he was this cynical, this suspecting and unloving. He couldn't quite pinpoint when it all started or what the instigating factor was, but he needed to shape up. Cynical dads raise killers and welfare cases.

Colson came by Jeff's desk, just to check on him, he said. He placed a hairy hand on Jeff's shoulder for effect.

"I'm doing well. Thank you for being so understanding," Jeff said. Colson didn't blink when Jeff took off at ten to run an errand. He needed to meet Gilbert to give the projector back. But why?

At home, Jeff yanked off the crimson and black blanket and saw the antique, dusty and scratched in all the endearing places. The chain whispered as he rolled it along the carpet and out to the front door. The lock, rusted and faithful, gave him a feeling of confidence. Gilbert coasted to a stop at the curb. His new Shark, Tony Glasicola, rode shotgun. Jeff met them at the curb. Tony gawked around, not meeting Jeff's eyes or greeting him, like he was pretending he and Gilbert stopped to admire the lovely neighborhood. Sunlight shot off Gilbert's greasy head and hurt Jeff's eyes.

"Let's do this, folks." Gilbert opened the back door to the van. "Where's it at? I brought muscle."

"You know, Gilbert, I've been thinking," and he thought about it some more, "maybe I don't need to give it back just yet." Tony, whose hands were stuffed into his pockets and admiring a neighbor's tree fort, gawked back at the mention of the projector.

"So you thought about it?"

"Yeah I thought about it," Jeff said. "Maybe I'll just keep it."

Gilbert looked from Jeff to Tony, whose neck craned at an extreme angle. "Maybe you'll just keep it."

"Yeah. Figured we can get down to it, you know." He toed at a rock near the curb. "With the visions and all that."

"Well, c'mon Ton'. Let's get gettin'." Gilbert slammed the van door over on his way around to the driver's side.

Tony walked over and pulled a wet hand from his pocket and shoved it out to Jeff. "Never got a chance the other day."

Jeff shook it and wiped the lint on his pant leg. Tony waved goodbye and hopped in the passenger seat.

"You know, I'm glad you thought about this, Jeff," said Gilbert. "*You're smart*; it only makes sense."

"Of course," said Jeff, wondering why he ever considered giving up in the first place.

Jeff and Kate rode to Audette's together after work. Kate changed into a cardinal red dress that teetered on her small shoulders. Jeff managed to throw on an aquamarine button-down that he decided not to tuck in. Tea candles blossomed all around the rustic venue as couples and parties murmured and shared appetizers.

"You know, Jeff," said Kate, tipping a glass of chardonnay to her lips, "I'm really happy."

"I'm glad."

"To be honest, I thought we were just old and married and that's how it was going to be." She drank again and swallowed thick and took a huge breath like she was preparing to jump off a cliff. "But you really came around. You showed love to me. That means something."

"I'm glad it means something to you. It does to me."

"I'm just," she held her glass and warbled it over the tea candle flagging in the middle of the table like it was a hanging cauldron, "I'm excited for the future. For us."

The pair made it home safely and fell into the bed. Jeff breathed and breathed, breathed to lower his heart rate and rest his mind. He rolled from the bed and to the bathroom where he, once again, checked the trash for signs of menstruation and found nothing but nail clippings and tangled wads of greying hair. The projector squeaked into the room and Jeff plugged it in, switched it on to its pretty whir, and cycled slides, unsure if a crumpled galactic rose or faded military cobalt spoke to him. He closed his eyes and breathed.

Night Seventy-Five

The dream came to him, overpowering his thoughts of insecurity, suspicion, and emptiness.

He was the gorilla. Charging forward, arms rippling under coarse, muddy fur, towards a quiet deer, and plowing into it, smashing through the front door of his home. He thrashed the deer around, it kicked back, hoofing into his chest and jaw, and he scrambled forward to chase again through the hall. He tackled it and chunks of the wall broke away, salting the two in white. The deer fled and he, once again, gripped and dragged and slammed it to the floor, against doors, into the bathroom. He took a leg off, and another, and pounded the body, warmth running over his feet and legs.

And then he caught a glimpse in the mirror. The gorilla's face was scratched out and shuffling, shaking, and on top of its head was a spider, red as God, its legs skewered into the exposed brain. And the spider was done with the gorilla and jumped off, and Jeff went with it, rattling along the floor, towards the bedroom. Nailed to the middle of the door in curling gold were the numbers "303." The spider and Jeff crawled up towards the keyhole to human screams. The dream ended just as the spider crawled through the keyhole and saw Kate, babbling in tears, clutching a baby loose in her arms.

Jeff's scream jolted him up. The first thing he noticed—the thing impossible not to notice—was the hurricaning cycle of slides, the mechanical surging as they clacked, clacked, clacked to the next and the next, vomit purple and molding orange, wilted cranberry, neon black. It painted the room in rapid redecoration, bleeding over the walls and glowing through the open blinds. The light bounced onto a man struggling in the trees, tied to them. Jeff recognized Tony Glasicola, strung up by thin ropes looped around his waist and chest and shoulders, untying the knots. Jeff wanted to smash through the window and choke him, punch him until his face became the bark of the tree, and then he noticed the last thing—the thing he should have noticed all along, that thing he missed those days away—Kate was gone.

Impossible. He knew where she was because the dream finally showed him. Jeff snatched his keys on the way out the front door and started his car, nude except for his underwear, and he sped off toward Gilbert's apartment. In the dark of the morning there was little traffic, so he fearlessly weaved to whichever side of the road he needed to be on. He ripped through red lights and around corners, hoping the useless police remained so.

Jeff screeched in the gravel, spitting it like a shotgun, out in front of the building, and his heart juiced to an impossible pace. Somehow, the dream made it real; an entire third floor of the building now loomed, decaying, as if it was there the whole time, five doors just atop the ones on the lower levels. And the door in the middle, 303, was wide open, the only lights on in the complex. Jeff scrambled up the steps, two at a time, then three, his feet catching splinters and his toes knocking the railings. Up again, and again, heaving, to the third floor and dashing to the middle and swinging into apartment 303.

Locks. Hundreds and hundreds of locks, maybe more. The room seemed bigger than was capable by the constraints of the whole building, and locks in safety deposit drawers, in wooden cabinets crammed into the dark walls, padlocks dangling from hooks, whole safes with wheels behind keyholes. There were thin, rickety-looking lockers with dozens of keyholes each, hidden safes on the floor and packed into the ceiling, ancient cupboards teeming with dust and simple, quaint keyholes keeping them shut. There were solitary jewelry boxes with stained glass tops locked secret, on top of locked dressers and foot lockers and cables wrapped and wrapped around oblong mysteries with a lock holding it all together.

And a baby on a covered table in the middle, alone, screaming. Jeff ran to it, wet and gooey, and stared. It was a normal, human baby, a boy, just like he saw on tv shows, howling for something it didn't know how to ask for. Jeff wrapped his big hands around its back and neck and screamed Kate's name. Over and over. The boy screamed at Jeff for something, anything. Kate had been here, he knew it, he could tell by the rumples of the cloth on the table and the locks and boxes shoved in a clear path to the door. But she was gone. Jeff held the boy. The boy screamed. He held the boy a different way, to his chest, to his heart, and the boy screamed and screamed and screamed.

Jeff slipped in so much sweat his feet slid across the metal doors and locks jutting out of the floor. He held the boy and looked at the door, open to the night. He walked over safes and lock boxes and around dressers and stepped to the newly appeared balcony his brain conjured. The boy screamed still, bright and right in Jeff's pounding ear. He took the boy to the car and couldn't decide if he should lay him on the seat or try to drive with him in his lap. He had to choose one way to go. Left or right. Kate could be left or right or anywhere by now. And he chose left.

And Gilbert walked up the steps, fully dressed, swimming in his suit jacket. He thumbed the keyring from his breast pocket and unclasped it, spinning it, skipping up the steps. He walked into 303 and saw the room of locks, and (he laughed as he thought of it) locked the door behind him. He took it all in, the drawers and doors and cabinets and safes. He fingered the first key on the ring loose and walked toward any lock he wanted and played, a thousand locks for a thousand keys and time and time to try them.

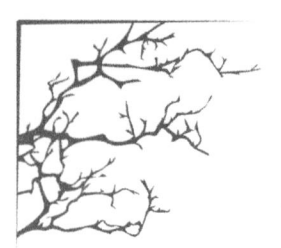

Epilogue

Where else would I go? The cops, like Jeff always said, were probably useless as an asshole on an elbow. Besides, what would I tell them? I don't even know what happened to me.

I never gave it much thought, surviving. You hear of tragic things every day: terrorist attacks, car accidents, earthquakes shucking neighborhoods to gravel. But it never happens to you. Until it does. I never considered what any of these people do once the unthinkable sneaks behind them and rearranges their unexpecting spines.

And then Mom died.

At some point, I had to itch my nose or go to the bathroom or simply walk because my leg ran fuzzy. And so I did. It's not 100 percent tragedy all the time. But it is 100 percent present in an abandoned lobe of your brain.

And when I woke up—my god, did I wake up on the wrong side of the bed. The wrong bed entirely, in fact. That hazy room, floor, walls, ceiling stuffed and cratered with safes and lockers like a lost Dali painting.

And that boy. A perfect, howling boy. He was there like Jeff's manifestation of love, or what he thought love was, or what love could be once he believed hard enough. But that wasn't my boy and never would be. I know something of love. I know when it's alive and when it's rotten and melting. That boy was neither. Not to me. Like a terrorist attack, a gasoline-licked bus flip, or a tsunami raging on the other side of the world, that boy was a tragedy. Someone else's tragedy.

So I left. Real quick. Didn't wait for an itch or a numb leg. Stubbed my toes and scraped up my heels real good on some of those tumblers mashed into the floor. Damn that boy. And damn that man. They say a woman is responsible for original sin, for stealing the apple, and from birth must work to repent the sins committed on her behalf. The Book of Katherine sings a different gospel.

The town was still dark. Nobody stopped. Why would they? That's a nightmare scenario. Stranded woman, limping along the road at 3 a.m.; you're likely to get jumped or worse for your kindness. I found my way, both relieved and disgusted that I was still in the town I'd lived in for decades. It betrayed me somehow. Things like this don't happen in sleepy, snowy mountain towns. Things like this happen in New York, in LA, in Japan, in Iraq. Ever since then I've carried pepper spray *and* a boot knife. A big one.

Phone, keys, wallet, every scrap of clothing that fit in my arms. The clean house, just like I left it, just like I remembered it. I ripped right by the paint studio without a thought. Damn that house. I hopped in the car and left. I didn't check the mirrors, didn't signal, didn't turn the headlights on 'til I hit the main road. I drove two towns over, screaming.

I thought of going to Daddy first. But what would I tell him? How could he not call an institution right then and there? There are certain levels of explanation required depending on the time of day you call for help. The 4 a.m.

doorbell won't settle for anything other than the full story. And I didn't have a story to give, other than a swirling gut, a hot head, and a crying boy in an impossible room.

For the first time I could remember, I couldn't sleep. I tried. I laid my head down on the motel pillow, smashed and limp from who knows how many occupants. When I closed my eyes I saw the boy on the table, jaw bent wider than I'd ever expected. I heard a jingling sound like a dull windchime or a custodian's overstuffed keyring. I had no idea what people did at 5 a.m. Personally, I decided on another drive. I stopped at a gas station with the brightest lights and filled up.

I thought about going to work, because what the hell else was there to do, but figured Jeff could find me there and try to say something. Try to come back again. Why did I let him back? I was sure he had to go. I was positive it was over. I wanted it done. And then I woke up one morning and saw the un-crinkled sheets on the far side of the bed and wondered where he'd gone, why he wasn't back, and why he left in the first place. Maybe some comfort. Maybe some spell. Something. Something floating. Something aching.

The type of call for help that doesn't need a full story is the 3 p.m. Claudia simply gave me the go-ahead, told me to bring my pajamas and asked what kind of pizza I liked. It's not a damn mystery to another woman. Daddy would take some work.

I did go back once. Just the one time. After I got my boot knife. I stalled in my car down the street. I looked for Jeff's car, or anything else out of place. It was just the street as far as I could tell, and my damn house. The grass sloshed with melt as I stomped over the lawn. I dug the knife out and hacked that flower up since Jeff seemed to give a shit about it. Cut every leaf and petal from the stem. And then it just burst out of me, a surge of hydraulic rage and I stabbed the ground over and over, more and more, my knife snapping on rocks and hurling dirt to the house and over my jeans. But the flower was dead and buried and I didn't look back when I drove off.

Now it's just what to do next. I haven't seen him since that night. No calls. I haven't tried his phone. He hasn't tried mine. Those asshole-elbow cops will want to know he's missing. And then they'll ask me what happened. What I know. Maybe think I'm responsible. And I don't know what the hell I'll say about that. Maybe I'll sleep on it. Think about it over a glass of wine and stretched canvas. Just like a man to start a fire and leave a woman to tend the hearth.

But let me tell you. The sleep. My god. I thought I knew sleep before. I thought I was the luckiest woman to rest her head. But now, it's like my whole life I was just dreaming of sleep, like I understood what sleep was supposed to be, and assumed I slept, too, just like everyone else. And this is the real thing, now. Now, it's like I've been nestled long enough for the eggshell to crack and see this new world from heights I could only dream of. Nudged from the nest and my wings took over on instinct. I survived.

And the dreams. The dreams. I could tell you about the beaming stars, the physical presence of warmth, angel smiles from heaven, how love is spoken from soft nuzzle of mother to cub, of dancing with unbreakable feet, but it's easier if I show you. I wake up each morning and slip through bliss just remembering my dreams, and then I paint them when I come home. I'll show you sometime. I can paint you the most beautiful dreams.

About the Author

Stephen Short is a native of the wintry Pacific Northwest. He writes fiction that ranges from paranoid and obsessive to childish and weird. His work is influenced by Quentin Tarantino and video games as much as it is by Raymond Carver and Denis Johnson. Stephen's fiction has been published in The Account: A Journal of Poetry, Prose, and Thought; is pending publication at The Lit Nerds journal; and has been nominated for Sundress Publications' Best of the Net. This is his first novel.

Milton Keynes UK
Ingram Content Group UK Ltd.
UKHW032316121024
449481UK00011B/337